# RAGGED EDGE

## DUSTYN MCCORMICK

SPELLHAWKS
PRESS

Dedicated to:

*Kelly, Jordan, Adela, Mac, and Keegyn*

*My Mom Karen, and Sister Wyndi*

*Mr. Brian Luther*

## Acknowledgements

So many people were involved in making this book possible there is no way I can thank all of them. That being said I'm going to try.

Allen Childers, he pushed and prodded and really lit the fire for me to publish this.

Toby Halverson, you know why, and hey twenty bucks is twenty bucks right?

I'd like to thank Jerry and Brandy Saulsbury. Jerry has been a great friend for many years and Brandy is one of my favorite test readers. She was a real trooper reading this chapter-by-chapter as it was written.

Clint and Michelle Hubler. You guys have always been there when I needed you and through some really bad times.

Sasha Kaplunenko, You've enriched my life in so many ways.

Ben Bills a great friend, and the inspiration for one of my favorite characters.

My writing group partners in Table for Eight.

Don and Glenda Leftwich

My Donors: Scott, Kelly, Kaitlyn, and Timothy Smith, Lenny Mannis, Allen Childers, Polina Tatrinova, James Cummings, Thomas Boaz.

All of you have helped make this dream possible and this book would not exist without your help. I will never be able to thank any of you enough. If I left someone out I am truly sorry and thank you all the same.

Finally, I have to thank my wife Kelly. She believed in me when nobody else did. Listened to me as I talked about the book almost non-stop while writing it and helped me through all the stress of the publishing process, refusing to let me quit the many times I wanted to. I love you Babydoll.

A very special thanks to you the reader.

In Memory of

*Elbert "Mac" McCormick – Dad*

*Mike Lebbert – Friend*

# CHAPTER 1

You don't actually lay on a psychologist's couch. I mean you can if you want but usually you just sit there, face to face, with someone that's trying to understand what is going on in your head. It's intimidating the first few times, then you get use to it and sometimes, for fun, mess with the headshrinker.

I wasn't having fun. My shrink likes sounding smarter than he is. He's full of nonsense phrases like "I see" and "that seems only natural" and, my personal favorite, "I understand." When he uses those phrases I want to reach out and break his nose then ask him if he still sees and understands and how natural does it feel. I haven't done it. Yet.

My shrink has me classified as "functionally deranged," meaning I'm delusional but not a danger to myself or to society as a whole. He's wrong of course, I'm not delusional and I can be, oh, so very dangerous.

1

# Ragged Edge

Sure, he didn't believe me when I told him what I am, and he doesn't believe some of the things that I say I do, but that's not important. It's just important to have someone I can talk to about the ragged edges of my life.

Those ragged edges, everyone has them, some people notice them, and most don't. Those are the edges where the reality you think exists clashes against the edges of the reality that truly exists. Seeing shadows out of the corner of your eye, strange lights in the sky, and hearing voices with no one around to produce them. Those are the edges people try to ignore, pass off as hallucinations or mental illness. The problem however, is that they are real.

Those edges brought me to this shrink. I have friends I could've talked to but I didn't want them thinking I was nuts, or worse, turn their backs on me. Dr. Johnson had become my closest confidant. I could tell him whatever I wanted with no worries about what he thought of me. Most of the time he didn't believe me anyway.

So that's how I ended up here, sitting on his squishy leather couch, looking at the books on his walls. Most of them were real but some only looked like books. He sat in a leather armchair across from me; a mahogany coffee table represented the neutral territory between us, decorated with just two cups of warm tea. He asked me how I was doing. He didn't mean just today of course.

"I had the dream again," I told him a neutral voice.

"Which dream?" he said, trying to sound like he cared.

"The one with the cabin. I always go back to the cabin."

"I see." Already with the clichés.

"It's just a plain log cabin; it sits in a clearing in the woods. In my dream, I was walking a path in the woods and came upon the cabin. It felt like I meant to go there, but once I found it I didn't want to go in."

"Why not?"

"I knew there was something waiting for me inside. Something I didn't want to see."

"What was waiting for you?"

"I didn't see it. The door was shut."

"Have you ever seen this cabin while awake?" He sounded bored. He wasn't paying attention. That's why he made a good confidant, I could tell him anything and he probably wouldn't remember it.

"Yes, I have. It looks like the cabin my grandfather owned. I use to spend my summers there when I was a kid."

"I see. Have you been thinking about your grandfather a lot?"

"Not much. I haven't seen him in years. When I got older I didn't visit him anymore."

"That seems natural; you became a teenager and had other things you thought were more important." I liked how he assumed I was like everyone else. I stopped visiting because I wasn't allowed to see him anymore. I didn't tell him that though because then I'd have to explain why I wasn't allowed, He'd see the reason as more proof of my derangement and try to mess with the medication he thought I was taking.

"I know inside the cabin that death is waiting for me, and birth." That raised his eyebrows. I think I surprised him.

"How could you know that if you couldn't see inside the cabin?"

"Intuition. It was a gut feeling. That's why I didn't want to go inside."

"How can death and birth be waiting for you?"

"One always accompanies the other, doctor. You should know that." I sounded more sarcastic than I meant to. Honestly though, sometimes these doctors surprise me with their ignorance.

"I see."

The short balding doctor was trying my patience today. Whenever confronted with something he didn't understand he always replied with "I see." It was damned annoying.

"Anyway that was my dream. I stood outside this cabin being overwhelmed by fear..."

"Of death?"

"Or life."

"Life?"

"That's what birth is right? It's life beginning; death is life ending. So maybe I was just scared of life."

"Do you think you're scared of life?"

"Why should I be afraid of life, doc? I'm living it, aren't I?"

He slowly leaned forward and took a sip of tea, and I studied him closely. Dr. Johnson didn't look healthy. His complexion was paler than usual, more of his hair had fallen out, and his beard wasn't as meticulously trimmed as usual. The smell of fear rose from him like a wave. Not fear of me, he considered me a harmless delusional. It was a quiet fear, a constant nagging worry.

"What about you, doc? Are you living life?" He sputtered, almost choking on his tea.

"I'm alive, aren't I?"

"Are you really?"

"I don't understand what you mean."

"I see," I said with a slight chuckle. "Well, doc, what I mean to say is what is wrong with you? You seem distracted."

"Don't be silly, I'm listening to every word."

"You're hearing them yes, but you are distracted." My voice came out low and filled with concern. The kind of voice you use when consoling loved ones.

"I was just thinking about my wife."

"What about her, Mark?" He didn't notice my use of his first name. He was really distracted.

"I've been thinking about cheating on her." His voice cracked.

"Why would you think about that?"

"She's been distant and withdrawn lately, and my secretary... I want my secretary."

I'd seen his secretary, and she was definitely attractive in an overdone, made with plastic kind of way. She had dark hair, blue eyes, and a nice figure. Then again, I've seen pictures of his wife. I think he had the better deal with his wife.

"Do you really, Mark?" This isn't the first time I've switched roles with Mark. He never remembered afterwards, which is a bit of a blessing. For me to help him I had to expose my true self and I didn't want him to see that.

"I don't know. I don't want to hurt her, but I feel like I can't control this thing inside me that wants Jezel," he said. He gazed at his hands clasped in his lap. He didn't notice that I was standing. He started rambling about his long hours, and thinking about Jezel most of the night. I let him talk and filled in my parts of the conversation with encouragement. His hands held his gaze while I removed my jacket. If he looked up now he wouldn't be able to see me. His mind would tell him that a bright glare of sunshine coming in the window made me appear strange for a moment. His subconscious would know what he saw, but he wouldn't believe it.

I slowly walked around and stood behind him, the sounds of the city around us muted. If he turned and saw me now he would probably faint. Most people do. I hit the intercom button on his desk that would summon Jezel. My instincts told me this sudden infatuation wasn't entirely normal, and I had to find out.

She sashayed into the office, bedroom eyes fixed on me.

"You called?" she purred. My hormones sprang to life, everything in me wanted this woman right now. I fought the urge and fixed a firm frown on my face.

"Succubus," I said.

"You figured me out? How excitingly lovely," she said, licking her lips and stepping closer to me.

To be honest I should've picked up on her sooner. A succubus was a demon that seduces her prey and then feeds on his or her life force. This wasn't something I wanted affecting my doc. I mean, he isn't the greatest shrink on the planet but he was my shrink. While giving the doc affirmative sounds urging him to keep talking I moved around the desk.

"Leave, demon, now," I growled. Fighting in the doc's office wasn't on the top of my to-do list, but maybe a stern warning would do the trick.

"And miss out on the delicious doctor? Surely you kid," she said, moving closer to me. She moved with a seductive feline grace, showing off her curves and trying to draw the attention of my eyes and, well, other parts of me also.

"Leave now and you live. This is my human," I said. Wings sprouted from my back and flames danced around my fingertips. She paused in her approach.

"Aww, the big mean guy doesn't want me to hurt his pet human. How cute." Watching her mouth move brought all sorts of thoughts to my mind. I pushed them away as best I could.

"Last warning, demon." I said, snarling as my doctor kept rambling. The easiest way to totally distract a human was to get them talking about themselves.

I moved into a defensive posture, my hands elongated into talons while the flames danced around them. Her eyes narrowed into slits and she slowly crouched down. Even this simple gesture was an attack. It allowed her to get into position to pounce on me while also forcing me to look down at her and the great work her plastic surgeon had done.

She expected me to throw a fireball at her. If we were outside maybe I would have, but inside I couldn't risk it.

# Ragged Edge

With any luck, she hadn't figured out much about who and what I am. I was never sure how detailed the notes were that my doc kept. I pulled my arm back as though I were about to throw the fireball she expected. Instead, I charged the short distance between us and brought one talon-clawed hand down across her face.

She didn't have time to react as I can move extremely fast when necessary. This was necessary. I'd fought a succubus before and barely escaped with my life. Since then I'd learned their weaknesses and right at the top of the list was their looks. My talons raked four long gashes into her face. Almost immediately her sexual spell was broken.

An inhuman scream escaped her lips as she pounced at me. Her fingernails lengthened into claws and she swiped at my throat. I pulled my head back in time to feel the air from her hand breeze past my neck. Using my other hand, I drew another set of gashes on the other side of her face as I rushed behind her. She wouldn't be seducing anyone for a long time.

"You can still survive this fight, Miss Jezel. All you have to do is walk away." I said in a calm tone as she turned to face me again. So far we still hadn't interrupted the doctor. It's amazing how well a little hypnosis and self-involvement can serve as a distraction. His ramblings had moved onto patient files and needing to take a vacation. He hadn't mentioned Jezel since my first slash across her face.

"Why?" she said, whimpering.

# Ragged Edge

"This is my human, my friend. Walk away now, send in your resignation, and I'll allow you to live to feed another day."

"What are you?" she asked.

"That's between me and the doc. Make your choice," I said.

"Fine," she said and began to walk past me.

I took a step back to allow her clear passage to the door never turning my back to her. As she got even with me one of her hands flashed out and sliced my stomach. Instinctually, I lashed out and ripped through her chest. I felt my talons scrape against her ribs as she spun away from me. To a human, that would've been a killing blow. From the succubus, it drew an ear-splitting screech of pain. The doc's rambling paused. I grabbed her from behind and clamped a hand over her mouth as I carried her out of the office.

"You've fed on your last human," I snarled in her ear as I snapped her head around, breaking her neck. I let go as her body slumped to the floor and slowly transformed into rose-colored goo. The doc's monologue continued from his office. Moving quickly, I cleaned up the mess left by the succubus' body. To keep her from returning, I had to keep a bit of it. I hadn't actually killed her so much as destroyed her body. If the goo was left whole, she would be able to reform a new body. By separating a bit, I could make sure she never reformed. The rest was sopped up in paper towels and thrown in a trashcan.

After throwing her away, I took her coffee cup and dumped it on the still damp carpet outside the doc's office door. Now it would appear to be nothing but spilt coffee. At her desk, I typed up a resignation letter saying she had gotten a call from another employer and had to leave immediately for Russia. I made sure to apologize for her abrupt departure.

With all that taken care of, I went back into the doctor's office and straightened everything up from our fight. My shirt was ripped and my stomach was oozing blood but the flow was stopping. My jacket would cover it. Picking back up my encouraging "uh huh" litany, I walked back to the couch and replaced my jacket before sitting down.

"So what do you think, doc, does my dream mean anything?" I asked, resuming my neutral tone and snapping him out of his hypnotic ramble.

"I think sometimes a dream is just a dream. It could be a result of your medications, or maybe you've been thinking about your grandfather a lot."

"I see."

"That's all we have time for today, Marcus."

"Alright, Doc. I'll see you in a few weeks."

He stood up and shook my hand as we walked to the door. I left his office feeling good. Mark was safe from the succubus, he wouldn't end up destroying his life chasing after the love of a demon and his focus would return to his patients. At least, once he found a new secretary. I made a mental note to pay closer attention to his next secretary.

# Ragged Edge

I guess at this point I should properly introduce myself. Dr. Johnson calls me Marcus Davidson. Most of my friends call me Joseph Stevenson, but my close friends and family call me by my true name, Sean Gryphon. I don't have any close friends. I stand about six feet four inches tall, my shoulders are linebacker broad, my frame is muscled though not overly so, my eyes are blue, my hair is long and raven black, and my wingspan is roughly twelve feet, tip to tip.

That's right, I said wingspan. I'm not human, or maybe I'm more human than a human, I haven't figured that part out. Oh, and I'm roughly seven hundred years old I look young for my age though so most people think I'm somewhere in my mid-thirties.

I also have a bit of succubus goo in my pocket. That's not normal for me but since it's there I figured I may as well mention it. Now where was I? Oh yeah, just left the shrink.

When I exited the office, the bright sunshine struck my face, making me smile. I don't care what you are; a beautiful sunny day will make you smile. Well, unless you're a vampire, I guess. I haven't met many creatures that smile while bursting into flame. I've always enjoyed them though, sunny days, not the flaming creatures. Most of the people walking past me on the street were smiling, some laughing. A general sense of goodwill pervaded everything. This only happens on certain days when the sun is shining brightly, but the day isn't too hot or too cold, a slight breeze keeps the air cool and carries the scent of millions of flowers and trees to your nostrils and everything gleams as if new. Honestly, how could you not smile on a day like this?

I put my hands in my pockets and strolled down the street whistling and enjoying the human race all around me. That's not always easy to do. Sometimes you guys make it almost impossible to enjoy your company. Seriously, there's the constant fighting and bickering, and then a huge number of you suffer from "poor me syndrome." I mean, just look around you sometime, open your eyes to your own race, and you'll see why it's so hard for a guy like me to want to help you out.

That's what I do see. I help you guys out like my shrink helps me out. Not by listening though; my help is a bit more proactive. I'm not the only one either. I know of at least a hundred others like me, and there have been thousands of us throughout your history. Don't bother with the history books, though, as we rarely get noticed and when we are, well, just ask yourself what I could be. I'm tall, handsome – OK, gorgeous, I know – and I have wings. The mortals that see us fill in the blanks, usually with flaming swords and thundering voices.

Sorry, I digressed a bit there. Where was I? Oh yeah, walking down the street. So like I said, it was a beautiful day. I was walking with my hands in my pockets, a bit of vampire goo in my left one, smiling, and, most importantly, minding my own business. You can never overlook the importance of simply minding your own business. If you don't, then you may find yourself in quite a lot of trouble. In my line of work, I could easily find myself dead. I always prefer not finding myself dead. It puts a terrible damper on the day.

# Ragged Edge

I knew the day was going too well. I hadn't argued with my shrink, no immediate threats on my life, and I was feeling happy. That's when I made a fateful mistake. I whistled. Never whistle when you're happy; the universe sees it as a challenge. A man appeared beside me. Normally, I don't care when people appear beside me, ghosts pose me no threat and, to be honest, I'm not always very observant of my surroundings. He appeared beside me, mimicking my tuneless whistle. He was an irritatingly good mimic.

His hands where in his pockets, like mine, there was a certain attitude in his walk, a little something that said he was happy and didn't care who knew it, like mine. Anyone paying attention could've mistaken us for brothers. I don't have any brothers, at least none that I know of. His outfit was pure business casual: black loafers, black slacks, pure white polo shirt. In short, disgusting.

"Having a good day, Sean?" His voice was eerily Walkin-esque, a strange lilt that made even regular conversation just a little creepy.

"I was, Darius." I replied, on my guard.

"What seems to have changed?"

"Well I was by myself, now you're here. No offense but I don't consider that a change for the better."

"I'm sorry you feel that way Sean. However, if you would return my calls, then I wouldn't have to be here and both of our days would look brighter." He was a patronizing bastard.

# Ragged Edge

Darius Sturmguard: trainer, mentor, coach, tormentor, patronizing bastard. He was my supervisor, a senior guardian, and a gift from the depths of Hell.

"I listened to your messages and I checked into the events you mentioned. They are all taken care of," I assured him with a smile.

"Is that so?" His eyebrow cocked when he looked at me.

"It is."

"Well then, would you mind explaining to me the manner in which they were taken care of?"

"As if you don't know."

"Exactly. Explain it as if I don't know." A hint of anger tinged his words.

"OK, so maybe not taken care of as such, but there was hardly a need for me."

We walked down the streets unnoticed, which was nice. I wasn't keen on any more attention than Darius'.

"So explain yourself, Sean." He reached out and grabbed my wrist. The scene around us began to swirl as he transported me with him. Now you may not understand this but try to stick with me. We have multiple forms of travel available to us just like you humans. We can walk, ride a bike, and drive a car – all of that is perfectly normal. We can fly, though most of us avoid it in cities. Too many buildings. We can also translocate. It's a sort of teleportation I guess you could say. Mostly we just step from one location to another and it takes just a fraction of a second. We can take other people with us and sometimes do, though doing so without permission is seen as exceedingly rude.

# Ragged Edge

My apartment replaced the street surrounding us. Not the place I would've chosen but I wasn't driving. I have a small apartment and decorated it in a style I refer to as single, thirty-something, crash pad. A broken down but comfortable sofa, wall-dominating flat screen television, and scratched and scuffed coffee table. An empty golden birdcage and a king size bed rounded out the main portion of the room. The fridge was placed conveniently beside the bed and started the kitchen. The only other room was the bathroom.

Darius stood in front of the TV. I was on the sofa.

"Look, Darius, did you even research those places. I mean, seriously?"

"Yes, I did research. I know exactly where I told you to go, the important people involved, and the reason for you going."

"Well yeah, but did you stop to see if I was needed?"

"You are a junior guardian; I wouldn't send you if you weren't needed!" Did I say there was a hint of anger in his voice?

"Well, OK, well, fine, you say that but seriously? First you told me to go to Maine, which might I say is a mean thing to do in the winter."

"But you didn't go so it doesn't matter."

"Well now don't be hasty. I popped in and guess what I found?"

"What did you find, Sean?"

"I found that the people of Maine are almost as strong as we are. They are accustomed to dealing with the exceedingly strange. I think they even enjoy it. So who am I to take away their fun?"

"Fun?"

"Yeah fun. If they enjoy the strangeness, why should I ruin it for them?"

"People died, Sean."

I stood up glaring at him.

"People always die, Darius. It's what these humans are good for. I can't save them all and really don't see why we should with the way they reproduce."

"How about because it's your job to save them. Your life is guarding them. At your age I shouldn't have to remind you of that simple fact." Patronizing. I think he thought it was fatherly but it was patronizing. I hate being patronized.

"What about Chicago, why didn't you go there?"

"That's easy. They have a wizard."

"What?"

"A wizard, you know, one of those advanced humans. They can tap into the world's powers? At your age I shouldn't have to explain this." I smirked at him. I'm a wonderful smirker. He chose to answer my smirk with a teeth-shattering backhand I never saw coming. I fell back onto the couch, clutching my jaw.

"I know full well what a wizard is, you petulant child. So you are telling me that you abdicated your duties to a human?"

"No, he is a wizard."

"He is still a human, stronger than most, but still human."

"He had it under control and didn't need my interference." Darius took a deep breath, calming himself.

"Sean, do you know why you are still a junior guardian?"

"Because, I'm incredibly good at it, and you love having me around." It was a shot in the dark. At my age I should've been a senior guardian or a trainer long before now.

"I won't approve you're promotion, Sean."

"Why not?" I honestly wanted to know but mostly I didn't want to talk.

"You are immature, arrogant, lazy, and, most important, you don't care."

"What do you mean I don't care? I'd love to be promoted, preferably to a trainer. I'm tired of living among these humans."

"Do you have any close human friends, Sean?"

I laughed. I tried to stop it but I couldn't help it. Darius could help it though. One of these days I'll learn how he moves so fast.

"I don't want any." I said, rubbing the other side of my face.

"Then you have a problem. You know you cannot be promoted without mating."

"Oh, I have no problems mating. Plenty of women will let you do that for the right price." I knew that wasn't what he meant but I hated this subject.

"That's not what I mean and you know it. You must have offspring. You must mate with a human and help raise that offspring until it becomes one of us."

"I know that, but what's the point. There are others happy to shackle themselves to a human. Why should I?"

"That is exactly what you need to learn before I approve your promotion."

Silence fell between us. He walked around the apartment, a short walk, and settled staring out a window onto the street below us.

"Sean, I am giving you you're last assignment." His gaze never left the window.

"What do you mean last?" I got up from the sofa and slowly approached him.

"I mean that if you do not complete this assignment, successfully, then I have no choice."

"No choice about what?"

"I have assigned you for final death." His shoulders slumped forward. His reflection in the windowpane showed his eyes closed.

"But . . ." I was speechless.

"I have to obey my orders just like you do."

"So the assignment, what is it?"

"You will leave this city, you will move to Kansas..."

"What? No way. Kansas?"

"You will go." More than anger, a threatening growl settled into his voice. He was serious.

"Why?"

"You will meet me at the residence of a Dr. Hillerman."

"Dr. Hillerman?"

"A professor of archeology. She has stumbled upon an artifact that has placed her in imminent danger. She knows of us."

"What?" This was almost unheard of.

"She knows of us. It seems she is particularly studious and has found our influence in more than a few places. I have told her that you will be coming to protect her."

"Bodyguard. Instead of guarding the entire race, you want me to protect just one woman?"

"Yes, Sean, I want exactly that and you will do it. Or you will die. Choose wisely and choose quickly." He faced me, wings spreading. His face shifted, nose and mouth elongating into a sharp eagle-like beak. He grew both in muscle and height. His hands sharpened into talons.

"Choose." No accent accompanied the statement. This was pure snarl.

"Fine, I'll go," I said bowing my head to him. There was a brief flutter of wind and I looked to find myself alone.

"Kansas. Just fucking great," I said as I grabbed the golden birdcage and my apartment began to shift around me.

# CHAPTER 2

As my apartment swirled around me, I allowed my body to shift. My kind have many different forms that allow us to perform our specific functions. Darius had shifted his to threaten me and I was doing the same thing. I figured, if I was going to have to protect a human, I may as well scare her with my fighting form. The physiological changes that take place are spectacular and sometimes painful. Darius is closely bonded with the eagles, but I'm more of a raven man myself. As my body shifted, my face took on the appearance of a rather large raven head, wings sprouted from my shoulder blades, hands and feet formed into sharply clawed black talons. My clothes melded into me. My musculature tightened on my skeletal frame while growing in bulk. In this form I am a fighting machine capable of ripping the throats from my enemies with one well-timed swipe of my talons. Although the timing in a fight is rarely good.

# Ragged Edge

During the change in form and location, I focused on Darius. He had told me to meet him at the residence of Dr. Hillerman. He neglected to tell me exactly where that residence was. So I transported myself to his exact location, or at least the general area around his exact location. OK, to be truthful, I showed up in the good doctor's house. Darius was outside. As the scene around me resolved itself into a well appointed living room complete with leather sofa, glass and metal coffee table, hardwood floors, and a black marble fireplace, I heard the telltale eagle cry that Darius emits while fighting, the shriek of a woman properly frightened, and the crash of a glass tumbler. From the smell I'd say the tumbler had been full of scotch.

I turned to my left and saw the doctor for the first time. I had expected an old wrinkled up hag of a doctor. I got a well-proportioned, medium height girl-next-door type of doctor. It was a pleasant surprise that I didn't have time for, not to mention I wasn't dressed to be courting my charge. I stood staring at her; outside, I could hear the unmistakable sounds of a pitched battle. Slowly, I leaned down and placed the birdcage on the glass table.

"Don't touch that." My voice came out rough and semi-high pitched. I was an overgrown raven after all.

She stared at me without replying. Under the circumstances, I thought that showed a strong character beneath the shock. Another eagle shriek pierced the air. I replied with a caw of my own and rushed to the door. Did you know that large talons aren't the best appendages for opening a door? I could've broken through it but considered that rude. I looked back towards the doctor and yelled, "Open!" She rushed over and turned the knob, opening the door. You can push open a screen with talons.

I hurried outside and took to the air. The battle was roughly a block away and moving further away. Darius hated fighting within a city. It attracted unwanted attention and we do like to keep ourselves hidden in the background. It looked like he was harassing his foes, keeping their attention on him and leading them away from the doctor's house. As for the foes, I didn't know what the hell they were. Their bodies were distinctly wolf like, yet also human, they alternated between running in bipedal movement and on all fours. Well, I've seen werewolves before so that wouldn't have surprised me, but all resemblance to werewolves ended at the neck. Their heads were truly gruesome given the circumstances: strong green armored skulls with the long jaws of an alligator. So I guess maybe they were were-alli-wolves or wolf-agators?

The important thing was that they were giving Darius a run for his money. Sure he hadn't fully opened up on them. He still had a ways to lead them to get out of the city. Lucky for us the doctor lived on the outskirts of town and not in the center. I headed in their direction as fast as my wings would carry me. I raked my talons along the back of the wolf-gator closest to me, felt the dingy matted fur grabbing at my talons and the strong armored skin underneath the fur digging into me as my claws dug into it. It was like raking them against a gravel road. The alli-wolf let out a piercing howl of pain as I shot into the air and out of the reach of its vice-like jaws. Darius shrieked again as he dove for a quick attack on the creature closest to him. I looked at my talons. I was bleeding. Anger rose in my gut. We continued leading the foul beasts in a southern direction where an open field was in front of us. Without speaking, Darius and I headed to the field.

A barbed-wire fence surrounded the field. Darius and I flew over it, and the wolf things jumped it. When inside the field's barrier, Darius shot vertically upward and came down with a flaming sword in his hands, large eagle wings being the only visible difference between him and a human. The sword severed through the neck of the last wolf-gator to enter the field. I wasn't anxious to put my claws into another armored back, so I formed a diamond with my hands, index fingers and thumbs touching. Boiling red energy appeared in the opening.

This part is hard to describe, the energy was like plasma contained in the shape formed by my hands. It looked like a rolling cloud of fire. I blew through the diamond and sent a jet of flame heading directly at the wolf-gator closest to me. In hindsight, I should have just used my claws. The fire burnt through the dingy hair covering the wolf-like body. The wolf-gator howled in pain but barely slowed.

To say that the smell of burnt dog hair filled my nose and the sight of a gator head attached to the now-bald wolf-shaped, gator-armored body gave me pause is an understatement. To be closer to the point, I received grass stains to my chin from my jaw dropping.

# Ragged Edge

It's not often I freeze in battle but I think this time I had a good excuse. I mean, imagine an alligator shaped like a wolf? Exactly, now pick your jaw up. The wolf-gator took advantage of my mental stutter and leapt at me, jaws wide open and aimed towards my neck. Reflexively, I put my talons in front of me.

All right, so it was less reflex and more pants-shitting scared blind defense. The creature hit me like a two-ton cannonball. I flew back roughly six feet before falling over, the wind knocked out of me. The thing reeked of burnt hair, rotted breath, and, surprisingly, swamp water. As my back hit the ground I felt a warm viscous liquid pour down my arms as an unbearable howling cry filled the night air.

My talons were pushed through the soft underbelly of the thing. I wiggled my fingers and the thing writhed in pain, its claws scratching at my midsection and forcing a shriek of pain from my lips. It was like having razor blades slice through me or a million paper cuts appearing at once. It seriously fucking hurt is what I'm trying to say. I rolled onto my side and removed my talons from the thing's guts. Thick gelatinous black fluid pumped from its belly as it lay dying. I stood watching it transform into the shape of a lovely young woman as Darius dispatched the last of the creatures. I allowed my own form to revert to its natural human-like shape.

I would like to say that I was no worse for the wear but who am I kidding, I just had my ass handed to me, and the serving platter was most definitely silver. I tried wiping my hands on my pants to get the thick black ichor off them. I wasn't positive but I was pretty sure having that thing's blood mix with mine wasn't a good thing. In short, I felt like I had been hit by a truck. Then it backed up and hit me again.

"What the fuck?" I yelled towards Darius, holding my midsection.

"They were waiting for me outside the doctor's house," he replied, unreasonably calm in my opinion.

"Good to know. What the hell are they?" I asked, a little shakily to be honest.

"Enemies, Sean." He really can be a bastard.

"Great. Who sent them?"

"The one who seeks to kill the doctor and recover the artifact."

"And that would be?"

"Another enemy Sean. I cannot give you all of the answers or you will not learn. Now, let's go meet the doctor."

"What about the bodies?" I asked.

"Watch," he replied, pointing at the nearest corpse.

I looked and watched as it seemed to age before my eyes. The skin quickly drying, wrinkling, and blowing away like so much dust. In a matter of minutes the corpse was gone.

"Hnh," I muttered.

"You get used to it." Darius said and started walking out of the field. I followed, holding my injured midsection as blood oozed between my fingers.

# Ragged Edge

I found myself sitting on the leather sofa that I noticed upon my initial appearance, my feet propped on the coffee table. Darius and the doctor were talking and ignoring my presence. I was fine with this. I had taken the torn and bloody shirt off and was examining my wounds. The wolfengators had torn into my stomach more than I thought and it felt like raw hamburger. Looked pretty similar also.

"I hate to be a bother here but, well, I am slightly injured," I spoke up quietly.

"Come on, Sean, you look fine to me," Darius said.

"Oh yeah, I really enjoy walking around with my guts hanging out. It's not uncomfortable in the slightest."

"Quit being a baby."

"Doc, I expect him to be a bastard, would you mind taking a look?" I tried for a smile; the good doctor's face told me I failed.

"I'm sorry. I'm not that kind of doctor," she said. Her voice was smooth and held a slight English accent.

"Sure you are. Dr. Hillerman, outstanding doctor of archeology. Well you happen to have a seven hundred-year-old artifact bleeding on your couch. Wanna do something about it?"

"I see no blood on my couch."

I could tell I was going to receive no sympathy from the pair of them, so I wiped my bloody hands on the couch.

"There, see? Blood on your couch. Now get me some damn towels or something so I can clean this mess up." I was losing my patience at this point. The doctor's mouth fell open as she turned and walked out of the room, presumably to get the towels.

"Now that we're rid of her, tell me Darius, what kind of danger am I in here?"

"Not mortal, at least not right now. Those wounds will heal just fine."

"Not what I meant."

"I thought not. Unfortunately, it's all I can tell you. When the doctor comes back the proper introductions shall be made and then I must leave. I've assisted you too much already."

"Too much already? Too much already!? Are you shitting me? You've told me nothing other than to show up here, and when I do I find you fighting three wolfengators, or whatever the fuck those were, and then I damn near get eviscerated. After all of that I get to watch what was once, presumably, a beautiful young woman fade to ash. With no explanation or help from you!"

"I did help you walk back here," he said with a smile.

"Oh gee, thank you so much for going so far out of your way to assist me, great captain."

"Don't push it, Sean. Remember, final death." The last word came out with an unmistakable threat to it. Darius was like that, sometimes I never knew if he liked me or seriously wanted me dead.

The doctor entered the room carrying a few towels. She paused at the door, sensing the tension in the air. I stood and walked slowly over to her, taking the towels from her hands. Darius spoke as I started wiping the blood off my midsection.

# Ragged Edge

"Dr. Ilsy Hillerman, though you've already met under most unfortunate circumstances, allow me to formally introduce—"

"Marcus Davidson at your service," I interrupted, bowing with a flourish while throwing the towels at Darius.

"Sean!" Darius shouted, the eagle scream lurking at the back of his voice. Apparently I really was trying his patience. Good.

"Fine, Sean Gryphon also at your service," I said with a glare at Darius.

"Your stomach," she said

I looked at my bare stomach. Aside from a few smears of blood, it was back to normal.

"Pretty neat, huh?" I asked, winking.

The doctor slouched to the floor. I guess maybe she wasn't ready for the entire truth of us. I don't know about the rest of her day but surely the past hour or so had been pretty stressful.

🐦🐦🐦

A few minutes later we had the doctor awake and sitting on the couch. Yes, the one I had just wiped blood on. She still seemed a bit woozy but I was pretty sure she'd make it the rest of the night.

"So," Darius said, "Dr. Hillerman, you've now met Mr. Gryphon. Please excuse his personality but he really is the best we have to guard you." He stopped and thought about this for a moment. "Or at least the best we have available at the moment."

"That's reassuring, thank you." Sarcasm laced her voice. This one had a backbone; I liked it.

"My pleasure. Now I'll leave you two alone. Sean, if you need any help please, hesitate to ask." He turned to leave.

"Wait, whoa, hold on, that's it?" I asked incredulously.

"What more do you want? Don't let her die, protect the artifact, and avoid dying. It's not that difficult, Sean."

"Ok, so what is this artifact? What am I protecting her from – other than wolfengators? And what happens if I die?"

"She will show you the artifact, you will protect her from any threat to her life, and I'm sure I needn't explain final death." Sometimes I really hated Darius.

"See, that's where I have a problem. Final death? Is this that serious? I mean no offense to the doc but can she really be that important? Wouldn't it make more sense for me to just protect this artifact thing?"

"Sean, the good doctor is more important than you realize now. Don't worry, my boy, I'm sure you'll figure it out. Now I must bid you farewell." With that he turned and stepped through the door. He has a flare for the dramatic on occasion. I turned back to the living room and collapsed in an armchair facing the doctor. She was staring at the golden birdcage I had brought with me. I let the silence surround us while I sized her up.

Like I said before, she was good looking. Curled raven-black hair framed her face. Her skin was fair except where freckles had popped up from too much time in the sun. There was strength evident in her hands and arms. Her eyes were as green as the Irish hillsides and some of the sharpest I had seen from a human, and she carried herself with a certain je ne sais quoi that projected unquestionable self-confidence. I had a feeling this woman didn't miss much, and from the attitude she had already shown, I knew she was going to be a handful.

"Why the cage?" she asked softly.

"Do you have many friends or family that like to visit?" I asked.

"Family no, but I do entertain friends."

"And do you have a boyfriend currently living with you?"

"No."

"So if one of your friends were to drop by sometime, how would you explain me?"

"You could be a visiting scholar or a relative that dropped by for a visit. Does it matter?"

"Or I could be a raven, in a birdcage, like a pet. At any rate, I need the cage. I didn't have time to search for a place to live while I'm babysitting you–"

"Excuse me!" She sat up straighter. I had struck a nerve.

"Fine, while I'm protecting you. Better? Anyway, I have spare clothes, weapons, armor, and research materials in the cage."

Her mouth fell open as she stared at the cage. Other than being golden it didn't look like anything extravagant enough to hold more than a bird, a few perches, food, water, and maybe some toys for the bird to play with. I thought about explaining how it worked but it was more amusing watching her try to figure it out.

"So, I will take up as little room in your house as I can, and you will listen to me and stay out of as much trouble as you can. Then, as soon as I can figure out what is coming for you and what this artifact is about, I can get rid of them and we can go back to our normal lives. Sound like a deal?"

"I take orders from no one." Attitude. I was quietly impressed though. She had already seen that I was anything but human and she still had enough testicular fortitude to stand up to me.

"Who said anything about orders? I just said listen to me. Though if you are attacked you will follow any orders I give you until we are out of danger."

"Look Mister 'I'm Too Good for This,' I didn't ask for you to guard me. I didn't ask to find this damnable artifact, and I didn't ask for your kind to get involved in my life." I could hear anger rising in her voice. That happens to me a lot.

"Are you sure?"

"What do you mean, am I sure? In the past few hours, I have had dogs with alligator heads try to break into my house, I watched a man turn into a seven-foot eagle and fight them, and then the Mothman appears in my living room..."

"Mothman?"

"That's what you looked like."

"Yeah, if you just look at the black feathers, but were my eyes glowing red? No, I don't think so. Believe me, if he was assigned to you, you'd be even more miserable."

# Ragged Edge

"Wait, he's—"

"Not one of us, no. Now please continue telling me how hard your life is right now."

"You smeared blood on my couch." There was venom in her voice now.

"I did ask for help first."

"Be that as it may, I still didn't ask for this and, yes, I am sure I didn't ask."

"Then maybe when you figured out that my kind exist, you should've stopped digging. Now the world is much bigger than you can comprehend and not everything in it is friendly. How did you find out about us anyway?" I was curious on this point. I mean we've been around for as long as humans, maybe longer, and yet very few humans ever find out about us.

She quietly stood and crossed the room to a bookshelf filled with old, well-maintained volumes. I thought she either had a maid or obsessively cleaned the place. She took down a book that appeared much newer than all the others and set it on the table in front of me.

"Those are my research notes. I started it as a hobby; it doesn't take much historical study to see similarities between all the different cultures. I just wanted to see where all the links were. Strictly personal you understand, professionally I'd probably be laughed out of the field. The research was like a game of cultural connect the dots. I started with the Sumerians and worked my way up. I didn't find out that my research was correct until after I found the artifact and Darius showed himself to me."

# Ragged Edge

I opened the book and read through her notes. The doc was meticulous in her research; the scary part is that most of it was right. In the old days, we frequently got mistaken for gods and the humans wrote about us. Sometimes their writings were about specific individuals like the Egyptian Horus, the Mayan Hurukan, and the Hindu Garuda. Sometimes they just lumped a few of us together such as the Sumerian Ahura Mazda. None of her research pointed to where we came from; it only showed that we had always been with humanity guiding, protecting, teaching, and on occasion destroying. We aren't all fond of the human race; there are those of us that believe humans should be as slaves to us. Those ignorant fools never think about the sheer numbers. Worldwide, there are maybe only a couple thousand of us, whereas humans number into the billions. Yes, we are stronger, yes, we can travel through space and time, and yes, we can do many fabulous and wonderful things. That said there are humans that can do some of the same things we can, their numbers out stretch ours, and you can kill almost anything with enough pissed off people and pitchforks.

She left the room and came back with a bottle of wine and two glasses while I read the notes. I was simply amazed at the work she had put into the research.

"I am stunned. You really traced us through all of this," I said as she poured the wine and sat back down on the couch.

"Like I said, cultural connect the dots. More than a few friends thought I was a little fruity, but I started with the simple basis that almost all cultures had bird-shaped gods, or beings with wings, fairies, angels, that kind of thing. So I decided there had to be a reason and started connecting the dots. Honestly though, it would've never amounted to anything without Darius. He confirmed my speculations and helped me figure out who was who. The one question I still have is, well, what the hell are you guys?"

"I don't quite think you're ready for that yet. Also, right now it's not important. What is important is this artifact. I'm going to need to see it if I have any hope of figuring out what we are up against."

Silently she stood and left the room. She was gone for about ten minutes then reentered the room carrying a metal box the size of a footlocker with a large padlock on it. She set it down, unlocked it, and opened it to reveal an antique-looking wooden chest. The musty scent of the ages rose up to my nose as it bloomed from the box. She reached in and carefully slid out the chest. This she set on the edge of the table and opened. Whatever was inside was wrapped in dark red velvet cloth.

"Did you put the cloth around it?" I asked.

"No, I found it that way, in the wooden chest. I know the velvet doesn't fit with its apparent age. That's not the only thing either."

"What do you mean?" I asked as she slowly unwrapped the cloth.

Inside the cloth lay a large vellum manuscript roughly three-feet long, a bit over a foot wide, and looked to contain about ten pages. "Where was this dig?"

# Ragged Edge

"That's the odd part. It was at a dig just outside of Shercock in Ireland. We thought we just had another Celtic settlement. This was found in what appeared to be a meeting hall of some type. The only thing I know for sure is that this thing had no business being there."

"The Codex Gigas," I said to myself as I reached out to grab the artifact. As my hands grasped it there was a thunderclap inside my head and the room went black. I felt as if a hook embedded in my frontal lobe was pulling me forward.

# CHAPTER 3

So there I was, everything was dark as if I had gone blind with a hook in my frontal lobe. To describe the feeling as pain would be doing it a gross injustice. Electrical bolts of screaming, piercing, stabbing pain racked through my body. I had no sense of time or space only a great sense of wishing for death. I have no idea how much time passed before the bolts of pain stopped, no idea when I first became aware of light around me. It was so gradual as to pass almost unnoticed.

I became aware of forms surrounding me. At least twenty shadowy shapes were in a loose circle with me and one other form in the center. They were chanting in a language I didn't recognize. The lack of recognition of the words did nothing to ease their foreboding tone. Every one of my instincts formed over hundreds of years screamed at me in one enormous voice: "DANGER!" For once, I agreed. I tried looking for a way out but beyond the shadows everything became foggy and darker. I tried to shift into my fighting form again. Nothing happened. I felt panic start to rise: a large acidic knot in the back of my throat, a ceaseless quivering weakness in my muscles. I hadn't even started my mission and I was already going to die. A warm fluid ran down my leg. I'm pretty sure I was so scared that I managed to cry my pants.

I was helpless. My entire being screamed for me to run away but I lacked any method to make that happen. I noticed the chanting was growing quieter. The figure sharing the center with me moved. I tried to jump back and couldn't. It's arms slowly rose towards it head. I could see its hands, or maybe claws. The fingers where bone thin, long, so white there couldn't have been any blood in them, and tapered into sharp pointed nails. The knuckles creaked as the perverted imitations of hands grasped what appeared to be a black hood and started pulling it back. I did not want to see under that hood. I tried squeezing my eyes shut. I felt my eyes shut. I still saw everything.

The hood moved back and revealed a bald head, the skin stretched so thin I could see the bones of the skull, even the lines where those bones met each other. The head was slowly moving up. I did not want to see this thing's face. I didn't have a choice. Dark pockets surrounded the red tinged eyes with large black pupils. A warthog like snout spewed tendrils of smoke. I started screaming because of the mouth, a long, forceful, silent scream. My lungs were going to burst if I didn't take a breath. I couldn't stop screaming and yet no sound ever left me. All I could hear was that damnable chanting. This thing in front of me had a normal mouth. Plump, violent red lips arranged in a grin. The eyes focused on me, and the grin widened into a smile.

From far away I heard my voice. It was still screaming. My throat felt like it was tearing from the endless silent scream. I felt more moisture run down my leg. Then I heard the thing speak.

"It is found." Its voice was nearly silent, like two sheets of sandpaper rubbing together. My scream stopped, my knees unhinged and I collapsed into the puddle of my tears.

The thing looked at me, raising its clawed hands to attack. I could only curl into a ball and watch as it knelt in front of me. My eyes attached themselves to its claws and my mind screamed its last word as it swung those claws toward my neck, "Demon!" I felt its claws tear into my neck. The world faded to black and I finally heard my scream in full force.

My ears were filled with the sound of screams. My throat felt as though I had swallowed a mouthful of glass shards. I felt my body quiver and two red stings of pain flashed across my face. My scream began to go silent, my chest felt near exploding. Then I heard the most beautiful, most awe-inspiring sound I had ever heard in my life. It was the simplest thing ever, yet more beautiful than the best poetry ever written. A sound that would make angels bow to their knees and weep.

# Ragged Edge

"Sean!" The sound was a voice.

"Sean!" The sound was my salvation.

"Sean!" The sound was my doom.

My eyes slowly opened, my vision was blurred.

"Sean!" A vague form stood in front of me. I jumped back away from it. All at once I became aware of several things: I was sitting in a chair that was toppling over backwards, I was back in Ilsy's house, she had been screaming my name, the artifact was no longer in my hands, and, finally, I knew this would be my last mission. I was going to die protecting this woman. Then my head hit the hardwood floor as the chair finished its backwards toppling.

"Fucking great," I mumbled, staring up at the ceiling.

I rolled myself out of the chair and stood it up. Ilsy was staring at me. I could see mild panic in her eyes. After the events of the evening I wasn't really surprised. Some humans have a remarkable ability to adjust to strange situations. Most do, to be honest. But there is always a limit and I believed we were reaching hers. Without a word I guided her to the couch, sat her down, and handed her a glass of wine. Walking back to the chair I saw a puddle on the floor, which explained why my pants were wet. I stared at it for a moment.

"Huh," I grunted.

"Some protector you are," she said quietly. I glanced at her, dismayed. A frown graced my face. I had to nod ascent. I'm sure none of my actions over the past few hours inspired her confidence in me. I appeared as an overgrown birdman. Okay, point in my favor on that one. I looked fearsome on our first meeting. Then I showed back up nearly eviscerated and hands looking as though I had put them through a meat grinder. Point against. Then I rubbed blood on her couch – not really a point either way but terribly rude in retrospect. A minor argument with Darius, followed by a fainting spell and crying my pants. I sat down.

"I can't believe you would say that." No reason to say I agreed with her.

"You pissed on my bloody floor." I sensed a bit of incredulousness in her voice.

"I didn't piss on your floor. If you were to taste that puddle it would be salty, as in tears. I was a bit scared." No sense denying the fear. "Don't lick it though, terribly unsanitary." No reason to test the crying theory.

"I wasn't going to. Can you call Darius back?"

"Yes."

"Good."

"But I won't." She stared at me angrily.

"I'm dead," she said. This was rhetorical and mostly to herself.

"Nope, you're still breathing, heart is still beating, and I assume your brain is still functioning, as well as normal anyway."

"Now listen, asshole. You come in here, scare the crap out of me, get blood on my couch, then pass out and piss on my floor. What exactly are you going to protect me from?" Now she was angry, but she was cute angry.

"Hell," I said flatly.

"What?"

"Hell. You know, fire, eternal damnation, souls of the wicked supposedly ruled by Lucifer but actually ruled by someone much worse."

"Hell?"

"Too big of a concept? Try the underworld, Hades, or settle on Satan."

"What's the difference?"

"Hell is a place, Christian in nature, and I wouldn't suggest vacationing there. The underworld is a bit more generic almost impossible to find a good martini. Hades is more of a mixture of the two, depending on the souls you're looking for it can be a pretty swinging place, or an absolute nightmare like internet customer service. Satan is a purely Christian creation taken from bits of mythology of other cultures but probably a pretty nasty guy to deal with, not someone you'd want as a babysitter – unless you didn't like the kids anyway."

"You're nuts."

"Says the woman who has had not one, but two birdmen in her house, who, incidentally, saved her from attacking wolfengators." I raised an eyebrow at her.

"Point taken."

"Right so I know what we're up against now, thank the artifact for that. Where is your bolt hole?"

"Bolt hole?"

"Bolt hole, hiding place, safe location away from danger? Chicken coop, panic room, hidey hole?"

"I don't have one." She sounded confused. Sometimes even the smart humans mystify me.

"Fine, we'll use mine, so new plan." I stood and grabbed the artifact off the coffee table, taking care to only touch the velvet cloth as I placed it back in its chest.

"What's the plan, fearless protector?" Man, she could be snide.

"Gather some clothes; we're going on a trip."

"Where?"

"To my bolt hole. Haven't you been paying attention?" My turn for incredulousness.

"Where is your bolt hole?"

"My apartment, but its out of state. It'll take awhile for them to find you and will give me time to find them. So come on, pack and let's go. Do you have a car?"

She stood and glared at me with her hands on her hips. I know she was pissed, but this pose made her incredibly sexy. Some women are like that. But in seven hundred years, I have at least learned that telling them they are sexy like this is a bad idea.

"Out of state? You really are nuts. I don't know you. I accept that you aren't human, fine, great even. Sure, I'm in danger from those dog alligator things..."

"Wolfengators."

"Whatever! The point is they showed me I'm not safe, but for all I know you and Darius could've sent them, and now you expect me to drive with you out of state. Are you fucking crazy?"

"My shrink would say I am, but I'm fairly sure he's wrong. Now let me break down the facts for you. Fact One: you uncovered the missing pages of the Codex Gigas or, if you like, the Devil's Bible. Fact Two: you are now being hunted by something. Fact Three: you would already be dead or a prisoner if not for Darius and I. Fact Four: of course I don't expect you to drive out of state. I'm driving. Last but not least, Fact Five: if you die, I die. Now pack a bag and let's go." I don't remember standing, nor do I remember allowing my wings to appear. It did help her calm down though.

"What do you mean, if I die you die?" she asked picking up her wine glass and walking from the room. I followed her down a dark hallway. I hadn't seen much of her house but she seemed to be fond of dark woods and apparently detested carpet.

"I mean what I said. Darius assigned me for final death. If I fail this mission, I'm done." She stopped and turned to look at me.

"Final death?"

"Look, I would love to stand here all night, drink your wine, and explain every detail of my race, but we don't have time for that. Will you please pack your bags?"

"I'll pack, you talk."

"Will it make this go faster?"

"Sure."

"Fine."

☐

# CHAPTER 4

"As you know, my race lives a very long time. I suppose to you humans, we live forever. You have to first understand that our physical appearance is not related to our real age. So physically I look in my thirties, which is pretty good for being seven hundred. Now, also understand that our physical age is not related to our real age. So, my physical age is seven hundred–"

"What's your real age?"

"I don't remember."

"How could you not?" she asked curious.

"You tend to lose track after awhile. Now hush, I'm not done." I hadn't even explained all of this to my shrink. The upside is that she was at least packing now. Her room was almost monastic in appearance. Bed, table, table lamp. At least the closet showed some color and was almost full.

# Ragged Edge

"Alright, in our first life we are raised amongst our people and have a short lifespan, usually only about fifty years. Then we die of old age. This is first death. Most of us make it through this first life with no problem. It's spent learning about our people, and the world around us. After first death our souls completely absorb all of the information we learned. So our first death is like a rest period. At this point we have little in the way of individuality. Our second life is spent amongst humans learning about your race and how you see the world around you. Generally in that life, we have an overall goal to achieve that is supposed to advance the human race in some way."

"So you grow up around us and then change our history?"

"No, we grow up around you and change your future. Usually for the better but sometimes, well, bad things happen. You weren't quite ready for nuclear power but Albert didn't know that. Then of course your race mostly ignored Tesla."

"Wait, so are you saying Einstein and Tesla were one of you?"

"Two of us, on their second lives. I could list them all night if you wanted but really it'd be very boring."

"Why?"

"Well it'd just be a list of names, most you'd recognize, some you wouldn't."

"No, I mean why affect our race?"

"For most of our lives it's our purpose. You have incredible evolutionary potential. Sometimes you just need a nudge. Now can I finish?"

"Yeah, go ahead." She sounded distracted.

"So after reaching our purposes, we die a second time and absorb that knowledge. Then comes our third life. This one is the longest with no set time frame. We usually die in battle. That's the life I'm on right now, technically. Within our third life we can die multiple times. Our purpose varies from individual to individual."

"What's your purpose?" she asked while zipping a suitcase.

"Right now? I'm a junior guardian. My job is to protect you guys from things like the wolfengators. Imagine it. Every fantasy creature you have ever heard about either exists or has at some point. I fight everything that would give you nightmares. I'm pretty good at it too, that's why I've lived so long. However, if I had been killed at some point it wouldn't have mattered much, my soul and knowledge would've been reborn into a new body and I would've continued with my purpose. In my field this would continue until I earned a promotion to either senior guardian or trainer, like Darius. In theory this continues until we become Elders. Most of us never make it to Elder. While there are thousands of us running around in our third lives and beyond, we only have twelve Elders at any one time."

"Alright, so it sounds to me like you are immortal."

"No, we can be assigned for, or choose, final death. Darius has assigned me for final death and the Elders have approved it. That means if I die while protecting you, I won't be reborn into a new body. My soul will move on to, well, whatever comes next. If I fail to protect you, then Darius will kill me. Same result." I stared at the floor while explaining this.

"So our lives are tied together," she said. I raised my head and looked into her eyes.

"Exactly. This is why I'm the best possible protector for you. Having my life on the line also ensures I will do everything in my power to keep you safe. Ready to go?" I asked cheerily.

"I guess," she said with a tone of resignation. I grabbed her bags and nodded towards the door.

"Lead the way, Doc."

We left her bedroom and headed towards the front door, pausing long enough to grab my cage and the box with the artifact. After locking up the house, she led me to a light blue Prius parked on the curb. A cool getaway car this was not. I put her bags, my cage, and the artifact in the backseat and walked to the driver's side where Ilsy was trying to get in.

"Nope, I told you, I'm driving." I said holding my hand out for the key.

"Why should I let you drive? Just tell me where to go," she said, a steel tension in her voice.

"It's not quite that simple, Ilsy. We have to go on some back roads that you won't be able to find." I tried to keep my voice calm.

"Seriously—"

"Look, for once tonight, just trust me. I have to get you to safety now and then translate those pages." I was getting irritated, I mean, how much floundering can one person do? It was getting old fast.

"Trust you? Where are we going anyway?"

"To my place; you'll be safe there. Now give me the keys."

"Where is your place?"

"A long ways away and the sooner we leave the sooner we get there. Keys."

She stared at me a long moment then heaved a monumental sigh of frustration before handing me the keys. I slipped behind the wheel as she walked around the car. Let me tell you something, six feet four inches of unbridled manliness does not fit behind the wheel of a Prius easily. I felt like I was getting a more intimate introduction to my gentleman's area than I wanted. I waited for her door to close then started it up and pulled away from the curb. Beside me, Ilsy fumed in silent fury.

I was glad for the silence as I drove taking random turns. My kind can translocate with vehicles as well as with people. It takes a lot more concentration and I didn't want her to freak out at the world blurring around us. If we had been in a vehicle capable of more speed, I might have done things different and saved myself some effort. As it was I had to make a series of short jumps. I knew I wouldn't be able to hide the fact that we had traveled thousands of miles faster than we could've flown, but I didn't need to throw it in her face either.

From her point of view the drive was simple enough, I made a right onto a road covered in gravel, drove another few miles and made a left onto a different paved road, another right, more lefts, and soon we pulled up in front of my apartment building. One long jump would have cost me much less effort but, like I said, protecting her sanity was a bit more important than conserving my energy. Without a word I turned off the car, handed the keys back to Ilsy, and got out to grab her bags, my cage, and the artifact. The corners of my mouth curved into a small smile. No matter what you are, there is nothing better than returning home after a life-threatening battle.

I led her up the stairs to my apartment. She took in her surroundings silently but I could hear the gears turning in her head. I'm sure she knew that we had left Kansas. I think she was trying to figure out how, and I could tell she couldn't recognize the city around her. This saved some uncomfortable questions until we were safely behind closed doors. As we entered she looked around, a small look of disgust disfigured her face.

"It's not much, but it's safe," I said.

"I think a hazmat team might question that assessment," she said. Okay, so I wasn't the best at keeping a well maintained, uncluttered, clean, empty-of-pizza-boxes living space. But, hazmat? I shrugged my shoulders and walked into the kitchen space and opened a cabinet full of specimen jars. Well okay, maybe they were mason jars. I took an empty one off the shelf and removed the succubus goo from my pocket, and placed it in the jar. Replacing the jar, I looked over the rest of my collection. I fancy myself as a bit of an entomologist. Only the specimens I collected would be visible to a handful of humans, maybe. So far, my collection spanned everything from the new goo to exploding roaches.

# Ragged Edge

Ilsy watched me with a dubious silence. I can see her point, she saw me take an empty jar from the cabinet, pull nothing from my pocket and put it in to the empty jar, then put the empty jar back in the cabinet. I guess for a lot of people that would be strange behavior. After dealing with the succubus goo, I gave her the grand tour – okay, so I stood in the middle of the room and pointed to the kitchen area, the couch, the bed, and the door to the bathroom. Like I said, it wasn't much. I never needed much.

"Where are we?" she asked as I reached into the fridge for a couple of beers. I handed one to her. Between the scotch she was sipping on my arrival, the wine, and this beer, I might be able to get her mind loosened up enough to accept what was happening.

"My place in the wonderful city of Portland, Oregon," I said a bit dramatically. She collapsed on the other end of the couch.

"That's... its... we... impossible," she stammered. If she was cute when she was angry, she was downright adorable when she was befuddled.

"You might want to change your definition of that word, Ilsy," I said as I took a drink. I watched her chug her beer before looking at me, an inquisitive eyebrow cocked.

"How?"

"Quantum travel, or teleporting if you prefer that term. I like translocating myself."

"What?" she asked. My shoulders slumped. I could tell I was going to have to explain everything to her. Some humans take everything at face value. Not so much interested in how something is accomplished, only that it was accomplished.

"Alright, take the world around you, the physical world. You should realize by now, I've already said it, that world is much larger than you think. With me so far?"

"Yes... I think."

"So if you want to go from point A to point B in the physical world, like Lawrence to Portland, you can get in your car, travel about eighteen hundred miles over about twenty-five hours, right?"

"I guess."

"Okay, so we did basically the same thing only we took less time. You see, time is distance and distance is time. You cannot travel in distance without traveling in time. Even a single step takes time. Maybe the smallest fraction of a second, but still, time. And in that time you travel the distance of a single step. Now in the case of quantum travel, you are performing the same actions – in our case, getting into a car and driving. Only you are using the energy that surrounds us all to bend the time and distance that you travel. In our case we drove for about two hours and covered eighteen hundred miles. I could've done it faster but I was worried about the effect it would have on your mind."

"Thanks, I think. Can I have another beer?"

"Certainly, help yourself. Mi casa es su casa," I said, propping my feet up on my scuffed coffee table.

"So what do we do now?" she asked from the fridge.

"Well, above all else, I think sleep is needed in the immediate future."

"Sleep?" she looked around my apartment and raised an eyebrow.

"Sure, you can use the bed. I'll crash on the couch."

"You mean I'm going to sleep – here?"

"Yes, on the bed or the couch if you prefer. It doesn't really matter to me."

"It's just, I mean, in such close quarters with you?" she asked, opening the new bottle.

"Oh, I see. In your case the "p" in PhD means prude. It's not like we'll be in the same bed, only the same room," I said, chuckling. Her face flushed.

"I am not a prude! Maybe I'm not comfortable sleeping in the same room with a man I just met."

"If it makes you feel better, I'm technically not a man. I'm just male."

"What's the difference?"

"Nothing really, just pointing out that we could split hairs and remember that we are from different species."

"After sleep what comes next?" she asked, then took another long drink.

"Ideally, I will translate those pages, find whoever it is that wants it, kill them, hide the artifact, and keep you safe in the shortest amount of time possible. Then we'll part ways, you'll continue your life, and I'll continue mine. Hopefully with a promotion, and we won't have to put up with each other a second longer than necessary. Is that satisfactory?"

"Yeah, I guess," she said quietly, staring at her half empty bottle.

"Good, now make yourself comfortable. I need to run a few errands." I finished my beer and stood.

# Ragged Edge

"I thought you said you were going to sleep?"

"Uh, no. I meant sleep for you. I have a few things to do first." I turned for the door and stopped.

"Umm, one more thing, since this thing was able to track you down, well, it might, that is to say, it could have figured out where those close to you live also."

"What?" she asked, suddenly worried.

"I mean, it's not outside the realm of possibility. So if there is anyone you would like me to check on... I mean it's outside of my area of responsibility, but I could peak in on them," I said.

"How? We're in fucking Portland!" she yelled at me.

"Do I need to explain travel to you again? Just write down their addresses and I'll take a quick peak. I'm sure everyone is fine." I said trying to reassure her.

She wrote down a list of names and addresses. Thankfully, it was rather short. In truth, I was in dire need of shuteye, but I knew she wouldn't settle down with me in the apartment. The only errand I had in mind was a quick fly through the city. It's something I enjoy doing at night when nobody is likely to notice me. Now I at least had something to do.

After I took the list from her I looked down the list of names. She had told me she didn't have any family that liked to visit her, but I noticed a few that shared her last name. I decided to pass on the question and headed for the door.

"Lock this behind me; open it for nobody," I said.

"What about you?"

# Ragged Edge

"One, I have a key. Two, I don't really need to open the door. So keep it locked, and keep the windows closed. If anyone knocks just ignore it."

"What about Darius?"

"He also doesn't really need a key. Though I doubt he'll be dropping by for a chat this late. Go on, get comfortable and go to bed. I'll be back in a couple hours," I said and walked out.

I walked out of my apartment, closed the door behind me, and waited for the lock to click home. I didn't think Ilsy would ignore me, but I wasn't going to take any chances either. After hearing the lock click, I left the building. I knew I'd have to do something about her Prius. Preferably something involving a junkyard, but now wasn't the time. I needed to think, I needed to calm myself, and I needed to plan. Most of all, I needed to fly, so I walked into an alleyway.

My body changed again, not into a fighting form but into one that I preferred. Walking around as a human is fine, becoming a giant raven-looking engine of destruction is cool, but my favorite thing is to take the form of a bird and fly. If you haven't guessed, when I am a bird I am a raven, perfectly indistinguishable from any other raven. This form allows me to blend in almost anywhere, travel quickly without the energy expenditure translocation uses, and scout out a city in a few minutes. Most important, it allows me to fly unnoticed. I can fly with my wings in my human shape but it tends to draw attention. Like this, I am just another bird.

Taking to the air, my mood soared. Let me describe the feeling of flight. I've talked to a few birds and I think they'd agree with me on this. In a word, flight is orgasmic. That doesn't do it justice though. Imagine if you will that you are a bird, the wind is rushing through your feathers. It's not a violent act though. This is like a lover softly blowing on your neck. The little hairs on your neck tickle your skin and you break out in goose bumps. A shiver runs through your spine and excitement rushes all over your body. Now imagine that feeling not just on your neck but over your entire body. The immensity of the sensation hovers on the border between pleasure and pain. Along with the physical sensation of flight, you have the view, unimpeded for miles and miles in any direction you care to look. People go to the top of the Empire State building for the view. I laugh at them. Nothing compares to a bird's view.

So I flew. The city spread out before me, thousands of car lights twinkled, streets unfolded below, and the great complexity and simplicity of human life engulfed my view. The view was enough to calm my nerves so I allowed my mind to wander. When you are faced with a difficult path and don't know which way to go, the best thing to do is to take a moment and let your mind find its own way. It will almost always find the right path for you. At this point I knew a few things. First, Darius knew what I was up against but wouldn't tell me, an asshole move if you ask me. Second, whoever it was knew where Ilsy lived, so Kansas wasn't safe for us. My bolt hole was safe for now. We had a couple days at best; at worst, we'd have to leave in the morning. Third, I was going to die. I tried not to focus on this point, but the knowledge of my impending death made everything I felt and saw that much sweeter. This could possibly be the last time I got to fly over this city. Finally, I was still missing pieces of this puzzle. I knew Darius probably held them but wouldn't give them up. So I'd have to find the answers myself. Why was this artifact so important, why this girl and, most important, why me?

The answers escaped me so I decided to track down those closest to Ilsy. I knew she'd be more cooperative if she thought I was checking on their safety. That little ruse got me a list of those most important to her. Perhaps they could provide clues as to why she was so important. With that plan decided on, I landed on top of a building and became human once more. By the flashing red altitude light, I read the list. It wasn't very long, and it looked like family members were listed at the bottom. I didn't understand her priorities but decided to follow her order. I memorized her list and took to my bird form once more. I knew that once I returned I was going to be exhausted but I chose to translocate in the interest of speed.

I focused on each person in the order she had written their name. Most of the people appeared to be friends. They were scholarly in appearance, and I saw more Priuses. Aside from the danger of leading terminally boring lives, they all appeared to be safe. With friends out of the way, I proceeded to visit family.

My first jump took me to Egypt. I appeared flying above a pyramid and, to be honest, dropped a few bird bombs in surprise. The heat and bright sun assaulted me. I also realized I'd have to be more careful, a raven wouldn't blend in as well here. I spotted the target of my attention immediately. An older gentleman, dressed for a different climate in a three-piece beige suit. More shocking than his attire was the automatic weapon in his hands being aimed at what appeared to be a mummy. A late model Mercedes stood between the man and his attacker. I circled overhead and watched the scene unfold.

I saw little bursts of flame erupt from the weapon, and heard the reports echo in the air. I laughed to myself. I've fought mummies and let me tell you, guns are useless against them. You cannot shoot a corpse to death. It just doesn't work. Apparently, the gentleman knew this for I received my second shock since appearing here. I watched the mummy burst into flames. Fire does work well against corpses, especially ancient corpses. When the fire started, the mummy burned like dry tinder and was nothing but ash in a matter of minutes. The man then walked towards it and used a loafer-covered foot to spread the ashes to the wind. I had to give him credit, he knew what he was doing. I decided I needed to know more about this man so I descended in a tight circle and landed beside his car.

I chose the side he had hunkered behind because it kept me hidden from his view. I shifted back to human form and realized I wasn't exactly dressed for the weather either. I had changed when we got back to my apartment and had chosen a black pullover, and black slacks. After all, I hadn't expected to visit Egypt that night. I sat beside the car in the hot sand and waited for the man's reappearance. His shadow gave away his approach before the sound of his footsteps. In fact I never heard his footsteps. He walked gracefully and silently like a stalking cat. I looked up as his shadow grew larger and hoped I had judged his height correctly.

If I had been anyone else I wouldn't have noticed that I startled him when he rounded the car. This man was calm, collected, and much older than I initially guessed. A white beard outlined his face. His face was spectacular. The man had just killed a mummy with incendiary rounds, yet his face was graced with wrinkles in all the right places to suggest good humor. A smile appeared beneath his beard and his eyes almost popped with a mischievous joviality that took me completely by surprise.

"Hello there," he said with culture dripping from his melodious baritone voice. This man was definitely from England.

"Good afternoon, sir," I said as I rose to my feet. His head stopped at my chest.

"Please forgive my rudeness, but I'm a very busy man," he said as he walked around me and opened the back door of the car. I turned to watch as he replaced the gun in the case on the back seat.

"I take it you're not a bird watcher then?"

"No, no, no goodness me. What a thoroughly boring hobby." He shut the door and turned to face me while pulling a white handkerchief from his pocket and wiping his hands. He then offered a hand to me.

"Sir Donovan Fry, at your service."

"Sean Gryphon. Pleased to meet you."

"Of course, the pleasure is all mine." He stood staring at me for a minute. While his eyes sparkled I could tell he was thinking at a furious pace.

"I don't mean to seem rude, Mr. Gryphon"

"Sean."

"Of course. As I was saying, I am a very busy man and I must continue on my way." He moved to step around me.

"Sir, please, all I ask is a moment of your time. If you are as busy as you say perhaps you would allow me to ride with you?" He stopped and considered my request.

"Oh, alright then, climb in."

"Thank you, sir." I said with a slight bow before opening the passenger door and sliding in. I had to hand it to the Germans, they sure knew how to design a luxury car. It had all the comforts of a limo with all the strength of a tank. I sat quietly as he sat in the driver's side and pulled on a pair of black driving gloves.

"Now young man, what is it you want with me?"

"How did you know how to kill that mummy?" I asked. I have no patience for sparing with words. Given what I had seen, I knew he had to assume I wasn't human. Since he had allowed me into his vehicle, I also assumed he had decided I wasn't a threat. This meant he thought he knew what I was, or he thought he could end me as easily as he had the mummy. Either way, there was no use acting like I didn't know what he was doing there.

"May I answer your question with one of my own?"

"By all means."

"Why did you give me your real name?" This one caught me off guard. I smiled at him and did my best not to lose my composure.

"What, what do you mean?" Smooth, that's me.

"Mr. Gryphon, you cannot hide your hand after playing it openly. I have only seen two other birds appear out of thin air, land, and become human." If not for his smile and the twinkle in his eyes I would've felt threatened. Instead, I was impressed. He had marked my appearance, even while being attacked by a mummy.

"Who were they?"

"Well the first was a madame that told me her name was Morgana, but she neglected to mention her surname. I can only assume this was a false name as she didn't react to it quite the same as one reacts to their true name."

"You said she?"

"Yes, she. As in a female, and not sidhe as in a fairy."

"I got that, can you describe this female?"

"Certainly, her hair was like yours, only shinier, she stood about five foot nine, weighed probably a hundred and twenty pounds, fair figure. If I had to guess I'd put her at maybe forty. Oh and she had the most amazing blue eyes I've ever seen."

"Mother," I said.

"Ah yes, she did mention something about that," he said.

"What else did she mention?" I grumbled.

"No need for that attitude. She simply said that I might be seeing you soon, and that you are protecting my dear niece Ilsy. Such a nice girl. Though honestly I don't see why you are protecting her. She has always been perfectly capable of taking care of herself."

"Come again?"

"My dear boy, do you know nothing of her?" he sounded surprised.

"Well, I know she is in her thirties, attractive in a girl-next-door kind of way, and has an independent streak a mile wide. She holds a PhD in archeology and currently teaches at a university in Lawrence, Kansas. Or will when classes start again in the fall. I also know that right now she should be sleeping in my apartment in Portland, Oregon."

"So then you know nothing of her," he said.

"I guess not."

"Well then, you'll want to go visit her father. He should be expecting you as well. Your dear mum told me that she was visiting at least four of us and that we should all direct you to Ilsy's father. She also said that we should urge you to skip the rest of your list. What list is she talking about?" I pulled out the list Ilsy had given to me and handed it to him. He read over it, chuckling to himself.

"What's so funny?" I was starting to feel grumpy.

"I have no idea where she pulled these names from."

"What are you talking about? Those are her friends and family, the people closest to her."

"I am sure she wanted you to think that. Until just a few weeks ago she was with me here. Then she said that she absolutely must return to Ireland. She didn't go into much detail though. I was a bit worried when she said she was going to Shercock. That's where her father lives, but then she said something about an important dig. This was after she spoke to a nice looking man in the lobby of our hotel. I assumed he was a colleague."

"Can you describe him?" I asked suspiciously.

He could, and he did.

"Darius." I spit the name out without thinking.

"So you know him?"

"He is my trainer and designated tormentor."

"So the young always see it with their teachers."

"Sir Fry, do you know what I am?"

"Of course young man, why else do you think none of this shocks me?" He made a fair point.

"What about Ilsy?"

"She is a young woman, of course, though I believe you did not mean that. To answer your true question, no I do not believe she knows what you are. Though I cannot in all honesty say what she has learned from her father's notebook."

"What?" This conversation just felt wrong, normally I was the one confusing humans and not vice versa.

"Go speak to her father, young man," he said as he pulled the car to the side of the road.

"I will, thanks for the ride," I said while opening the door.

"One more thing." He grabbed my arm. "Please give him my love and tell him that Uncle Nebhotep is now resting peacefully."

"Um, sure." I said. He let go of my arm and I got out of the car and closed the door behind me. I started walking and then I shifted into the raven and flew off.

# Ragged Edge

My head was spinning as I jumped from Egypt to Shercock, Ireland. A slight drizzle was falling when I appeared and looked at the old estate below me. The hills called Ilsy's eyes to my mind. I circled down and landed on a windowsill. Her father lived in a stately mansion. Made out of stone, it looked as though it would be claimed by ivy within the next century. I looked in the window and saw a large library filled with books, a fireplace centered on one wall, and two comfortable looking chairs faced the fireplace with a small table between them. I could read some of the titles from the window. It appeared that her father liked old and rare books.

As I was looking in the window I heard a door open below me. I craned my head down to see who was coming out. I took one look and flew off the sill, changing my shape to prepare for a fight. Two of the wolfengators stalked out of the door, each taking a position to the side of a stone walk as a man stepped out. He was bald with paper-white skin. He smelled musty and his clothes were dirty. His eyes were milky white as if he were blind. I slammed to the ground with wings spread above me. The wolfengators and man were roughly thirty yards from me. They stopped and stared at me. I had landed with my right hand on a large stone, beneath my palm the stone's shape changed. I called into mind a stone sword I had seen in my grandfather's cabin, and the stone in my hand took on a rough approximation of that sword. A little longer than a short sword, the blade was finely edged and the hilt fit perfectly in my grip. I stood and walked a little closer. The gator things stared at me hissing, the man simply stood watching me with a malevolent grin on his face. I stopped and planted the sword in front of me.

"Who are you?" I asked.

"A visitor of poor Sir Hillerman." His voice infected my ears like nails on a chalkboard.

"What is your business here?"

"A friendly social call I assure you." His grin widened.

"Leave this place," I said.

"Gladly, except you seem to be blocking our path."

I stepped to the side and pointed towards the road with my left hand.

"The way is clear. Now leave."

"Very well." He started forward followed by the gators flanking him on each side.

I stood my ground with the sword ready to defend myself. The wolfengators snarled as they passed and the man chuckled. They passed behind me and continued down the walk without a glance back. Once they were out of sight I proceeded cautiously to the front door, still standing open. The hallway looked as though a bomb had exploded. Broken furniture and glass littered the floor. Paintings hung askew and the carpet bore rips and tears. I changed to my human form, keeping my wings, and entered the house.

"Mr. Hillerman!" I shouted.

# Ragged Edge

Rooms that were opened to my right and left and were in similar states of disarray. I smelled blood on the air and hoped I hadn't arrived too late.

"Mr. Hillerman!"

The house was eerily quiet and felt empty. The smell of blood told me it wasn't.

"MR. HILLERMAN!" I was now loud enough to make my voice crack.

I heard a whisper in the room to my right. It appeared to be a bedroom. This room was oddly in order, but on the bed was an old man. His face was crossed by multiple claw marks. One eye was gone the other was the shade of Ilsy's. He moved an arm. The other appeared to be attached by just a couple threads of skin.

"Mr. Hillerman?" I asked quietly. He nodded in return. I walked to his bedside. It wasn't until I was beside him that I realized he had been stripped naked. His stomach was flayed open and bleeding profusely. I lay my hands over it, a blue light flooded from them. Sweat beaded up on my forehead and the room swam before my eyes. I felt exhaustion flooding into me. The light from my hands dimmed, the wounds on his stomach were mostly closed though blood still seeped from a few open cuts. He took a large breath and blew it out.

"Thank you, good sir." His voice was barely above a whisper.

"I'm sorry," I said, looking into his eye.

"Ilsy," he said.

"She is in my care, sir."

"Bring her."

I nodded and started to leave then stopped. A blanket was folded at the foot of his bed. I used it to cover him, then tore the sleeves from my shirt and tied one around his missing eye. The other I used as a tourniquet for his almost severed arm. He nodded to me and mouthed the word thanks. I walked out of the room and jumped to my apartment.

I didn't bother with the door. I just appeared in the middle of my apartment. Street lamps lit the otherwise dark room. My body quaked with exhaustion and the room swam before my eyes. I stumbled towards my couch and collapsed onto it. I had pushed myself too far. I had to push further. Ilsy's father didn't have much time left and he wanted to see her. I had to get her to him.

"Ilsy." My attempt at her name barely qualified as a mumble. I took a deep breath and let it out slowly before trying again.

"Ilsy." I managed a bit more than a mumble but nowhere near loud enough. I listened to her soft breath on the bed. I hated waking her up for this. It had to be done.

"Ilsy." A little louder. She shifted on the bed. I took another deep breath.

"ILSY!" I managed a brief shout. She sat up on the bed frantically looking around her.

"Huh?"

"Ilsy, it's me, Sean." I tried keeping most of the fatigue out of my voice. She scratched at her head and yawned deeply. If looks could kill I wouldn't be standing here today.

"What?" she growled.

"We have to go."

"What?"

"Now, we have to go now."

"Why, where?" she was fully awake now.

"No time, just get dressed." I stood and stumbled towards the fridge. Redbull doesn't actually give you wings, but it does give you a temporary energy burst. I watched her climb out of my bed in the same clothes I left her in.

"That saves time," I said before drinking the entire can.

"What's going on?" she asked.

"No time, come here and take my arm." There was an edge to my voice that she apparently didn't want to argue with because she did as I asked with no question. I put my free hand over hers.

"This is going to be a little jarring for you, and I'm sorry but I can't help it." I summoned up all the energy I could muster and sent us to her father's house.

# CHAPTER 5

I heard a gasp and squeal as my apartment dissolved around us. I blocked it out and focused on her father's bedside. I felt a tremendous headache starting just behind my eyes and knew this was the last jump for me until I had some sleep. I'd be lucky to manage a brisk walk. Her father's bedroom started taking shape in front of us.

"Daddy?"

I ignored her and focused on finishing the jump. Normally this was something we can do without even thinking about it. Today, I had to maintain intense focus. If I let it waver it was hard telling where we would end up and in what condition. When I could feel the hard floor beneath my feet, hear the gasps of the dying man in the bed and smell the blood around us, I knew the jump was complete. I felt Ilsy's hands let go of my arm, the room went gray before my eyes and I slumped to the floor with my back against the wall and closed my eyes.

"Dad." Her voice wavered.

"Ilsy." The response was whispered.

"What happened?" she asked.

"They came for me, dear."

"Don't talk, daddy, I'll call an ambulance." I heard the tears in her voice.

"Ilsy, I'll be dead before they get here. I'm sorry dear."

I wanted to leave the room. I could've probably done it unnoticed if I could've walked. I felt wrong listening to this. I was out of place and ashamed that I could do no more for the old man.

"Daddy, what do I do? She sounded like a little girl now, no hint of the steel I knew was within her.

"You carry on, dear, you remember your education, and you trust in Sean." The old man's voice was getting weaker. I could feel Ilsy's eyes on me and I tried to shrink into myself.

"Daddy, are you sure?"

"Yes dear, it is time for you to take your place in the family. As for Sean, I wouldn't be talking to you now if not for him. He did all he could and brought you to me."

"I'm ready, daddy." Her voice cracked and she let out a heart-wrenching sob.

"So tired." His voice was barely a whisper.

I heard Ilsy's sobs as her father's breathing slowed and eventually stopped. She let out an inhuman sounding cry forcing me to open my eyes. She had thrown herself across her father's bed. I stood slowly, using the wall for support. Not knowing what to do I stepped forward and closed her dad's eye. I softly put a hand on Ilsy's back and stood beside her. I didn't know what else to do. I don't know how long we stayed that way. It felt like hours. Eventually, she started calming down and stood beside me. Tear streaks ran down her face, her eyes were swollen, and the light had gone out of them.

"I love you, daddy." She whispered and bent down to kiss his forehead. Then she walked out of his room. I followed her. Her eyes took in the destruction as she picked her way through it towards the stairs.

"Sean, will you wait down here please?" she asked. I didn't think she should be alone but her eyes held a promise of violence if I argued.

"Sure, Ilsy." I said softly.

"I won't be long," she said and gave me a soft smile.

I watched her walk up the stairs. The strong woman I had first met was hiding. She had broken down and the day had gotten the better of her. I understood she wanted time to pull herself together. I also understood that we weren't completely safe here. I didn't think the wolfengators would be back but I wouldn't be able to do much against them if they did return. As she disappeared from my sight, I walked towards the front door that still stood open. I pushed it closed and sat down against it facing the stairs.

# Ragged Edge

I don't remember dozing off but the next thing I knew Ilsy was shaking me awake. I jumped to my feet and collapsed against the door as the room grayed out again. She grabbed my shoulders until I was steady. Beside her were two suitcases leaning against the wall. She had cleaned her face and seemed more composed. I rubbed at my eyes and looked down at her.

"You okay?" I asked softly.

"No." She shook her head and squeezed her eyes closed as tears welled up.

I pulled her to me and held her head against my chest. She tried to fight before collapsing against me. We stood that way while she composed herself again.

"I'm sorry, Ilsy, I got here too late," I whispered.

"It's okay," she said, sniffling. "I wouldn't have been here without you." She gave me a pained smile.

I looked at the bags on the floor.

"Are you ready?"

"Yeah, are we going back to your place?" she asked as she bent for the bags. I stopped her and took them myself. They were heavier than I expected.

"Actually, not right now. Is there a hotel or something nearby?"

"Yeah, in town. Why?"

"I can't transport us until I've had some sleep and maybe something to eat." I felt ashamed admitting this to her.

"I see. Daddy should have a car we can use," she said and led me outside. We walked around the house to a large garage in the back. I laughed when she opened the door. I had expected a luxury car of some sort, maybe even a sports car, instead I saw another damn Prius, this one black.

"What is it with you guys? At least your Uncle Fry has the good sense to drive a Mercedes, even if it is twenty years old." She chuckled a little.

"Daddy didn't care about cars, he wouldn't even have one if I didn't pick this out for him." She walked to the back wall and pulled the keys off a peg. I loaded the bags and climbed into the passenger seat.

"So you met, Uncle Fry?" she asked getting behind the wheel.

"Interesting fellow, told me to give your father his love and tell him that Uncle Nebhotep was resting peacefully now. How old was your father?" She chuckled again.

"Nebhotep isn't really an uncle, dumbass. He was a mummy Uncle Fry had been chasing for a few months. I was working with him shortly before, well, before my life fell apart apparently." She held onto the wheel and hung her head. I remained silent until she looked up and started the car.

"So, what's in the bags?" I was grasping at straws but the air was charged with so much sadness it made me uncomfortable. The last thing I wanted was silence.

"Sean, I'll explain when we get somewhere more private. For now, well, do you mind if we don't talk?" she asked, looking me in the eyes.

"Sure, Ilsy." I smiled at her then looked out the window. Before I knew it was happening I was asleep again.

# Ragged Edge

I woke when the car stopped. Looking out the window I saw we were parked outside a nondescript hotel. Ilsy held up a door key.

"You weren't lying about being tired. I've already checked in." She got out of the car as I rubbed the sleep from my eyes. I climbed out, headed for the trunk, and grabbed the bags before following her into a room.

"Just the one?" I asked cocking an eyebrow. She laughed.

"Are you turning prude on me? At least here we have two beds," she said as she led me inside.

There were indeed two queen size beds in the room and a small television. I took off my torn shirt and collapsed on the nearest bed. Ilsy walked to the far bed and sat down.

"I thought you wanted something to eat," she said.

"In the morning. For now sleep. We should be safe but please lock the door – and don't leave." I opened one eye and gave her the sternest possible look I could muster while drifting towards sleep.

"Sure, Sean." She got up, locked the door, and then climbed into her bed. I watched her quietly for a while before drifting off. Several times during the night I awoke to her quiet sobbing. She was obviously trying to be silent, I pretended to still be sleeping. Overall, I would have to say that our first night together hadn't gone very well and I only hoped that it didn't set the tone for the rest of our association.

# CHAPTER 6

I awoke before Ilsy and climbed into the shower. Next to flying, a good hot shower is a wonderful cure all. I let the steaming hot water pour over my body and thought over the past day. Clearly there was more to Ilsy than I had been told. Her family was familiar with the same ragged edge I walk every day. How much she knew about I wasn't sure but intended to find out. For some reason my mother had gotten involved in the situation. This wasn't good. Normally, a mother should have the best interest of her child in her heart. My mom wasn't exactly normal. I didn't even know that she was still alive, to be honest.

The whole Ilsy situation aside, there was still the matter of the damned artifact. I also wasn't sure how to get the time to work on it if the damn wolfengators were going to be killing off Ilsy's family members. In a perfect world they wouldn't have even been aware of her family.

# Ragged Edge

This isn't a perfect world. Now I was going to have to work fast or protect her family. Too many eggs in the basket would definitely cause something to be overlooked. According to Darius, my main concerns should be keeping Ilsy safe and keeping the artifact safe. Beyond that, I realized I knew nothing.

As I washed, I ran through my options. I could focus on Ilsy and her family. I could focus on the artifact. I could run the risk of talking to my mother and finding out what she knew, but to do that I'd have to either stash Ilsy somewhere safe or take her to meet Mom. My apartment was the safest place I knew but her car had been parked in front of it for the past twelve hours. It would be foolish of me to think it hadn't been spotted. I knew my apartment could keep the wolfengators out in the short term. In the long term they would eventually get in, and I couldn't risk her being there when they did. For that matter we needed to go back and grab the damned artifact. I rinsed off while realizing my options were limited. I had one decent option that wasn't good.

I stepped out of the shower and dried off. I wiped off the mirror and stared at myself while I dressed. I didn't do this out of vanity or at least not totally out of vanity. It was mostly to look myself in the eyes and make sure I was firm in my decision. I didn't like what I saw. I saw indecision, I saw confusion, I saw fear, and I saw weakness. I'd like to say I couldn't believe my eyes, but eyes never lie if you know how to look. I snarled at myself and tried to force that door closed.

# Ragged Edge

I left the bathroom to find Ilsy awake. She was staring up at the ceiling with tears rolling down her cheeks. I stared at her for a moment, unsure of myself.

"Shower's free," I said quietly and walked to the window. I couldn't look at her like this.

"Thanks," she said, sniffing. I continued staring out the window. While the room was basic, the view was first class. It held rolling green hills, a pond in the distance, and a little roadway going past. Mostly I focused on the hills, the color of her eyes.

"Not to sound heartless but you should shower fast. We need to eat and run."

"I'm not hungry." The life had gone out of her voice. I sensed this mission becoming a lot less fun.

"Fine, shower and we'll go." I tried to keep my voice flat.

"Where?"

"Back to my place; we need the artifact."

"I can shower there."

"No time, we'll grab and go."

"Where?"

"A safe place. Just get moving." I closed my eyes and turned around. When I opened them she hadn't moved. I sat at the edge of her bed.

"Just leave me alone, Sean." She turned away from me.

"I can't do that, Ilsy."

"Why not?"

"In the first place, I'm here to protect you. That's easier to do if I'm with you."

"Why me?" I think this was rhetorical.

"I don't know, you found the artifact, that's all I know."

"So take the artifact," she mumbled.

"I have to protect you and it. Now get up and let's go." I let anger slip into my voice. I was hoping she would respond to it.

"Sean, my dad just died. I know you probably don't understand how that feels. I'm sure yours is still running around somewhere, but it fucking hurts. Now leave me alone." Well she responded with anger. It was better than the monotone.

"Ilsy, you're right. I don't know how it feels. Not because my dad is still alive though. I mean, I guess he could be, but I never actually knew my father."

"Why not?" She turned towards me. I couldn't look in her eyes for long. I saw curiosity, but I also saw pain.

"It's just how we are. Children are raised by their mothers and, if possible, grandparents. I was raised by my grandfather." I stared at the floor. I don't know why I opened up to her, but it seemed to help.

"Where was your mother?"

"I don't know. She wasn't exactly the loving type. I think she resented what she was. She hated my father for leaving her at home while he continued fighting and protecting you humans. The Elders had a hard time with her. The last I knew she was assigned for final death. She is still alive though."

"How do you know?" she asked, sitting up.

"Your Uncle Fry told me. She told him to send me to your father. If not for that I wouldn't have been able to bring you to him."

# Ragged Edge

"Maybe she's changed."

"I don't know, but I'm gonna find out as soon as I get you safe." I looked back into her eyes. We sat that way for a long while. I broke the silence first.

"Who are you, Ilsy Hillerman?" I asked without looking away.

"What do you mean?" Her cheeks turned red and she looked away.

"First off, I don't talk to humans like I do you. Well, I mean, except my shrink of course. Secondly, your father seemed to know who and what I am, your Uncle Fry definitely does. So who are you?" She looked up at me briefly then grabbed one of the suitcases we had brought with us.

"I'll show you mine if you show me you yours." Her eyes sparked with a glimmer of her old fire. Finally we were getting somewhere.

"Agreed, under one condition." I had to proceed cautiously. Usually we don't reveal much of ourselves to humans, not even humans that believe in us and have seen some of what we can do.

"What condition?"

"You have to understand that for your safety and mine I can't tell you everything." I looked at her sternly.

"What can you tell me then?"

"I can tell you about myself, my history, and my lives. I can tell you a little about my race. Just understand that if I leave something out I'm not hiding it, I'm protecting you."

"I see, and when can I know the parts you leave out?"

"Never."

"Never?"

"Well, maybe on your deathbed."

"I see."

"That's my condition, take it or leave it."

"I guess I have no choice." She sighed and unzipped the bag.

"I don't have much to tell really. I grew up here in Shercock, studied at Oxford, and I've traveled through most of the world."

"Why don't I surprise you? The wolfengators would've had most humans a gibbering mess yet you only worried about the blood on your couch."

"It's a nice couch."

"You're dodging the question."

"Alright. First, look at these." She pulled out three books. I studied their covers. I knew the books, they were required reading for junior guardians in training. They were all bound in black leather. Their titles were marked in gold leaf. These copies were very old and held the spicy musty scent of old libraries. Inside, they all appeared to be hand copied. I knew they weren't the originals but the handwritten scripts impressed me. They were The Necronomicon, the real one and not the Lovecraftian tale of fiction, The Tibetan Book of the Dead, and The Egyptian Book of the Dead.

"Interesting collection," I said slowly.

"My dad translated and copied them."

"Why?" I was curious and more than a little worried. These were not happy books. People used the knowledge in these books for very nasty business.

"Partly because it was his job, partly because he enjoyed a lifelong quest for knowledge of all forms. Purely theoretical, mind you. He never tried to use it."

"His job?"

"Yeah, he was an archivist, or a librarian if you prefer." I was caught off guard. I hate it when that happens.

"I think you should start at the beginning."

She put the books back in the suitcase and closed the zipper.

"Not here. You mentioned a safe place. Is it also private?"

"Fairly private, yes."

"Good, let's get you fed and pick up the artifact. Take me to this safe place and I'll tell you the whole story." She was becoming more of herself and I was glad to see it. It could have been my charming personality, but I was pretty sure it was the chance to tell me her story and to hear mine. I just had to figure out how much to tell her.

We ate at a local pub then jumped back to my place in Portland. My apartment appeared untouched. I looked out the window and noticed that Ilsy's car had been towed. That could be good and bad. On the one hand, it was no longer in front of my apartment to give away our location. On the other hand, the city never towed cars that fast. Either way, it wasn't important right now. We needed to get the artifact and go to the one place I knew would be safe.

"Before we go to the safe house, I want to make sure you are clear on something."

"What?"

"When we get there, you cannot go outside. You have to stay in the house no matter what."

"What kind of safe house is that? It sounds like a prison."

"It's not that. Okay, to be honest I haven't told him we're coming…"

"Who?"

"My grandfather. His cabin is the safest place I can think of. It's the only place I know nothing can get to. There is a catch though."

"What's the catch?" she asked dubiously.

"Technically, humans aren't allowed."

"But–"

"And strictly speaking, I'm not supposed to go there either."

"Sean, in your seven hundred years, have you ever looked at a dictionary?"

"What's that supposed to mean?"

"You do realize that a safe house is supposed to be, well, safe?"

"Granddad's cabin is safe."

"Not if we aren't welcome!" She had a point.

"Well technically that's true, but I know Granddad wouldn't hurt you. If I could talk to him, I would ask before we went but I can't."

"Why not?"

"It's just not allowed. Not yet anyway."

"I don't like it, Sean." I couldn't blame her. I threw up my hands and plopped myself down on the couch.

"Fine, we'll talk here, but stay close. We may have to leave at any moment."

"Okay," she said, looking around nervously, then sat beside me on the couch.

"My story begins back when the Celts ruled Ireland. The Hillerman family has its roots in the Brigantes tribe on the southeastern edge of Ireland and in Northern England. Obviously, our surname has changed much since then. I believe it was my grandfather that first changed it to Hillerman but we'll get to that. The story that has passed down from one generation to the next is that in the year 72 AD the head of our tribe, Teyrnan, rescued a Druid priest from a fearsome beast. The descriptions of this beast make it sound as though it were a red-haired dire wolf. In gratitude, the priest assured Teyrnan that his tribe would find favor with all the friendly creatures of the land, and they did. For many years their cattle were the sturdiest and healthiest in all of Celtic Ireland.

"The size and health of the Brigantes cattle brought much renown to the tribe and it steadily grew. It also drew the attention of the Aen Sidhe, or people of the hills, also known as the Tuatha Dé Dannan–"

"The true Fairies?"

"That's how they are seen now, but at that time they were the gods of Ireland. So one day while Teyrnan was walking in the woods, the goddess Danu approached him. Teyrnan was dumbstruck seeing a being of such beauty before him and dropped to his knees prostrating himself before her. Danu commanded him to rise and asked him for a favor. The gods were holding a great feast and were in need of many heads of cattle. Teyrnan, wanting to please the goddess promised her all that she wanted. Danu asked for more than three hundred of his sturdy cattle. At this Teyrnan hesitated, for as much as he wanted to please the mother Goddess he had little more than three hundred. At that time a man's wealth was measured by his cattle.

"After much thought, Teyrnan agreed and asked when and where he should deliver them. Danu told him they would be needed in a fortnight at the great hall, Tara. Teyrnan promised they would be there. When he returned to his home he called his clansmen together and told them of the deal with Danu. The tribe was outraged that he would promise such a thing without asking anything in return, but Teyrnan knew that any favor given to the Aen Sidhe was a favor owed. If the tribe was patient they would surely reap the benefits.

"So it was that in a fortnight the largest herd of cattle seen up to that time in Ireland was standing before the great hall of Tara. Danu, looking more beautiful than on her first appearance, stood before the hall with arms opened wide. She offered her thanks and asked the herdsmen to move the cattle into the hall. Teyrnan passed the order and one spoke up demanding of Danu to tell them what they would receive in payment first. Teyrnan chastised the impudent herder but the others picked up the demand. In the end they all refused to help with the cattle until a payment was discussed. Teyrnan hung his head in shame.

"Danu asked the herders what payment they would like. They showed their greed and demanded wealth greater than the wealthiest kings. This show of greed angered the Mother but she promised the men the wealth they had asked for. The men rejoiced and quickly moved to herd the cattle into the hall. Only Teyrnan held back. The Mother approached him and asked him why he would not help. He answered her that he did not seek wealth and was ashamed that his clansman would demand such of a goddess. She then asked him what it was that he would like in payment. He told her he expected no boon and would accept whatever she felt proper to give.

"The goddess smiled on Teyrnan and kissed his forehead. She told him that the gift he would receive would continue with his family throughout all the ages. It was a gift worthy of the gods and would make him the wealthiest of all his clansmen even if he were struck poorer than the lowliest peasant. As she spoke her appearance grew in beauty so that it drew tears from Teyrnan's eyes. All around the hall he began to notice men and women of such indescribable strength and beauty. He asked the Goddess about the newcomers and she told him they had always been there. Then taking Teyrnan by the hand, she walked him around the hall and introduced him to each and every one of the Aen Sidhe.

"Danu dismissed Teyrnan's men to return to their homes and invited Teyrnan to stay for the feast. He accepted and was granted a seat beside her at the head table. During the feast a great bard entered and told the assembled gods of Teyrnan's bravery, generosity, and humility. The gods were much pleased and each added a blessing assuring the gifts would pass from generation to generation as long as the world turned. Teyrnan was humbled and graciously accepted each blessing even though none of the assembled gods or goddesses presented him with anything. After the feast Danu accompanied Teyrnan back to his hall.

"During the walk, Teyrnan turned to Danu and told her that he did not understand: all of the assembled gods had promised him such gifts that would continue throughout the entire line of his family but none actually presented him with anything. Danu smiled and assured him that it was well he did not understand for through confusion we seek answers, and that even if we do not find the answers to our questions, we always find wisdom. She told Teyrnan that all of the secrets of this world were open to him and his family if they but sought for them. So it was that Teyrnan was humbled again for he did not consider himself a wise man. He was king through the luck of his birth, he was never confident in his decisions concerning his immediate family let alone the entire tribe, and he had learned to rely more on his blade than his mind. In telling this to Danu, she simply smiled and laughed. He asked why she laughed. She told him that with the secrets of the world he would find many reasons to raise his blade and that the truly wise always question their decisions for only the foolish have total confidence.

# Ragged Edge

"So it was, hand in hand, Teyrnan returned to his village with Danu. He was greeted by his wife and children who each knelt and paid respects to their great visitor. Danu kissed them each in turn and bestowed them with the gifts each god and goddess had given to Teyrnan. It is said that Danu returns for the birth of each generation and bestows them with the same kiss.

"In the years after the feast, Teyrnan frequently saw the gods and goddess and they always accepted him as a friend. When his clan went to war, the Tuatha marched beside him. It was Teyrnan that discovered and dispatched the first werewolf of Ireland. Now his relationship to the gods and his sturdy cattle brought him much respect even as his tribe fell into disarray. For the wealth that was promised to the greedy herders that day did not come in the form of gold, silver, and other riches. No, it came to them as sorrow, grief, and hardship – of these they had a wealth greater than any king that had walked the land before them. Such as it was, the gift of Danu was their curse. Generous goddess that she was, she did not place this same curse upon their undeserving progeny. For the offspring of these men had ample opportunity to learn generosity and humility at the hands of Teyrnan, who did all that he could to ease the suffering of the greedy herdsmen." Throughout the story Ilsy's voice had been strong. She sounded like a teacher talking to a student. It was wonderful to hear. A tear dropped from her eye as she finished.

"That's how my dad told it to me anyway." She smiled and wiped the tear away.

"So what happened after that?" I asked eagerly.

"The years passed as they tend to do. Each generation received their blessing from Danu and the family learned more and more of the world. You said that the world was a much bigger place than I thought it was. I didn't correct you at the time, I mean if you want to be a pompous ass that's your business, but it's really not much bigger. So far, only you and those wolfengators are new to me, and even you aren't that new."

"What do you mean?"

"Well I already knew your race existed, I just don't know what you are."

"That's true I guess. Go on."

"Okay. The next part of our story starts in 1888, London. Specifically at about three-forty in the morning on Friday, August thirty-first..."

"That's when the body of the first Jack the Ripper victim was discovered," I said.

"Correct. The family name had changed from Brigantes to Heeley. Rowan Heeley was an investigator for the London police department. A special investigator. Truthfully, had he been present at the beginning the Ripper murders would've never made headlines. At the time he was in Dublin fighting alongside his brother Owen against a roving pack of werewolves. They had been terrorizing the city for months. Coincidentally, if you believe in coincidence, the pack alpha was a descendant of one of the first herdsman that spoke up in Teyrnan's time. Owen had been tracking the pack for a month and had finally managed to locate their lair. The pack was much larger than he had first thought and he asked Rowan to take time off if he had it to come help.

"There were ten Heeley's present for the attack on the wolf den. Owen and Rowan were the only survivors. Five were killed in the battle and after the fifth fell, the Aen Sidhe joined the battle and helped make quick work of the den. The other three died of their wounds. This highlighted a mistake the family had been making. Previous to this fight only childless adults were allowed in battle. The attack on the wolf den showed the brothers the folly in this thinking. From then on, family members were kept from battle until they had offspring; this way it was ensured that the family wouldn't be wiped out in one battle.

"Anyway, Rowan returned to London after the third victim had been found. He showed up to his office with a broken arm that eventually had to be removed. He worked on the murders tirelessly and discovered the culprit. A succubus had lost its mind. Under normal circumstances a succubus feeds from sexual energies. Normally they don't kill their victim and rarely ever in so violent a manner. The succubus went on the run after Rowan had identified it. The Heeley name was getting known in supernatural circles. Rowan, being ill from his wounds and exhausted from long hours spent investigating, sent word to Owen. It was Owen that tracked the succubus to Egypt and ended its life. Meanwhile, Rowan's arm was removed. He retired from his official investigating job and became the family's first archivist. He traveled the world collecting texts on the occult and worked tirelessly translating them. Owen and his oldest son took on the task of fighting what threats they could find.

"After Rowan and Owen Heeley, the family became more organized. We were never a large family and after the battle of the wolf den our numbers had been depleted badly. The family focused mostly on Ireland and Britain. In the early 1920s, my grandfather Desmund came to America and changed his last name to Hillerman. He found a country rife with the things he had been fighting in Ireland so he convinced other family members to join him. Before long there was a small clan of Hillermans settled in Manhattan. Slowly they spread out through the country but we've never been as numerous here as in Ireland.

"Desmund had four sons. My father Albion, Patrick, Brian, and Aidan. He had one daughter, Brigit, she married Uncle Fry and he joined the family fight. Sometimes those that marry into the family choose to stay out of it even if they are told about it. Uncle Fry was eager to join and has an aptitude for stumbling onto little pockets of evil. In all honesty, it's possible that somewhere along the line he's related to us. For the most part, the family has always been honorable but every family has a few black sheep so there have been illegitimate children throughout the generations. We haven't traced those in the records, so it's hard to tell.

"Anyway, that brings us up to me. I was in training to take my place on the front lines but haven't had children yet. In the meantime I've had to commit our family history to memory and recreate my father's original research about your kind. In truth, it was him that put the idea into my head. I didn't know it was a test at the time. I'm also not sure if I passed." She looked down at her hands folded in her lap and another tear fell from her eyes.

"Ilsy, you impressed a member of the race you were researching, I'm sure your father would be proud." She looked up and smiled at me.

"So, I showed you mine. Now show me yours," she said. I thought I saw a new glimmer in her eyes. One I hadn't seen there before, I can't be sure if it was there or not though. At the moment my eyes caught the strange sparkle in her eye and I started to study it, there was a knock on the door. Three soft raps followed by a smooth, comforting voice.

"Hello? I believe you can help me." We both stood and stared at the door. I walked towards the door motioning for Ilsy to keep quiet, and looked through the peephole. Standing in the hallway was a man about medium height. His gray hair was pulled back into a braid and he wore a black cassock with smudges of dirt near his feet.

He looked at my peephole, if I didn't know better I would've sworn he could see me.

"Mr. Gryphon, please open the door." It was a simple request, totally reasonable. My hand was moving towards the knob before the hairs on the back of my neck pricked up. There was no reason for me to open the door, and no reason for any priest to know who I was. I stepped back from the door and motioned for Ilsy to grab the box with the artifact. I grabbed my birdcage in one hand, Ilsy's with the other, and focused on my grandfather's house.

My apartment swirled around us as the soft knocking came again at the door. For just a moment everything around was dark and then the world swam back into focus. We hadn't gone anywhere. The soft rapping continued.

"Mr. Gryphon, I know you and your friend are in there. Perhaps before running we could talk?" The voice sounded so reasonable.

"Why don't you let him in, Sean?" Ilsy asked as she let go of my hand and approached the door unconcerned about my failure to transport us anywhere.

I watched her hand stop as she reached for the doorknob. She took a step back then came returned to my side, a look of grim determination on her face.

"What is it?" she asked.

"By all appearances, a priest. Though I'd wager that he is no normal priest," I said quietly.

"Where were we going? Why did you stop?" she asked.

"Grandfather's, and apparently I'm blocked."

The knocking came a little more forcibly now.

My mind worked at a furious pace recalling everything I knew about the Codex Gigas. Written in the thirteenth century by a Benedictine monk, the legend says he promised to write the bible in penance for an unspecified crime against his order to avoid the fate of being walled up in a room condemned to die of thirst or starvation, whichever came first. Given twenty-four hours to write a book containing the entire knowledge of the known world, he knew he would fail and sold his soul to the devil. That was the legend and it was much closer to the truth than the current theory that it was written by a hermetic monk named Herman the recluse. I decided to try my luck.

"Brother Herman, if you're standing at my door you certainly aren't much of a recluse." I said loud enough for him to hear me. The rapping stopped for a second. I guess I struck a nerve.

"We all must grow and change with age, young Gryphon." His voice remained calm and reasonable though a slight edge of threat crept in around the edges.

"Sean, who is that?" Ilsy asked.

"He wrote those pages you hold. I'll tell you about it once we've escaped."

"What do you want, Herman?" I asked.

"I want the rest of my work," he answered.

"I don't see that happening. Have your people call my people, we'll do lunch and fail to come to an agreement."

"You're a funny man, Mr. Gryphon." He answered as my door shook like it had been smashed with a battering ram. A large crack ran down the center of it.

"Now, Herman, you should know that beating down the door to a man's castle is a sure way to make an enemy."

"You are no man." His voice came out as a crackling croak like a toad breathing fire.

"Seems that makes two of us," I said, mostly to myself but eliciting a chuckle from Ilsy.

# Ragged Edge

"Stand behind me Ilsy, keep hold of the suitcases, artifact, and my cage just in case. I have one more place we can go but it's kind of a last resort." I spread my wings wide and stared at the door. Ilsy did as told without question. Either she was in shock or recognized our danger. Given the story she just told me, I leaned toward danger recognition.

"Villainous swine, I command thee to leave this dwelling!" My voice rang out clear and commanding. I felt Ilsy move around behind me then lean slightly against me. She was a quick study, apparently already figuring that we had to be touching to jump together. The pounding on the door stopped. I could approach it and look out the peephole again, a good way to get shot or stabbed through the door. I could try jumping again, grandfather's cabin was out but literally everywhere else had infinitely fewer threats to our lives.

"Winged vermin, hand over the manuscript and I will leave." It's amazing how clearly a croaking, crackling voice can carry. With the door between us there was nothing I could do. The problem was trying to figure out how to get the door open without presenting an opening to be attacked. So far the best I could think to do was stall.

"Who are you to demand my obedience, unclean one?" The key was to not deliver a specific threat. It's always better to let their imagination form the threat. I was answered by another bang on the door, the crack lengthened. As much as I didn't know what he was going to do, he likewise had no idea what I was doing. I pulled my right arm back like I was preparing to throw a football. My fingers began to glow red, I started moving them in a rhythmic order starting with my index finger and ending with my thumb. In my palm a ball of fire formed. My fingers kept it formed and ready to be thrown.

Another boom and loud cracking noise demanded my attention. I could see an eye peering through my door. Old weathered hands reached into the crack and started pulling the door apart.

"Last warning, fallen one!" I shouted as I felt Ilsy's body press tighter against my back. I reached behind me with my left hand and grabbed for her arm. With a sudden screeching and ripping of wood, my poor door was ripped apart. Standing before me was a man of interminable age. His calm young face belied by his gray hair and weathered hands. Still, for someone older than me, he looked incredibly handsome – except for the flames dancing in his eyes.

"Leave this place NOW!" I readied my throw.

"Give me the book." It was a standoff, neither of us willing to make the first move. We were both stalling, and we both knew it.

"Ilsy, close your eyes, hold tight to everything."

"What?" she hissed in my ear.

"I don't want you getting sick. Close your eyes and hold tight." Without taking my eyes off the man, I started to jump, making it as slow as possible. The priest took one step across my threshold; I pulled my arm back farther. A second step brought him fully into my apartment. Everything blurred except the priest. I threw the fireball just as he flung his hand toward me, releasing a gelatinous black blob of energy in my direction. I held the jump until I saw the ball strike the man full in the face, flame splashing around his head. An earsplitting shriek tore through the air, I finished the jump.

Darkness surrounded us as our feet touched ground. I heard Ilsy wretch followed by a splatter on the pavement beneath us as I slumped to the ground, my chest feeling as though I had been hit by a wrecking ball.

"I told you to close your eyes," I said as I brought another fireball to life in the palm of my right hand. I let go of Ilsy's arm and reached into my pants pocket. The light from the fire revealed a large garage. Steel walls surrounded us, dark gray pavement on the ground, the only thing in the garage was a car. A black and red 1971 Pontiac GTO with darkly tinted windows. I crawled to the driver's door, unlocked it, opened it, and reached in to turn on the headlights. The light flooded the garage. As Ilsy continued puking I examined my chest. My shirt was torn to rags, and a large black and purple bruise encased my rib cage. After poking at it I decided the damage was minimal and pulled myself to my feet.

"Have we learned anything tonight?" I asked, leaning against the hood and crossing my ankles.

"Shut up, Sean," she said weakly as she stood and wiped her mouth on the back of her hand.

"No, Ilsy, you followed my instructions perfectly right up until the end. Lucky it was nothing more than a jump."

"Lucky?"

"Yeah, you ignored my warning and then turned yourself inside out. Unpleasant, but not fatal. Maybe we would've had to run. If you ignored me or froze then, well, you could be dead. Or worse," I finished quietly as I rubbed my still sore chest.

"Point taken," she said looking down at her throw up. "Where the hell are we?"

"My parking garage at the docks."

"What happened? You tried to jump but failed. Why?" Always a student.

"I tried going to grandfather's. I knew I wasn't supposed to go there, but I didn't realize I was actively blocked. I need to talk to him, and I don't want to drag you into a fight."

"You are such an arrogant ass, do you forget that I've been trained to fight? I can fight with you," she said, jutting out her jaw.

"Absolutely not. Tonight it was one, maybe he had backup in case we tried to run and maybe he didn't, but if you noticed, I wasn't too eager to engage him."

"What's your point?" she said as she looked at me for the first time. Her eyes lingered on my bruised chest and torn shirt.

"Get in the car, Ilsy, we've got a long drive." I didn't feel like arguing right now. I needed to drive past my building, I thought the flame had stayed on the priest, maybe even killed him but I doubted I would be that lucky. Some of it could've splashed off and set the apartment on fire. If so I could at least call the fire department.

"No," she said, moving to a spot on the floor away from her mess, then sat down.

"You're acting like a child." Anger was rising in me.

"I don't care. Tell me why I can't fight beside you."

"In honor of your family, I can't allow it because you have no children. In interest of your safety, I can't allow it. Death can come quickly in a fight; I can't watch you constantly. If I fall then you will most likely be outnumbered. If you are injured, I have to defend you and deal with that distraction."

"I'm not afraid to die in battle, Sean."

"Nor am I. I don't, however, relish suffering final death because I was dumb enough to allow you in battle." I knew now that I had other reasons to not allow it. I just couldn't admit it. It was more important to me than ever to finish this job quickly before things got worse. I turned away from her and walked to the trunk of my car, grabbing our belongings on the way. After stowing our things, I pulled a spare shirt out of my bird cage and put it on.

"Ilsy, come on, we need to move and get to safety. I have a cabin in the mountains, we'll go there for now and I'll call my grandfather and maybe Darius. We'll figure out what to do after that, alright?"

She stood and walked over to me. I had a full foot in height over her; she didn't care. Without warning, her fist slammed in my stomach doubling me over, the other followed swiftly into my chin, knocking me on my ass. She stood over me as I fought to catch my breath.

"Sean, you can say yes, no, or maybe as much as you want. The fact is you can't stop me even if I have to handcuff myself to your wrist. Now get in the car and drive, really drive, no more of that jumping shit." Her accent came out thick and strong, her eyes blazed fiercely as she stared back at me. Wordlessly, I got into the car and waited for her.

"Why the hell do you have this gas guzzler anyway?" she asked as she climbed in.

"Because it eats Priuses for breakfast, because it's old like me, and it's strong like me. This car is the closest friend I have." I looked over at her and smiled weakly. "Pretty sad isn't it?" I turned the key and the engine roared to life. I pushed a button on the remote clipped to my sun visor and the door in front of us started opening.

"If we make it back here, you're cleaning the floor," I said, then laughed as I pushed on the gas and the car jumped out of the garage.

You can say what you want about global warming and the rising cost of gas. There are simply no modern vehicles that can match the joy of driving a monstrous hunk of steel, molded into a work of art, that rumbles and roars with the slightest push of the gas pedal. It's a joy that comes close to the joy of flying and that's why I picked up the car. I could've jumped us to my cabin, but I wanted to drive. It was that simple, sometimes you just have to drive.

# CHAPTER 7

**W**e drove past my apartment building, and from the road we could see no sign of the violence that had taken place there less than an hour ago. That was good. I had no way of knowing if the priest was still in my apartment or not and didn't really care. I lived simply and had nothing that couldn't be replaced. Everything important to me was with me in my car and there was no way for him to follow us. I was sure we'd get at least a couple day's reprieve.

We spent the first couple hours driving in silence again. I spent most of the driving time thinking about how we related to each other. It seemed we could get along fine if we were talking about her family, or what I am. We had a conversational connection but it seemed to get severed anytime my position in relation to her became apparent. I could understand. She came from a family that had spent many centuries fighting the same evils I fought, but she had never been tested. The mandate that no member fought without first having offspring made perfect sense in a way. They were just one family and it was easy for a family line to end. At the same time, it left ones like Ilsy itching for the battles they had grown up learning about but constantly being left in the background.

It had to be a hard position, and while I was sympathetic to her desire to prove herself, I also knew that I wouldn't be able to protect her in a full-on fight. For some reason Darius had demanded that I protect both her and the manuscript. I could hide them easily enough, but I was worried about her staying put wherever I placed her. I could find her if she left but she could be dead by then. If she ended up dead, then I would be dead. I could keep her by my side, but eventually we would end up in a fight and she could still end up dead. I knew we would have a few days at the cabin alone so maybe I'd be able to learn more about her in that time.

"What did he do to you?" Ilsy asked, breaking the silence.

"What do you mean?"

"Your chest, it looks like you got hit by a damn baseball bat."

"Just before we jumped, while I was waiting to see if my fireball hit, the fucker threw a ball of ectoplasm at me. Judging from the feel, I'd say it was made from dead energy," I said.

"Dead energy? You mean the monk is a necromancer?"

"So it would seem," I said, rubbing at my still sore chest.

While his magical abilities posed no extreme threat to me, having the energy of the dead smack into you leaves lasting pain no matter what you are. I had the distinct feeling Brother Herman had learned more about me than I had about him, and I wasn't happy about that.

"Why do you need to speak with your grandfather?" she asked.

"What?"

"At your apartment, you said you needed to speak with your grandfather. Why?"

"Do you know what those pages are, Ilsy?"

"You said something about the Codex Gigas, the Devil's bible, right?"

"Exactly. For centuries there have been ten pages missing from the bible, most scholars believed they were simply the rules of the Benedictine order. Others thought maybe it held some kind of spell or ritual."

"Which is it?" she asked.

"Damned if I know. Never read the original."

"Why does he want just these ten pages? Why not the original in Sweden?"

"I imagine he doesn't need that one, besides that isn't the original. My people have the original. The one in Sweden is just a copy, almost an exact replica."

"Almost?"

"There are some things people don't need to know, like the distinction between Satan and Lucifer. Two different guys. If Lucifer had written that thing for the monk, then none of this would be happening. Satan is a bit more dangerous."

"Why?" One word questions, they get annoying after awhile. I simply shook my head and drove on in silence.

"Guns," I said, breaking the silence.

"What?" she asked.

"Guns. Can you use them?"

"Yes," she said, sounding like I was a simpleton for asking.

"I've been thinking."

"That's a surprise." I ignored the jab.

"When we get to the cabin, I'm going to call for grandfather and Darius. It'll take at least two days for them to get here."

"Can't they just jump to us?"

"Probably if I was going to use a telephone, but my cabin doesn't have one and cellphones don't work there."

"Then how are you going to call them?" Yeah, she definitely thought I was an idiot.

"Bird phone," I said simply.

"What?" She was moving toward exasperation.

"I use my raven cry. A special call that carries to all ravens in the near vicinity, they repeat it, other birds pick it up, and it travels around the world. It will take at least two days for the word to spread to Darius and grandfather. They might come right away or, if they are busy, they will come as soon as possible."

"Okay?"

# Ragged Edge

"So we will have a lot of time on our hands. Now, we can spend it arguing, which I don't enjoy, or we can spend it learning."

"Learning?" She was interested now.

"Well, if I'm going to allow you to fight alongside me, I need to know you can handle yourself so I'm not having to worry about you." I knew I'd worry anyway but maybe this would placate her.

"You mean when I fight alongside you at a time of my choosing." Then again, maybe not. Discretion being the better part of valor, I ignored this.

"Also, you showed me yours and I told you I'd show you mine, as much as I could anyway." I looked over at her.

"Really?"

"Well you deserve it, besides we'll have to keep entertained somehow."

"What do you mean?"

"Well, my cabin is pretty basic: four walls, a bed, a couch, an icebox, a gas stove, and a fireplace. That's pretty much it."

"What about water? A bathroom? You know, the simple needs of life."

"Well, I have a water pump, and there is a nice clean spring within a mile. I also have a camp shower, but you have to heat the water on the stove if you want a hot shower." She heaved a sigh and stared out the window. I thought I saw slight smile on her face though.

"So anyway, I thought we could spend our days sparing so I can see how well you fight and get in some target practice so I can see how well you shoot. The evenings and nights can be long though. Now on a normal trip here, I fish during the day and listen to the birds in the evening. At night I'll jump somewhere fun and then jump back when I'm ready to sleep. We need to lay low though, so I figure at night we can tell each other stories."

"What about the book?"

"With a little quiet time it shouldn't take long to read that. Besides, it'll be hard to read at night with just the fireplace and candles."

"We'll see," she said, looking at me and smiling.

"I mean it's that or we spend our nights bored and then end up going at each other like howler monkeys," I said, grinning.

"What?" she asked incredulously.

"You know – scream, yell, throw poo at each other. I've heard it can be rather messy, but maybe it'll be fun." I said.

"Absolutely not," she said with a laugh.

"Go at each other like rabbits?" I asked.

"I think we'll stick to stories," she said, shaking her head.

"Suit yourself, I only have six hundred and eighty-four years experience." I winked at her with a grin on my face.

"Good pickup line. Every woman dreams of sleeping with an ancient old man," she said, smiling back.

"I'll take that as a no," I said.

"Very perceptive."

# Ragged Edge

We drove on while making occasional small talk. When we got close to the cabin, I pulled to the side of the road.

"What are we doing here?" she asked.

"You need to drive. There is a store coming up and we need to stop for supplies. You're a stranger here, I'm not so I have to hide myself from sight."

I reached into my back pocket and pulled out my wallet. I flipped through it and handed her a few bills.

"We'll need food, ice, and toiletries. I'm going to be with you but only you will be able to see me. If the place is being watched, I don't want us seen together. They might mistake you for someone else. With my height I tend to stick out a bit."

"Okay?"

"When you get out, leave the door open so I can slide across and get out. Act like you are having a hard time shutting it. Remember, nobody can see me except you, so don't talk to me. I'll point at the things I want, you pick up what you want but this isn't a shopping trip. We need to be quick about this."

"Alright."

"Let's go then."

I settled into the passenger seat and she drove like a bat out of hell. I hated shopping but this trip was fun. I never realized how amusing it could be to let one person see you then act stupid and try to make them laugh.

# Ragged Edge

After shopping we proceeded to the cabin. It sat in a clearing in the woods and was very comfortable for one person. For two it was going to be a little cramped but then so was my apartment. I opened the door and snapped my fingers together. The fireplace sprang to life. It had been awhile since I had last been here; a fine coating of dust covered everything. I started unloading the car while Ilsy familiarized herself with the cabin. Not that there was much to get familiar with. I think there are hermits that have more convenience than I do at my cabin.

We had collected a large amount of things since leaving Kansas. I brought in her suitcases, my golden cage, and the box with the manuscript and placed them in one corner. I set the groceries on the kitchen counter and filled the icebox. This was an old refrigerator that used ice to keep everything cool. In a couple days we'd have to get more ice but for now it worked fine. After putting everything away I reached into one cabinet and pulled out a couple of beers. I offered one to Ilsy.

"Cozy," she said, taking a drink.

"That's the general idea," I said as I flopped onto the couch. A fine cloud of dust sprang up around me.

"One question though."

"What's that?"

"Where's the bathroom?"

"Behind curtain number one," I said, pointing to an old Navajo rug I had hanging from the ceiling. She walked over and looked behind the curtain.

"I see a shower, but where can I, you know, do my business."

"Oh yeah," I said, hesitating as I sensing another ass chewing coming on.

"What?" she said. Her eyes flashed dangerously.

"Well, okay, so I normally come here alone."

"Sean."

"And because I can telelocate, it's easy for me to come and go as I please."

"Sean." Anger was rising in her voice.

"So, that is to say, I never actually built one." I winced and waited for the yelling.

"Great, so you want me to hold it for a couple of days?" she said, yelling now. I knew this was going to happen.

"Well you could use big John."

"Who? What big John?"

I nodded my head toward the front door where a shovel leaned against the wall.

"What am I supposed to do with that?"

"Dig a hole of course."

"Oh, how silly of me, of course." She flopped down on the couch beside me. "You really don't deal with many humans do you?"

"Nope," I said and then took a long drink of my beer.

"Why not?" I knew that question was coming.

I sat staring into the fire for a minute collecting my thoughts. I wasn't sure how to explain that I didn't desire contact with humans as a general rule.

"Ilsy, I'm seven hundred years old."

"So you keep saying."

# Ragged Edge

"Think about it, Ilsy. Imagine living seven hundred years surrounded by people that don't even live a quarter of that."

"So what, you're afraid of attachment?"

"Not exactly. I mean, yes, I don't relish seeing friends die of old age while I remain ageless to them, but it's the way of things. Death is inevitable. I know that, hell, I've experienced it a few times."

"It's not the same," she said quietly.

"You're right. I come back. Still, I come back in a different body, and if I managed to learn anything my personality might change also. So it's a death and a rebirth. Same soul, different person." I watched the flames dance. I didn't really want this conversation, not now.

"Look, it's late. We should sleep so we can get started tomorrow. I'll go call grandfather, and Darius."

She watched me silently. I stared into the fire refusing to meet her eyes. When Darius told me of this mission I had no idea of the dangers involved. Now that I did know, I wanted nothing more than to punch him in the mouth.

"Okay, Sean," she said. I nodded and stood up, then turned to look at her. She was staring at her beer.

"Ilsy," I said, "I'm sorry I couldn't save your father."

She looked up at me, tears welling in her eyes.

"I'll go make my call. I'll be back in a little while. Stay inside please." I put my hand softly on her shoulder. There was so much more I wanted to say but couldn't. I squeezed her shoulder lightly and walked outside taking the shovel with me.

# Ragged Edge

I shut the door behind me and leaned the shovel against the wall of the cabin. I shifted into my raven form, flew to the top of the nearest tree, and looked at my cabin. A full moon shone on it with bright bluish light. The smoke from the fireplace wafted in the still night air and the firelight danced merrily in the windows. Ilsy was right; my cabin was cozy. From this distance the scene looked happy and serene. The fact that it wasn't hung heavily on my heart. For the first time that I could remember, I was truly sad. I chastised myself and proceeded with my call.

Making a birdcall like this was both simple and complicated. Birds talk to each other all the time. People hear it as birdsong and random chirps. In truth, their language is almost as complex as any human language, but the main difference is that birds are more blunt. They don't dress up their meanings. I think that's just one reason you've never heard of a bird writing poetry. In plain English, what I said was simple.

"Grandfather, Darius, I need to speak with you. At my cabin. Bring Ilsy's Uncle Fry. I am Sean Gryphon, and I speak plain." Anyone that doesn't speak bird – Ilsy, for example – heard a cacophony of raven caws. My call trumpeted out of my beak much louder than any normal raven could manage. It was then picked up by all the ravens in our near vicinity and spread out. It would take a couple of days for them to answer. Maybe even three since I told them to bring Ilsy's uncle. I was both dreading and excited at the prospect of a couple quiet days alone with Ilsy. After making the call I watched the cabin from the trees for a while. I was hoping to give her enough time to go to sleep.

I saw the door open and the soft light from the fire pour through the opening, Ilsy silhouetted in the doorframe. I silently flew down and landed on the roof of the cabin then walked to the edge and looked down at her. She had changed into an oversized t-shirt and loose shorts.

"Sean?" she called. I stayed silent as she grabbed the shovel and walked into the woods. I followed close enough to keep an eye on her. She dug a hole and I turned my back. Soon I heard the shovel filling in the hole and she walked back to the cabin. Before entering, she looked up at the moon and smiled.

"I miss you, daddy," she said softly, then walked inside and shut the door. I flew into the yard and reformed into my human shape, wings spread, and watched through the window. This time if Ilsy looked, she wouldn't see me. I watched her climb into bed and curl up on her side. I could hear her sobbing through the window. I wanted to help her but didn't know how. Darius hadn't said anything about comforting her, and I honestly wasn't good at it. I had seen many humans die in the past and normally only felt frustration at my failure to protect them. Or sometimes anger at their ignorance. This time was different though. I wasn't told to protect Ilsy's father, and I didn't fail to protect him. She did get to tell him goodbye and from what I understand most people find some comfort in that.

# Ragged Edge

I don't know if the wolfengators were looking for something or if they killed him merely to serve as a distraction. I don't know if they found anything but they definitely brought up one hell of a distraction. Here I was watching this young woman mourn the death of her father, hidden away in a cabin that was obviously uncomfortable for her. What I should've been doing was reading those pages, figuring out why the priest wanted them now, and what role the wolfengators played in the whole mess. I should've been finding out why my mother got involved and exactly what the hell Darius knew. I needed to find out why Ilsy was so important that I needed to protect her. Surely she wasn't the last of her family line. Thinking these thoughts, I turned from the window and proceeded to waste most of the remainder of the night. I figured it might make Ilsy more comfortable.

# CHAPTER 8

I woke the next morning to the smell of bacon and eggs. The sizzling sound reached my ears a second after the smell wafted into my nose. I smiled, stretched, and opened my eyes. I jumped off the couch and looked around me. Ilsy was at the gas stove cooking and humming softly to herself. The layer of dust that had covered everything the previous night was gone and freshly picked flowers stuck out of a beer bottle on the small table that designated the dining room.

"Morning, lazy bum," Ilsy said when my gaze returned to her.

"What did you do?" I asked, startled.

"I woke up early and was bored. So I cleaned this place up a bit. I should be asking what you did last night but I already saw it. Instead, I'd like to know how you did it." She was smiling a little this morning. The swiftly shifting emotions she had displayed were starting to get disconcerting.

"The same way I telelocate, or created the fire in my hand, or lit the fireplace," I said, walking over to the table and looking around the room again. An old sheet hung over a new doorway beside the Navajo rug. I smiled and shook my head.

"Forgot the door, didn't I?"

"Considering you built a working bathroom in a night, I'm not complaining. Seriously though, how?" she asked.

"Alright, my people have a special relationship with the things around us. In ancient times it was considered magic. I guess now it still would be. Someday your people will figure it out. To put it simply, we tap into an object on the molecular level and coax those molecules into a new form. So the new bathroom is made of three trees that I turned into the walls and floor. The toilet is made of a few large stones I found and reshaped. The pipes to drain the toilet are simply tree roots; they run into a small pond about fifty yards from here. Don't worry though, I dug the pond so we aren't contaminating anything." She brought a plate of bacon to the table and put a couple eggs on a plate then set it in front of me.

"Well, thank you," she said. I smiled and waved her off, trying to hide the jolt of excitement that ran through my body. She turned and walked back to the kitchen. I got up and followed her, poured a couple glasses of orange juice and settled back down at the table and waited for her to join me.

"So, now that you have a bathroom, what do you think?" I asked in an attempt at small talk.

"It's more comfortable than camping in a tent, but not as good as a hotel," she said, placing a couple more eggs on a plate and then joining me.

"Quieter than a hotel though," I said.

"Agreed."

We sat talking and eating. Eventually, the food was gone so we just talked. We talked like we were both human. Like her father hadn't just died. Like we weren't staring at death in the near future. I'll always remember that morning.

After breakfast I finally dug into my birdcage. I pulled out all sorts of jeans and t-shirts. She took a suitcase into the bathroom to change clothes. After the cage was empty of my clothes, I put on a pair of loose fitting sweats and started hanging all the clothes in the small closet. I laid a loose-fitting black t-shirt on the back of the couch. After finishing with the clothes, I started digging out spare armor: gauntlets, grieves, chainmail shirts, and two full sets of padded leather armor. Ilsy came out of the bathroom as I was arranging the armor.

"Sean, why do all your shirts have holes in the back?" she asked as I started pulling weapons out of the cage. My back was to her so instead of answering, I grew my wings. When my wings grow the skin on my back opens almost like a cut, and from these openings my wings grow and unfurl. Aside from being seven feet long tip-to-tip, they are identical to my raven wings. Long ago I started cutting holes in my shirts to avoid ripping them when my wings grew.

"That's why I wear a jacket all the time," I said, looking over my shoulder as I folded my wings back up.

"I see," she said.

I didn't carry many guns in my cage. Two P-250 .45s, a twelve-gauge shotgun, and one automatic rifle. Ilsy looked them over as I pulled out ammunition for all four guns.

"Is that it?" she asked.

"For guns, yes. I don't normally use them," I answered.

"What do you use?"

"These mostly," I said as I began pulling out an assortment of swords and knives. There were long swords, a couple katanas, and one great sword mixed in. The knives were throwing knives, perfectly balanced, and stuck into a sheath that strapped around my stomach.

"If not one of those then I use my talons, and of course my beak adds a certain something to head-butts," I said smiling.

I let her look at the weapons as I took my old shirt off to put on the t-shirt, my chest still sporting a large purple and black bruise. Fucking necromancy. Even for someone with my healing abilities, it takes awhile to coax cells that believe they should be dead into living again. I shook my head and started strapping on the leather armor. She looked at me and laughed.

"What?" I asked.

"You look silly in that getup," she said, still chuckling.

"Yeah well, you're going to show me how well you can fight. I'm only going to be going at about forty percent. I want you coming at me full speed and strength. I know we'll be in fights for real soon, and I'd rather not start them already banged up."

"Told you I'll be fighting, glad you smartened up. Also, you're already a bit banged up," she said.

"We'll see about that," I said, ignoring the comment about my chest, and walked outside.

"But you said we'll be in fights soon," she said, following me.

"Sometimes shit happens, Ilsy. At least now if it does before I get you safe, I won't have to worry about you so much." I stopped halfway to the trees and turned to face her.

"So how have you been trained to fight?"

"Mostly hand to hand, some swordplay, and marksmanship," she answered.

"Good, let's start with hand to hand."

"Alright."

I stood facing her and held my hands behind my back.

"Whenever you're ready," I said.

Without a word she came at me slowly. She kept her hands open but raised them in a defensive posture. I stood still as she moved in and simply watched her. Her form and technique were good but she moved much too slowly. Nothing like when she struck me in the storage locker. In a fight against a vampire in full dark, she'd be dead already. When she got within striking range, I waited for her to tense up. I expected her to telegraph her move and wasn't disappointed. When the punch started, I telelocated behind her and shoved her shoulders. The momentum from her punch and my shove threw her off balance and she fell to the ground.

"You're dead, Ilsy," I said.

"You teleported," she said indignantly as she got to her feet.

"You telegraphed your punch. Now come again, and move faster like last night. Remember, if we end up in a fight it will be against creatures that are supernaturally fast. You must move quickly and decisively." She nodded and moved in on me again.

She threw a punch without telegraphing it but it was still much too slow. I dodged it easily but then she showed me she was about to kick. I caught the kick and pushed her onto her back.

"If this is you at a hundred percent, I wouldn't dare take you into battle. Hell, I wouldn't feel safe with you in a bar fight. Again."

We kept at it for a few hours. As I suspected she hadn't started at full speed or strength. I had to anger her before she would get there. Lucky for me, that wasn't much of a problem. When she got riled up, she started fighting smarter and anticipating my moves. I had to give her credit for skill. At the end she came at me with a right hook. I telelocated behind her again and was caught off guard by a leg sweep. She had learned to watch for me starting to blur. When I did, she cut off the punch and fell into a leg sweep. She couldn't move as fast as I could teleport but she did manage to sweep one leg out from under me. Finally, we broke for lunch.

Over ham sandwiches, we discussed fighting techniques and general abilities of potential opponents. I didn't know much about the wolfengators. She listened intently without interrupting me. I was surprised to discover that I actually enjoyed teaching her and wondered if this was what it was like to be a trainer. We went back outside after lunch. I walked over to a pile of wood for the fireplace and grabbed two short pieces and formed them into blunted training swords. I then handed one to Ilsy.

"Same as before. Come at me."

The sword training persisted until sunset. She seemed more confident with a sword than she did with hand to hand. I made a mental note to find a sword her size. I still didn't think I wanted her tagging along in a battle – too dangerous, too distracting – but I wanted her to be able to defend herself if the battle came to us. Perhaps it's unsportsmanlike of me, but I always agreed with whoever said, "If you find yourself in a fair fight, you screwed up." I didn't intend to fight fairly. When I found where the damn priest and wolfengators were located, I intended to hit hard, hit fast, and leave a flaming wreckage behind me.

We went inside at sunset. Ilsy wanted to take a shower but wasn't sure about it being cold. I thought about suggesting I help her warm it up but held my tongue. This is why I don't like being alone with attractive women because, human or not, I am still male.

# Ragged Edge

Instead I took a couple pans out of the cabinet, filled them with water and put them on the stove to boil. I just hoped she could shower fast.

After the water boiled, I turned it off and poured it into the tank for the camp shower I had setup. She waited a little while for it to cool. She was fidgety. A nervous energy seemed to radiate off her. I decided it was probably the past couple of days finally getting released from her system after a day of hard physical exertion. There were a few times she looked at me as though she wanted to say something, then she'd close her mouth and pace the room. I sat quietly lost in my own thoughts as much as I could be. To be honest, she made me a little nervous. Finally, she went into the shower and I went outside.

I busied myself digging out a small fire pit and gathering large rocks to set around it. I ended with an earthen depression roughly four feet wide and about six inches deep. Not quite as small as I intended but it would work. I gathered up small sticks for kindling then stacked a few logs on it. I placed my index finger on one of the sticks and concentrated for a moment, I felt heat gathering in the tip. When I was sure it was hot enough, I released the heat into the stick and it immediately popped into flame.

I know my kind are supposed to be attuned to all of the elemental energies, and I am. I just use fire more than most. I mean, when you think about it, fire is dead useful. It can be used to create and destroy, heal and kill, provide warmth, light, and ambiance. Okay, so I really liked fire. In this case it allowed me to build not just something that Ilsy and I could cook our next meal on, but also something to sit around and set the proper mood for what I was about to tell her. I'm not a good storyteller, I don't have years memorizing a story so that I can tell it by rote and draw the listener in like she did. So I have to make sure the atmosphere is proper.

By the time Ilsy joined me, I had a metal grate over the fire and a couple steaks cooking. She offered to make a salad to go with the steaks. I was suspect of her Irish heritage and expected her to suggest potatoes of some type but I agreed to the salad. The nervous energy seemed to be washed off her in the shower and I had no intention of causing discord. To be honest, that one day was more special to me than any of the others in my seven hundred years. I was happier than I had ever been; there was no fighting, no bickering, and nobody was trying to kill me. I also had to admit that it was spent with some of the most pleasant company I had had in, well, it was just the most pleasant I could remember.

The food was cooked and devoured, sparring all day can give you a voracious appetite. I went into the cabin and brought out two skewers and a bag of marshmallows. I handed a skewer to Ilsy, and we roasted marshmallows in silence for a while. I sensed she was waiting for me to speak and I was content to let her wait. I had to gather my thoughts. Until now, my shrink knew more about me than any human alive. That was okay because he thought I was nuts. I was about to let Ilsy delve even further than he had, and I knew she would believe everything I said. She had seen proof of it repeatedly in the past two days.

# Ragged Edge

Half a dozen marshmallows later, I felt ready to begin. I laid my skewer aside and stared into the fire. She watched me with baited breath and leaned forward as if she knew what was coming. I took a deep breath and began.

"The story of my people and, ultimately, myself goes back almost to the beginning of life itself. Within our ranks there are a few different theories on how it started; in that respect our races are very much alike. I don't know if we are a step up on the evolutionary ladder or simply a step over onto a parallel ladder. What is commonly accepted is that we and humans started basically the same way. We are definitely on the same tree of development; we just went on one branch while humans went on another.

As for what caused that divide, I think only the gods can answer that. At any rate, while both of our species were developing intelligence and the ability to use tools, we were equal. At that time we weren't as attuned to the elements as we are now. As far as is known, we also only had the one life. The first noticeable difference in our races came with the development of societies. You humans organized into villages first. We spent more time in the trees. Then the language development separated us further. You humans developed your own form of speech; we continued to mimic animal sounds. It is believed that we were able to talk with the animals even then.

As humans became more centralized, congregating into bigger and bigger villages, they began to lose their link with nature. Likewise, nature began to forget about them. Like I said, we stayed in nature and it seems nature held us even more closely. We began to feel what we now know is the molecular makeup of everything. We learned to manipulate it. Most importantly we learned to hide from your race. We had no desire for conquest or war. We desired knowledge and understanding of the world that surrounded us. The primitive humans tried to fight with us as their cities grew larger. So we hid. Sometimes we hid in plain sight, integrating with human tribes. We became shamans, healers, medicine men, and women. Through this blending we tried to learn more of you humans. We learned your languages, and we learned that you were blind to the world around you.

So it went for centuries. Our races grew together as they grew apart. Then came religion and our abilities became suspect. We were driven from the human villages that we were once welcomed in. So we went in search of a place to hide. To grow on our own. We still tried to blend in with your race but we now had to go unnoticed. We were forced to hide our abilities. We were still infants in the world. We learned new abilities at an alarming rate. We spoke to the animals and learned to act as them. Then our race split for the first time. What you would call mutants started to show up. Children being born with animal characteristics. Babies were born with the heads of bears, or the gills of fish, some with the wings of birds.

It may sound cruel but these children, the heralds of our future, were often put to death. They were viewed as abominations. We refer to this as our dark ages. We were so supremely arrogant in our knowledge of the world that we couldn't imagine anything different. Imagine it. We walked amongst gods and the creatures of your mythology. Hell, we became some of your gods and myths, yet we felt superior to all. All of this came even before written language, Ilsy. Then came the day of the great gift and great curse. It seems that nature will only put up with a race of children twisting it to their means for a short while.

All of us, no matter where we were, suddenly blinked out of existence. Our people appeared in a place that is indescribable. They were met with a face. Nothing more, just a face. A face made of mud, eyes of fire, and hair of water. Its words came out on great gusts of wind. This face chastised our people for our arrogance. We were becoming a danger to ourselves, to you, and to it. Those of our race then were struck ignorant. They had no words. Then we were offered a choice.

We would not be given dominion over the world, that was reserved for your race. We were to protect you, to guide you, to teach you if we chose to accept. Some of our race then accepted. The ones that denied simply blinked from existence. Broken down into their smallest particles, they were inhaled by the great face and ceased to exist."

"So the gift was your life?" Ilsy asked.

"You would think so, but no. We were told that our race would always be small, so we would need the ability to travel quickly. We were granted our telelocation ability. We were told we would have need to fight, to see things from above, and to hide from our human charges. So we were granted our shape-changing ability. We were allowed to keep our knowledge of the world and how to manipulate it at the molecular level. Then we were told the cost of our gifts. To make sure we remained a small race, we were told that our women would bear no more female offspring. To mate and bear children, we had to mate with a human. This a male of our race could do only once in his life. The child that was born would be one of us," I paused. I couldn't explain why but I didn't tell Ilsy the other side of our mating: that the woman who bears our child also becomes one of us.

"Go on" she said.

"Then we were told of our lives. How we would have multiple lifetimes to learn and pass on that knowledge. When asked how we might die, the voice smiled. Our oldest and wisest members, twelve Elders, one ancient, would be able to grant death. It was not explained how this knowledge passes down or what happens. This is what we now call final death. Some more of our race then denied the gift and ceased to exist. We were left as a race of thirteen. The original twelve Elders and ancient."

I stood then and went into the cabin. I returned with a couple of beers and handed one to her.

"So that's how my race began. At least that's the story that was told to us. I have no reason to doubt it but I wasn't there in the beginning so I can't swear to it. The facts fit though, so I see no real reason to question it," I finished lamely.

"Wait a minute," she said, looking at me suspiciously.

"What?" I said, taking a drink.

"If you have no females, how is your mother still alive?" Damn, I had hoped to gloss over it.

"She comes from very hardy stock?" I said hopefully.

"Sean."

"Okay. Yes, none of us are born female. We do have to mate with humans to have children. It's just that once we do impregnate a human female, she becomes one of us."

"So if you sleep with a woman she turns into one of you?" She sounded amazed, but there was something else in her voice. Something I couldn't explain.

"No. It's a bit more complicated."

"How so?"

"Do you believe in soul mates, Ilsy? That you are meant to be with one person for your entire life?"

"It's a nice thought and fodder for the hopeless romantics. I don't believe in it though." She hesitated. There was definitely something going on here I wasn't comfortable with.

"Well for us it's true, in a way. We can only mate with select humans. I mean we can have sex with any human we want, even marry them if we wish, but only certain ones will get pregnant."

"How do you know if you've found the right human?" Her interest in this part of us seemed a little unhealthy.

"I guess you could call it animal instinct. I've been told we can sense it."

"Then why mate with one that can't have your child?"

# Ragged Edge

"I don't know, Ilsy. Mating is biological; it's easy to understand. You screw, the sperm fertilizes the egg, and boom a baby grows. For you humans it can be done with anyone, which is very obvious when you see some of the ignorance in the world today. For us, it's more specific. Only a few of you have the proper genetic mutation to make you susceptible to becoming one of us. As for love, plenty of you humans are in marriages that can't bear offspring." I wanted to say more but I was getting irritated for some reason. I felt like I was having to defend myself to her. I looked away from her and back into the fire.

"What?" she asked, reaching out and touching my arm. I looked at her hand on my arm then back into her face.

"Love isn't about offspring. It's about two people, two beings, two animals that have found someone they don't want to live without. The poets are fond of saying that love is about wanting to die for someone. I never understood the point of that. I'd rather live for someone than die for them. What good am I dead?"

"But death isn't permanent for you," she said with a smile.

"It is if you die," I said and looked back into the fire.

I'm not sure why the turn in our conversation got to me. A confusing jumble of thoughts had launched a mental attack on me. My parents were proof that you could have children without love. I don't know what my dad felt about me as I never knew him. Until recently I always thought my mother was indifferent; that was why grandfather raised me. Now I was forced to reassess that opinion. It was, after all, my mother that sent me to Ilsy's father. If she knew the attack was going to happen, then it allowed me to find a friendly footing with this human. I don't know why she would've sent me there if she didn't know of the attack. Then again, if she knew that attack was going to happen, why send me there? Maybe she thought I could stop it. Maybe she expected me to get there sooner. The wolfengators didn't seem surprised to see me so maybe they knew I was coming.

I felt Ilsy's hands take hold of mine as a tear rolled down my cheek. I hadn't realized I was crying. We sat like that in silence until the fire died down. Then I stood, grabbed a bucket of water and dumped it on the hot coals. Before we went back inside, Ilsy hugged me. I knew it was stupid, I knew I should've stood as a wall. It was a weak moment but I hugged her back. Then we went to bed. Well, she went to bed. I laid down on the couch and listened to the night outside lost in my thoughts. The only thing I don't remember from that day and night is falling asleep.

# CHAPTER 9

The next day went much the same as the first except that I didn't light a fire that night. While the first night had been great, it was also scary. I was almost willing to admit that something about Ilsy made me want to consider her a friend, rather than a nuisance I had to protect to save my own skin. I didn't want a human friend. My shrink was fine with me. So that night we stayed in the cabin and she ate her dinner at the table. I sat on the couch with the manuscript in front of me. I knew Latin but it made no sense. It seemed to be a running description of something. I just couldn't tell what.

Ilsy finished eating, walked over, and sat beside me. I acknowledged her with a brief glance and went back to staring at the stone. We sat quietly for a few minutes. I could tell she wanted to talk again and I was trying to avoid it. At this point I was staring through the pages not really seeing them.

"Sean," she said.

"Yeah?" I asked, not looking up.

"You didn't tell me anything about yourself last night."

"Well, you got all sex obsessed on me." That got her attention.

"I what?"

"Come on, you were all over me. I could've snapped my fingers and had you naked in a second." I tried to laugh but it sounded false even to me.

"Whatever. It's not like I really wanted to know anyway." She stood and walked over to the bed.

"Then why'd you ask?" I said, looking up finally. When I saw how she looked at me, I was honestly surprised I hadn't gotten hit yet. For some reason, I had to keep pushing her.

"Maybe because we're shut up in this rat trap cabin with nothing to do in the evenings. Maybe because you said you'd tell me after I told you about me."

"Did you tell me about you?"

"Well, no, I guess not."

"See? We're even."

"Fine."

She lay on the bed and stared at the ceiling. I went back to staring at the pages. When I thought she was asleep, I went and stared out the window. I was almost hoping to see Grandfather, Darius, and Uncle Fry appearing at the edge of the woods. I'd be lying if I didn't admit that a part of me hoped it would take them longer to show up. Even though her attitude was less friendly that night, I still enjoyed it. Smiling to myself, I put the manuscript back in its box and laid on the couch. I was starting to drift off when I heard Ilsy crying quietly. I tried to ignore it. I knew I should have kept my mouth shut. I couldn't stop myself though.

"Ilsy?" I asked softly. She ignored me. I wasn't all that surprised. A part of me argued that her ignoring me gave me an excuse to say nothing else. At least I tried right? Instead I sat up.

"Ilsy?" Again, no response.

That was two attempts. Was it my fault she didn't want to answer me? I had reached out, and she had to know I knew she was crying. If she chose to ignore me then it was her problem. But I got up and walked over to the bed where she was turned facing the wall. I knelt beside the bed.

"Ilsy?" This time I reached out and put my hand on her shoulder.

"What, Sean?" At least it was a response.

"Why are you crying?"

"Like you fucking care."

"I asked, didn't I?" I clinched my fists at my side. I felt both concerned and angry.

"What's your point?"

"If I didn't care, I wouldn't have asked. I'm only supposed to protect you, not blow sunshine up your ass." Sometimes, my mouth moves faster than my brain. I winced after those words escaped.

"Sean, go away." I could hear her teeth were clenched.

"I'm thinking that's not going to happen."

"I don't want to talk to you, Sean." I knew that, hell, I understood that. I don't know why I didn't get up and walk away.

"Too bad I'm the only one here for you to talk to."

"Why won't you leave me alone?" Now that was a good question. I answered it the only way I could.

"I don't know." I didn't say it was a good answer, but she did turn to look at me. I could see her eyes were swollen with tears. I was almost positive there was snot on the sheet behind her.

"You don't know?"

"Hey, I only said I was old, never said I was wise," I said.

"That's true," she said, sniffling.

"Come on, what's wrong?"

"Why are you such a bipolar ass?"

"What?" I knew what she meant, but wanted to stall for time.

"Yesterday we got along great. It was almost like we were becoming friends." I nodded in agreement. "Then tonight you totally ignore me and act like an arrogant jerk when you do talk. I mean, what the hell is wrong with you?"

I still didn't have a plausible answer. I shifted positions so that I was sitting on the floor. I pulled my knees up and wrapped my arms around them.

"Look, Ilsy, I'm not bipolar, and it's not you. You just have to understand that in all my life I have never, and I mean never, been close friends with a human. If we ever go back to Portland when we don't have the damn priest or wolfengators chasing us, I'll take you to some of the humans that consider me a friend. You'll see that none of them even know my real name. What kind of friend is that?"

"But I do know, Sean. Hell, I know where you came from now and still don't know what the hell you are. Why tell me if you didn't want to be friends?"

"At first, because it was the easiest way to get you to do what I wanted. Then, I don't know. I wanted to help try and take your mind off your loss, get you back to yourself again. Then I realized it was kind of nice having someone to talk to." I was staring at my knees.

"Then why the jerk act?"

"It's dangerous, Ilsy. That's why I didn't want you fighting along side me. If we're friends then I have to watch your back. If I'm watching your back, I'm not paying attention to mine."

"You're right, I'll be paying attention to it. That's what friends do, Sean. They watch each others' backs." She was right. I nodded my head in agreement, unwilling to let this line of conversation go further.

"So, I'm the reason you were crying?" I asked as I buffed my fingernails on my chest.

"Don't flatter yourself," she said. "It's all just so overwhelming. I mean, three days ago I had a nice artifact that was a bit strange. Then Darius showed up, then those damn wolfengators, and then you. In the past two days, my life has been turned upside down, I've left my home, I've traveled halfway around the world, twice, my father has been brutally murdered, and I never know if the guy protecting me is going to be nice or a complete jerk. I'm sorry but," she said, letting out a deep shuddering breath, "it's just a lot to handle."

I sat quietly for few moments and then looked at her. I was sympathetic, really, I was. I mean, hell, in the past two days I'd met a human that I couldn't help but like, been told I was going to die permanently if I failed, had my head raped by some pages from a book, and had a hell of a lot more questions than answers about anything.

"At least the sky isn't falling," I said.

"What?"

"The sky isn't falling. So things could be worse. Look, soon my grandfather will be here along with Darius and your Uncle. Then maybe we can move forward. For now, how about getting some shuteye. We have another day of training tomorrow, you are still super slow," I said.

"Fast enough to smack you around a little."

"We'll see. Goodnight, Ilsy." I stood and looked down at her.

"Goodnight, Sean," she said looking up at me, a slight smile on her face. I nodded to her and went back to the couch. My head was starting to throb right behind my eyes. I had a feeling it wasn't my sinuses.

The morning began with another Ilsy-prepared breakfast and more time pretending to be human. I don't know how good this was for her mentally but it was fun for me. After breakfast we went back into the yard for more fight training. I had decided to go faster and harder with her, but I had not made her aware of this decision. If I was going to let her fight at my side, I had to know that she could quickly recognize changing situations and adapt to them. When we got out to the yard, I tossed her one of the wooden training swords we had been using.

"No hand to hand?" she asked as she caught the sword.

"No, I was thinking today we'd go free form. Basically, Grandfather, Darius, and your Uncle Fry could show up at any time now. I don't know how long that little meeting will take, but after today our little practices will have to stop. So, I want you to give me everything you've got today."

"I'll give you everything," she said with a twinkle in her eye.

I took a fighting stance in front of her and waited for her to come at me. She moved in cautiously but not too slowly. I could tell she expected me to teleport behind her. She was half right, I did teleport just a few inches away from her. She was already turning to slash at where she thought I'd be. I reached around her, grabbed her sword arm, and forced the tip of the sword to just below her chin.

"You're dead, Ilsy." I let her go quickly and decided grabbing her had been a bad idea.

I picked up the other training sword and resumed my defensive posture. She looked at me before returning to her attack stance. There was something in her eye I couldn't identify, but it failed to make me comfortable. She attacked again while I was distracted. This round lasted much longer. I simply dodged and deflected her attacks until she started falling into a pattern. I could tell she was distracted, lost in thought much like I was. I could've stopped her so we could talk about it, but in real life the enemy never calls time out. Instead, I went on the attack.

I switched up my tempo and the directions of my attack. She managed to block most of them but a few smacks got through, but I kept pushing forward going faster and faster, then slowing down. She tripped over her feet and fell to the ground, her sword falling from her hand. I bent over her, placing my sword to her throat.

"You're dead, Ilsy," I said. I was answered by the sound of pistol being cocked. While my brain was trying to identify the sound, I felt cold metal placed against my right temple.

"You're dead, boy," a smooth, cultured, Irish accent whispered in my right ear. Ilsy's face lit up.

"Uncle Fry!" she said as she wiggled out from under me and stood up. I placed my hands on my knees and stood bent over as the object was removed my temple. I barely registered the removal though, I was still thinking about Ilsy wiggling under me. I gave my head a shake to clear it then stood up and turned around.

Darius was standing behind Sir Fry, and an old man with long silvery hair, piercing glacier blue eyes, and strong hands wrapped around a walking stick stood behind Darius. I nodded to Sir Fry, who was busy holding onto a crying Ilsy, and walked towards my grandfather and my mentor. I felt a tear rise in my eyes as I looked at my grandfather. It had been almost three hundred years since I had seen him. I didn't know how much I missed him until I saw him standing with Darius.

# Ragged Edge

Darius stuck out an arm to stop me from approaching my grandfather.

"The ban is still in affect, Sean," he said sternly. I blinked hard and looked up at the sky. I hadn't realized how hard this reunion was going to be.

"Darius, will you please thank Elder Gryphon for answering my call?" I said, looking my grandfather in the eyes and trying to convey everything I felt through mine. Darius turned to repeat what I said and my grandfather held up one of his hands.

"I heard the boy very well with my own ears, as I suspect he can hear me perfectly well with his own." His voice was strong, deep, and defied his apparent age. Darius bowed his head.

"Very well, Elder Gryphon. In this meeting I am merely a figurative messenger." He took a step back. I tried to approach my grandfather but Darius stopped me again.

"The Elder will approach if he wishes, Sean. You will stay." A clear threat laced his words. I never wanted to hit Darius as much as I did at that moment. I felt my muscles tensing preparing for the attack, then I felt a small hand in the middle of my back. I looked and saw Ilsy standing beside me. I gave her a small smile.

"Ilsy, you've met Darius." His name leaving my lips like poison, I held my hand out towards my grandfather. "This is my grandfather, Elder Atlas Gryphon." My grandfather bowed towards Ilsy and walked forward. Ilsy extended a hand; he took the offered hand and kissed the back of it.

# Ragged Edge

"Aphrodite herself would be jealous of the beauty walking the earth as Ilsy Hillerman," he said softly. A furious blush rose in her cheeks.

"I thought you grew up with him, Sean." She looked at me.

"I did." I said, confused.

"Didn't learn anything did you?" she asked with a smile.

"Young lady, my grandson is graced with an overly hard head."

"I've noticed sir. After only three days I've become well acquainted with some of his less desirable characteristic. And some of his good ones," she said. Her eyes gained that strange quality as she looked at me again.

"Don't worry, miss, he grows on you."

"Like a bad fungus," Darius said.

"Alright that's enough picking on Sean," I said, flustered, "Grandfather, this is Ilsy's Uncle–"

"I know Sir Fry well enough already," he said, extending his hand to Ilsy's uncle.

"It is good to see you again, Atlas." He bowed his head.

"Fair enough, let's go inside so I can tell you all why I called for you," I said, gesturing towards the door.

My grandfather led the way and we went inside.

Once inside, my grandfather took a couple logs from beside the fireplace and crafted them into extra chairs. Everyone sat down as I passed out bottled water to everyone. I took a long drink from my bottle and then stood in the center of the room. I addressed each of the listeners in turn starting at the lowest ranked among us, Ilsy, and moving up to my grandfather. I then knelt and asked my grandfather for permission to speak the story of the past week. He rolled his eyes.

"Don't waste our time with silly ceremony; just say what you have to say," he answered with a hard glance at Darius. I loved my grandfather.

I began by telling them of my meeting with Darius, him informing me of my mission, and the threat of final death. I moved on to the fight outside Ilsy's house, my vision from the manuscript, and everything else that had happened until we came to the cabin. I left out the talks Ilsy and I had, the feelings I had stirring in me, and everything that had happened once we got to the cabin. While talking, I saw Ilsy's uncle looking around the cabin, and Darius' glance bouncing between Ilsy and myself. I think he sensed much of what wasn't said.

"So that brings us to now. I was hoping to get help translating the manuscript and figuring out what we are up against. I'm not familiar with wolfengators. Darius refused help at the beginning. As my job is to protect the book and Ilsy, I feel the situation has reached the point where I can't do so without assistance."

"Are you an idiot?" Sir Fry asked. I turned to look at him.

"I like to think I am not, sir," I said through gritted teeth.

"The answer to your wolfengators is right here in this room. Just open your eyes, boy."

I looked around me; it was my cabin. I saw his finger pointing toward the rug hanging over the door to the shower. I stared at it in silence for a minute, my mind working furiously. Then I slapped my forehead as the answer came to me. I should have guessed it right away.

"Naagloshii," I blurted out.

"What?" Ilsy asked.

"Skinwalker, dear. Though in this case I doubt they are true skinwalkers," Grandfather said.

"Why?" I asked.

"For one thing, boy, there are too many of them in too many places. So I imagine you're dealing with one main guy and a bunch of underlings," Sir Fry said.

"What does that mean?" Ilsy asked.

"It means you've got one nasty creature giving his, or her, abilities to a bunch of people. Probably very young and dumb enough to believe promises of power. Normally, they choose just one shape. Yours has decided to combine them," Darius explained.

"Yes, you see a skinwalker gains their shape-shifting ability from a coat made of the furs of the animal it wishes to turn into. They then gain the abilities and appearance of that animal. In this case the coats are part wolf and part alligator. You said the young woman you killed decomposed and turned to dust in front of you. That means their lives have been extended by some power. So your main skinwalker is probably very old," Grandfather said.

"Why would they be interested in a holy book?" I asked.

"They could be working with the priest, or they could be unrelated," Sir Fry said.

"If they aren't working together, why are they after Ilsy?"

"Our family has many enemies, boy. Look what they did to my brother. This priest asked for the book; did he mention Ilsy?"

"No sir."

"Then I would lean toward them being an enemy of our family. If that is the case, then it is a family matter. We will take care of it and you can leave Ilsy's care to me," Sir Fry said and began to stand.

I felt white-hot panic rise in my throat. For all my complaints, I had gotten used to having Ilsy around. I wasn't as anxious to be rid of her as I acted. Now that she might be leaving, I felt like a scared child.

"Don't be hasty, Sir Fry. This is just supposition, she could still be in danger," I said, holding a hand out to stop him. I felt Darius' eyes boring into me. Ilsy was looking up at me in shock.

"We are always in danger, Sean. Our family is equipped to handle it. You are a single man, a remarkable man from a remarkable people, but still just one man. She is safer at our compound," he said firmly.

"But," my words failed me. I had no argument to stop him. I nodded my head and turned away. He put a hand on my shoulder.

"If you need help with the priest, boy, just give me a call. I'll fight beside you." He patted my shoulder. "Come on, Ilsy, we'll wait outside for Mr. Darius."

"No, Uncle," she said. I felt a knot clench in my throat.

"What?"

"I'm staying with Sean." I turned to look at her, and she was staring up at her uncle. Neither moved nor spoke for what felt like an eternity.

"Are you sure?" he said finally.

"Yes, Uncle. I will call if we need you." She stood and hugged him.

"Very well." He moved to leave.

"Sir Fry."

"Yes, boy," he said, turning towards me.

"I swear to you I will protect her even at the cost of my life. Though it would be easier if you were there. Stay, Sir Fry, fight alongside us."

"I can't stay just now. I have business to take care of since my brother..." he said, looking down. "Call me, and I'll be there."

"We will," I said.

He nodded to me and walked outside.

"Darius, take the knight where he needs to go. I will wait here."

"Elder Gryphon, I'm not to leave your side," Darius said as he stood and headed towards the door.

"Don't argue. Just do it."

"Yes, Elder Gryphon," he said and waved a hand to us as he walked outside.

I sat on the couch beside Ilsy and smiled at my grandfather.

"Brother Herman. You've gotten yourself into quite a mess, Sean. Let me see this book and we'll see about getting you out of it."

# CHAPTER 10

Ilsy grabbed the book and took it to my grandfather. He carefully held onto the velvet cloth surrounding it. He studied the vellum, moving his lips as if reading it. For all I know, he was. Ilsy and I sat in silence and watched him. I couldn't stop myself from looking at her out of the corner of my eyes. She glanced my way occasionally, when she did the lines in her face were softened and that indescribable look was still in her eyes. I thought I knew what that look was. I was sure it was the same way I looked at her when she wasn't looking.

After a furtive look at Ilsy where our eyes met, we both smiled, or rather grimaced in a vaguely smiling manner, and quickly looked away. I caught my grandfather looking at us. A smirk sat on his lips. He caught me looking and smirked a little wider before continuing reading. I went into the kitchen and grabbed another bottle of water. The silence was starting to wear on my nerves. I tried a couple conversational gambits but Ilsy and Grandfather didn't seem interested.

What seemed like hours passed, I was about to go outside when my grandfather finally looked up. He closed his eyes and sat quietly for a moment. Now I knew he was testing my patience. I walked back to the couch and sat down preparing myself for a long wait. Ten minutes passed before he opened his eyes again. Without a word he stood and walked outside. He was old in appearance but not in action. He left the walking stick beside his chair, and spread his large wings as he crossed the threshold. Ilsy stood to follow him and I caught her arm.

"Just sit. He'll be back." She sat down beside me and sighed. The waiting was obviously taking a toll on her as well. After five minutes we heard a loud echoing series of harsh caws that could've only come from a crow.

"He's calling someone." I said, my nerves on edge. "Who?"

"I have no idea." We sank back into silence.

Another five minutes passed and the call was repeated, then my grandfather walked back inside and sat down. He looked at the two of us sitting side-by-side, almost close enough to be touching, and shook his head while chuckling. I was about to say something when an uproar of owls reverberated around the cabin. A frown passed over my grandfather's face, but he nodded and let out another caw.

"What was that about?" I asked.

"The terms of our separation have just been changed. You are now allowed to come to my cabin."

"Really?"

"Yes, provided of course that you are grievously injured and in need of aid."

"So not just for a chat."

"No," he smiled wanly.

"Still, at least we have a place to run if necessary."

"A bolt hole." Ilsy said.

"Exactly," Grandfather and I said in unison. He smiled at me more warmly and then reached forward for the manuscript.

"Sean, my dear grandson, before I reveal to you the meaning of this book I must give you a warning. As an Elder it is my duty to inform you that the contents of this manuscript, and the use the priest has for it, are most dire. This has gone beyond a threat to dear Ilsy or to you. This is a threat to the entire human race. As a junior guardian, you are not deemed qualified to handle a threat of this magnitude and are allowed to turn away from it without consequence." He paused and stared at me solemnly. I nodded, acknowledging my understanding.

"As my grandson, I feel you are able to meet this threat with at least average odds of surviving. Furthermore, I strongly urge you to continue your task and face whatever happens. I believe, if you are successful, your triumph will convince the council to lift the curse of final death from you, and possibly even to promote you. Finally."

"So, I can turn it down, but nothing changes. Or I can accept and possibly die," I said, standing and pacing the room. I didn't want to die, but I wasn't a coward either. Sure, I bitch about the humans and I find their ignorance to be tiresome and supremely irritating. That doesn't mean I wanted them to die horribly at the hands of some mad necromancer monk. I also thought that if my grandfather believed I might survive then maybe I could handle it. At least he wasn't telling me I would probably die. Then again, he was my grandfather. He raised me through my first life, greeted me at the end of my second life, and trained me at the beginning of this life. He was supposed to be supportive. I looked at Ilsy for a long time. If she fought beside me and I fell, she would be condemned to death – or worse.

"Will you tell me what the book says before I decide?" I hedged.

"No."

"Figures. Am I allowed to have help?"

"You may have whatever assistance you feel that you require, excluding the Elders. We will not take part in this."

"Great." I looked at Ilsy, my eyebrows raised. She looked into my eyes and nodded slowly.

"Alright, I'll do it." I felt the conflicting emotions of a weight being lifted from my shoulders and a larger weight being added on.

"Sean, you know about the original Codex Gigas. We managed to get a hold of it years ago and place a copy in its place. That original was missing ten pages when we got it. So the copy is also missing ten pages. As

# Ragged Edge

I'm sure you've figured out, these ten pages are from the original. If you can't tell that just from the history then you can taste the pages. Go ahead." Grandfather held the pages out to me.

I took them from him and moved them to my mouth slowly. Under normal circumstances I refuse to taste any ancient books. Some of the things they made book covers and paper out of long ago didn't exactly taste good and, even in their aged state, couldn't possibly be good for you. My tongue touched one of the pages and I immediately pulled it away from me.

"What?" Ilsy asked with eyebrows raised.

Before answering her, I brought the pages back to my face and smelled them, then handed them back to grandfather with a sigh.

"Human flesh. And blood." I said while trying to wipe the taste off my tongue.

"Exactly. Most of the first book was written with regular velum and ink. These ten pages are human flesh and blood," Grandfather said.

"Why?" Ilsy asked.

"Who knows? Maybe to add a layer of sacrilege to the Devil's bible," I answered.

"Or because the author knew that the church would never allow these pages to remain so it would be easier to take them," Grandfather said.

"The writing on them though. That isn't Latin." I pointed to the writing. Most of it was in Latin just like the rest of the book but some words comprised multiple languages with letters varying here and there. Some words were in a completely different language. If not for the age, I would have thought someone had simply cut letters and words out of magazines to glue on the page like a ransom note. These were all written in the same handwriting though.

"To understand that you must understand the history of the Codex." Grandfather said. From his tone I could tell he was about to slip into a lecture.

"In the thirteenth century there was a monk, most likely Brother Herman, that had broken the vows of his order in a particularly horrendous way. The leaders of his order sentenced him to be walled up inside his chamber to eventually starve to death. Pleading for mercy, Brother Herman promised to write a book containing the Old Testament, the New Testament, and all of human knowledge to that point. Somewhat sadistically, the leaders of the order accepted this with the condition that he had twenty-four hours to do it. No man can write a book of that magnitude in a day. Brother Herman set to work writing as fast as he could but around midnight he realized he could never finish." Grandfather stopped to take a breath and a drink of water.

"It was then that he decided to make a deal with the devil. Or so he thought. A figure appeared to him as he made his plea to Lucifer. The figure listened to his plight and agreed to write the Bible for him, for a price."

"His soul," Ilsy said matter-of-factly.

"You would think that. Maybe if it really had been the devil that would've been the price and we wouldn't be here. No, the figure demanded Brother Herman's undying loyalty. Again not something that would normally concern us. Except this particular figure had the ability to make the undying bit a reality."

"Who was it?" I asked. I could count the amount of beings that could give a human eternal life on both hands, the ones that actually would give a human eternal life on one hand, and of those I couldn't think of any that I actually wanted to deal with.

"We don't know. All the manuscript said was a figure in shadows, which of course enhanced the Brothers' opinions that it was in fact the Devil. We know that Lucifer, in fact, had nothing to do with it. He wasn't even in the area at the time."

"What about the Devil or Satan?" I asked.

"At that time Satan wasn't quite strong enough to do anything of the sort. As for the Devil, you should know better than that, Sean. He doesn't want to deal with humans any more than you do."

"What do you mean Satan wasn't strong enough yet?" Ilsy asked.

"Well, he's more of an ideological creation," Grandfather said. "Purely human in origin. Sometimes, just sometimes, the belief of a thing can make that thing real. At that time, there hadn't been enough belief or worship of Satan for him to have enough power to do anything like this. Whoever did it, though, certainly believed."

"Why do you say that?" I asked.

"When you dig through the mixed languages in these pages, it's pretty simple. These pages dictate a ritual to open a gateway."

"What kind of gateway?" I asked slowly.

# Ragged Edge

"One that holds back all the hordes of hell," Grandfather said in a deep, overly dramatic voice before returning to his normal voice.

"Or, less dramatically, one that will open a doorway to one of the lower levels of the spiritual realm."

I sat back silently to process this information. Darius came barging in the door. Ilsy let out a short shriek. I stood, shifting from human to fighting form in the process. What I saw shocked me and I switched back to human form to walk over to Darius. He was bleeding badly from multiple wounds, his eyes roaming around the room crazily. I got to him as he started a swoon. I reach out to catch him. As I did I glanced out the open door and saw Ilsy's uncle laying just outside, apparently unconscious. I started to speak but my voice caught in my throat. Underneath my hands I felt a warm liquid oozing from two twitching stubs.

I carried Darius to the bed and laid him down on his stomach. Grandfather ripped off his shirt and we both stared at him in shock. The stubs were protruding from Darius' shoulder blades. I whispered to grandfather about Ilsy's uncle. He left and walked outside, telling Ilsy to help me. I sent her to grab towels and bandages as I placed my hands on Darius' stubs. I held onto them and blue light flooded from my hands. I felt the blood slow then stop. Ilsy appeared at my side and handed me a towel. I wiped off the blood and checked for more wounds. Aside from light scratches around the base of his stubs his back was fine.

I had Ilsy help me roll him over and started healing as many of the wounds as I could. Deep claw marks dug into both thighs, a bite had been taken out of one bicep, his chest and stomach were covered in slashes, and his face bore three grooves that had to have come from claws. I was able to take care of the cuts on his thighs and the bite in his arm. Black spots started floating in front of my eyes. I had Ilsy hold pressure on the rest of wounds and walked into the kitchen slowly and grabbed more water from the fridge, then reached into a cabinet and pulled out a bottle of rubbing alcohol.

Walking back to the bed, I could see his eyes were open again, tears trickling from the corners. He inhaled sharply as I poured the alcohol on his chest and stomach. I told him to close his eyes and he did so silently. I used a corner of the towel to clean the grooves in his face. His jaw tightly clenched – the alcohol had to have burned like a bastard on his face but he never made a sound. I bandaged the clean wounds as best I could. He opened his eyes again and looked at me for the first time.

"Thank you, Sean," he said, then closed his eyes again.

"Welcome," I said.

"What happened to him?" Ilsy asked.

"I don't know," I said and took a deep breath.

Then grandfather came back in, supporting Ilsy's uncle.

"Uncle!" she said and rushed to his side.

"I'm alright, Ilsy. Atlas took care of what ailed me. I'm just tired is all."

He looked it. Dark circles encased his eyes and his shirt and pants were stained in blood and torn to shreds.

Ilsy and Grandfather guided him to the couch and he collapsed into it. I sunk into one of the chairs and watched Ilsy dote over him.

"What happened?" I asked.

"We were ambushed. I don't know how they snuck up on us. We went to my house so I could pack some clothes and weapons. There was a commotion downstairs. I rushed down and saw him surrounded. Fifteen, twenty maybe. They were all over us. I got to him as fast as I could and we fought together. One of the damn things jumped on him from behind and chewed through his wings. That was when he grabbed me, next thing I knew we were here." His eyes closed and he slowed his breathing.

"We would've died had he not brought us here. Too many of them," he mumbled.

"Too many what?" I asked although I already knew the answer.

"Wolfengators."

Ilsy shot a glance at me. For the first time I saw a touch of fear behind her eyes. Two attacks I could accept as coincidence, but three attacks had to be more. How did they know Darius and Sir Fry would be there? They had to have known that Darius would be with Ilsy's uncle, otherwise why show up in such numbers? They also seemed to know what Darius was, that's the only reason to have made a concentrated effort at chewing off his wings. My mind whirled with the possibilities, my brain thrummed with fatigue, and a headache pulsated right behind my eyes. Sir Fry was snoring softly on the couch and Darius was asleep on the bed. I quietly stood and walked outside. I felt frustrated anger boiling in my stomach, radiating a nervous energy throughout my body. I needed to move.

Ilsy and my grandfather followed. I was happy to have them there even though I mostly wanted to be alone. I reached down and scooped up a handful of rocks then started throwing them into the woods as hard as I could. Sure, it was a little childish but it helped relieve a little of the tension and didn't hurt anyone. When you can easily hurl fireballs, throwing rocks is usually preferable. After throwing the last rock, I let out a roar of frustration. A flock of birds took to the sky, hurling insults at me for scaring them. Then I felt a soft hand on my shoulder. I turned and saw Ilsy standing behind me with Grandfather by the cabin door. Looking at Ilsy, the pain and anger broke loose.

Without a word she pulled me down into a hug. My head rested on her shoulder as I softly wept. So, maybe I am an overgrown child. I had never seen Darius this badly injured, and that alone was enough to send an electrical jolt of fear coursing through me. Ilsy had almost lost a second family member since I entered her life and again there was nothing I could do about it. To top it all off, I had just accepted the charge of stopping some insane monk from opening a gateway to what he thought of as hell. The damn wolfengators kept coming from all sides, and I still didn't know where they fit. So the confusion, the fear, and the pain of seeing Darius so grievously injured finally got the better of me.

We stood that way for a long time. My weeping subsided and I pulled back from Ilsy. I tried to thank her but my mouth just moved uselessly. There was so much that I needed to be say but now was not the time. So I nodded my thanks. I put more logs into the fire pit and lit them before sitting down and staring at the flames. Grandfather and Ilsy joined me.

"How did they know?" I asked.

"I don't know, Sean. We can't be tracked when we jump around. Perhaps Donovan is correct and the skinwalkers are a family issue."

"Then why attack with so many? There were only three at her house and only two at her father's house – and some guy."

"What guy?" Ilsy asked.

"Medium height, slight build, nasally voice, bald, his skin was whiter than white, dirty clothes, and he looked blind." I wished I had paid more attention to him.

"Blind?" Grandfather asked.

"Yeah, his eyes were a cloudy white."

"What did he do?"

"Well he didn't run screaming into the night, nor did he offer me a fight. He said they were paying a friendly social call to Mr. Hillerman, I told them to leave and he said I was blocking their path. I stepped aside and he walked past me. He was chuckling when he did."

"What did the skinwalkers do?"

"They snarled at me and that was it."

"You were not the target."

"I know. If I had known what they had done to Ilsy's father, I would have killed them. I hadn't been inside yet though."

"I will be back," Grandfather said, and before I could say anything he took a step, transformed into a crow, and flew off. I followed him with my eyes until he winked out of existence as he reached the top of the trees.

"Wow," Ilsy said.

"It is pretty cool, isn't it?" I said, smiling.

"What's he doing?"

"If I had to guess, he didn't like my description."

"Ok, so?"

"So he went to see for himself."

"What?"

"He went to watch what happened."

"Like watch watch?"

"Yeah, I guess if I had looked around I would've seen him."

"How can he?"

"Basically, the same as when we travel from place to place. He's going back in time to watch everything unfold." I picked up a stick and held it in the fire. It was mild fun to watch it catch fire in a natural manner. Depending on who you talk to, my way of starting fires is also natural but somehow I don't think it's quite the same.

"Could he stop it from happening?" Ilsy asked. I knew the question was coming but dreaded it all the same.

"Physically, yes, he could."

"Then why didn't he?" she asked, anger and pain painting her words.

"It's not allowed."

"Not allowed?" I could hear the anger rising.

"Right, that's why he left as a bird. It's the only way he can watch but make sure he doesn't change anything."

"But he could save my dad's life!" She pounded a fist on her leg.

"No Ilsy, he can't. It's not allowed."

"What do you mean, it's not allowed?"

"It's one of our laws. We have the ability to travel backward in time. If we do so in our human form, we could accidentally alter the course of history. In theory, it could've already been altered and we would never know. That's a discussion for another time though. The point is if grandfather were to go back and save your father, then he would be alive when he isn't supposed to be. In the big picture that could be good or bad, we have no way of knowing. Which is why it's safer if we just don't mess with it."

"Then why go back at all?" Her teeth were clenched.

"Usually to learn. In this case, he will see the man I spoke to leaving your father's house. Maybe he will recognize the guy. Then we might know who or what we are dealing with. It might also tell us if the monk and wolfengators are working together."

"What if the guy was the one in charge? Maybe if your grandfather killed him before he killed my father, we wouldn't have this problem."

"He won't do that, Ilsy. To interfere would be inviting death. If we could alter the past then we would have saved our homeland long ago. We simply can't do it."

"What happened to your home?"

"A mad monk trespassed on it. You were there, remember?"

"Not what I meant."

"Our homeland was destroyed by a volcano. What modern scientists call a super volcano. Our original home was an island. On one side was a fertile plain where crops of all types grew abundantly, and in the center was the mountain. In a way, our island was actually two islands with water separating them and the mountain was in the center. It was a beautiful island. Then one day the earthquakes started. Our scientists knew about the volcano because previous eruptions were why our plain was so fertile, kind of like Vesuvius. Those of us alive at the time knew it was going to explode so we abandoned our homes. When it finally exploded, they gathered the dust and debris from the sky and the larger pieces from the sea and assembled them into equal-sized pieces at the four points around the globe." I saw a light behind Ilsy's eyes. She had heard this story before. A number of humans had read about our homeland and thought it was only myth.

"Is that the story or is it fact?"

"Fact. The first trip to the past all young ones of my race make is to visit the homeland. We see it as it was before the volcano exploded, and we watch the explosion happen. The hellish force of the explosion is indescribable. When I saw it happen I wondered why we didn't stop it. With our connection to the elements, we should have been able to take the thermal energy away from the explosion, make it a weaker volcano like Kilauea in Hawaii. The Elders said that would have gone against the way things were supposed to be."

"Destiny?"

"Basically. I don't put a lot of stock in it myself normally, but one can't really argue with the Elders. I mean in the grand scheme of things, what does it matter if the future changes? Think of it: if Hitler had been killed before rising to power, millions of people would have lived normal lives."

"What about the good things he did?"

"What about them? He invented the autobahn and saved a country from a depression. In some ways, the war he started rescued the world from the same depression. Does that mean those millions of people had to die for it to happen or would someone else have come along and done the same thing without the murdering?"

"It's not unrealistic," she said slowly.

"The same is true for the opposite. We can't predict the future so we don't change the events of the past. The Elders say everything happens for a reason. I think it's basically easier to learn from the past. Eventually your father would have died anyway, why take the chance of something catastrophically bad happening if he didn't die that night?" I tried to say this as softly as possible. I knew it was rather blunt but she didn't need to push this subject. I had already gotten in trouble with time travel once and I didn't even change anything. The Elders get pissy about the issue being pushed. I tried to get them to stop my father from leaving.

"I think I understand," she said as a crow appeared in front of us. Before landing, it turned into my grandfather.

"What did you see?" I asked.

"We will wait for Darius to wake up. I will say that I do know the man, though I do not know why he was there and how he yet lives."

Darius and Ilsy's uncle slept for hours. We sat outside and grandfather showed off his hunting skills. Or rather, he borrowed my car and drove to the grocery store. In the modern world anyone can be a good hunter if they can get to a supermarket. I would deem his hunt unsuccessful: he brought back hot dogs. We skewered them and had roasted hot dogs for dinner. In a way it was fun. It took me back to times when I was young and we would go camping. In all of my lives, I think those were some of the best times. I always learned something on those trips. That was how he taught me to make a fire, and on one memorable occasion how to put a fire out with water from your fingertips. That's also how I learned to enjoy the simple pleasure of sitting outside and listening to the world around you.

If your ears are open you can hear everything the world has to say. It's something even my race takes for granted these days. Humans move through the world at breakneck speed, never once asking if they are actually getting anywhere. My race is picking up the same habit. On a whole, this is bad. We are what we are due to our natural bond with the elements of nature, our link with the quantum plain. Slowly we are losing this. I haven't interacted with many of the young ones but from what I've heard, we are getting weaker. Perhaps it's for the best though. Nature hates stagnation and we really haven't changed, ever.

Eventually Darius stumbled outside. He looked awful. Most of his wounds had healed already but he had a sullen, morose quality to him I had never seen before. I can't say I blamed him though. I wouldn't be too thrilled with having to live as a human until my wings grew back. He sat by us without a word and I handed him a hot dog on a skewer. He chuckled once and held it over the fire. By the time his dog finished roasting, Uncle Fry came shambling out. Night had fallen around us. Uncle Fry had a limp and held onto the ribs on his right side. Whatever gifts the Aen Sidhe had given Ilsy's family, the ability to heal quickly apparently wasn't one of them.

With a groan, Sir Fry joined us by the fire, and Ilsy handed him a skewer. He shrugged his shoulders and started cooking his dinner. For a time all five of us just sat by the fire silently collecting our thoughts. Drinks were gotten, bathroom breaks taken, and the silence stretched out far into the night. I don't know about everyone else, I never asked, but to me it felt like the world was taking a great breath. A giant inhale before blowing a candle out in a strong sudden puff of wind. Something big was coming, something life changing.

# Ragged Edge

Every particle of my body vibrated with anticipation yet I sat calmly by a fire enjoying the companionship of the group I had brought together. I'm glad I didn't know what was awaiting me. I'm sure I would have gone insane.

It was midnight when conversation started again. Grandfather took Darius into the woods leaving Sir Fry, Ilsy, and me to entertain ourselves. I learned that not only was Sir Fry a knowledgeable man and a skillful fighter but also an excellent storyteller as he regaled us with tales of his younger years. He told stories of Ilsy's father, a rebellious young man that often found himself in accidental trouble, and of a young Ilsy, most causing her to blush an impossible shade of red. I made up my mind that if I survived the coming battles that I would add on to my cabin so that events such as this could take place in happier circumstances.

Darius returned before Grandfather. If anything, he was looking more dour than he had when they walked off. I knew the coming talks were not going to be pleasant from the look on his face and the avoidance of my eyes. I couldn't remember the last time he refused to look me in the eyes, I think it was probably the time he caught me in a compromising position with a female djinn. She decided that rubbing lamps wasn't the only thing I was good for. That time it was embarrassment that caused him to avoid my gaze. This time it was something ineffable.

# Ragged Edge

Grandfather joined us after about ten minutes. His wings were spread and he stood behind Darius. All small talk ceased, a collective breath was taken and held.

"Darius, tell him what you told me." There was a hard edge in Grandfather's voice that I hadn't heard in a long time. Darius stared at the ground.

"Sean, tonight when I took Donovan to his house, I caught a glimpse of someone. I ignored it at first. I think now I shouldn't have." He spoke so quietly we had to lean forward to hear him.

"Who?" Again I knew the answer before he spoke. Some sadistic part of me had to hear it.

"Your mother." Ilsy gasped, Sir Fry groaned. I slowly let my breath out.

"What of her?" My voice was hard like stone.

"I think, but I can't be positive on this, that it was her directing the attack."

"Why would she do that?"

"I know it was her Sean; I went back. The attack started on her signal. It also ended on her signal. These two escaped because she apparently didn't want them dead," Grandfather said.

"What?" three voices combined into one.

"I don't know. I saw Darius and Donovan fighting for all they were worth. The skinwalkers acted in concert as a true wolf pack would. They had no chance of survival. At the very least Darius should have brought one or two here latched onto him. After his wings were ripped off, the attack stopped. They were allowed to escape. After they vanished, the walkers gathered around your mother. I saw the man from Ilsy's father's house also. The entire group linked hands and left."

"So who is this guy?" My world was spinning out of control.

"Darius knows." Darius winced at my grandfather's words. We all watched him expectantly.

"His name is Arik, Arik Sturmguard. He's your brother." He finally looked up at me. The pain in his eyes was unbearable to look at. I looked away. Sitting next to me, Ilsy felt my body tense. She placed a hand firmly on my arm.

"It happened after your father left. Your mother had already left you with Atlas. I never told you because I thought he was dead."

"Tell me now." I stared into the fire, the flames growing higher.

"Your father and I were best friends, Sean. You look so much like him. We were inseparable for hundreds of years. Then your father met your mother. He could tell she would produce a child for him but I think he was truly in love with her. The kind of love Greek poets used to write about in their tragedies. There was something about her that made me uneasy. He wouldn't listen to me though, eventually they were wed and you were born. Your mother had an independent streak a mile wide. As a human she was the daughter of her clan's chief. She was accustomed to receiving anything she wanted. Hers was a clan of warriors and she fought right alongside the men. So when she became one of us, she couldn't accept simply teaching others to fight."

# Ragged Edge

"They fought endlessly and he eventually left. In the human world this isn't uncommon, but for us it's almost unheard of, as you know. As far as I know, it's still unknown what happened to him. He hasn't been seen or heard from since. There have been times that I've thought I have glimpsed him, I don't know for sure. After he left, your mother was heartbroken, thrilled, and in a rage all at once. Since her husband had left, she saw no reason to abide by our rules. That's when she left you with Atlas. During your second life she came to me looking for your father. I hadn't seen him and told her so. She hung around and one night, well, I think you can guess what happened. She stayed with me until the baby was born."

"There was a terrible storm that night, the likes of which I haven't seen since. The baby came and he was the most extreme white. If he hadn't been screaming I would have believed him to be dead. I knew this child was not one of us, but what it was I wasn't sure. I demanded we take it to the Elders. She attacked me. When I woke up, she was gone with the baby. She left a note telling me not to seek them out. That was when I learned of his name. I didn't know what to do so I went to Atlas—"

"You knew of this?" I asked my grandfather.

"I did," he said

"You never told me?"

"It wasn't for me to tell."

"I saw your mother again just after I had been assigned as your trainer. She told me the child had died. So I saw no reason to tell you. You were already showing her rebellious streak, and I didn't want to make it worse. For what it's worth, I'm sorry."

I kept staring at the fire. I couldn't make sense of the emotions boiling around inside of me. Before I knew I was doing it, I had yanked my arm free of Ilsy and did a short jump intending to strike Darius. Instead I reappeared to meet the granite of my grandfather's fist. A bright white light flashed before my eyes. For me, the night was over.

# CHAPTER 11

I woke the next morning with a throbbing jaw. Confusion and pain made the previous night a jumbled mess of images. I tried following a coherent thread but couldn't find one. I then tried the next best thing: ignore it all. The one constant with all the threads was the night's end with my grandfather's granite fist smashing into my jaw. The momentum of my jump, the force in his swing, combined to create one bone-shattering collision. If I had been human, I would've woken up needing to eat through a straw. As it was my jaw still hurt and felt a little swollen.

I looked around the room. Sir Fry was on the couch snoring softly, a crow was roosting on a support beam, and Darius was laying on a pallet on the floor. I didn't see Ilsy at first. I thought she had gone to the bathroom so I sat up in bed and rubbed my eyes, gingerly feeling my jaw. It wasn't shattered still, not even broken, but eating breakfast was going to be an adventure in pain. I

# Ragged Edge

felt movement behind me and turned quickly. My head spun when I did and a wave of nausea coursed through me. I closed my eyes until it felt like my stomach was going to stay firmly in place. When I opened them again, I found Ilsy in the bed beside me. I couldn't do more than shrug and get to my feet.

As quietly as I could, I stripped off my shirt and grabbed new clothes from my closet. I snagged a towel on my way outside. The morning smelled crisp and clean with a minor nip in the air that almost made it chilly. If we had been alone I never would've left the cabin without Ilsy. But she had protection, even if two of the warriors were wounded, so I took a walk. My bare feet made little sound as I walked into the woods. My people have an innate ability to walk softly and quietly; if we make noise in our movement it is almost always intentional. The ground was cool beneath my feet and felt good. I walked the full half-mile to the spring I normally used for water. The water this morning was still enough to resemble a pane of glass.

I stripped naked at the water's edge and dove in. The spring was roughly twelve feet deep and six feet in diameter. Not much of a swimming hole but an excellent place to soak and let the frigid waters caress the cares from your body, which is what I did. The icy water felt awesome on my jaw so I made repeated dives to the bottom. I felt the tension cleansed from my body as I bathed in the spring. My jaw finished healing and I began to feel more myself – until a hand grabbed my hair as I surfaced and yanked me from the water. Without thought, I transformed into my fighting form and I heard a laugh before my eyes focused. I was being held a good thirty feet off the ground by a woman with dark hair, shinier than mine though streaked with gray, a fair figure, and beautiful blue eyes.

"Mother?" I gasped.

"Yes, child, mommy has come for you," she said and flung me by my hair toward a tree. I used the momentum of the throw and jumped just behind her, driving my fisted talons into the small of her back. She let out a yelp and snarled as she transformed to fight. In my form, I resemble an overgrown humanoid raven, I couldn't immediately identify what bird she resembled but it struck me as some kind of vulture.

"What do you want?" I snarled. She speared towards me and slashed at me with six-inch talons. I proved the more agile of the two of us and dodged the blow. Her speed carried her past me and we turned to face each other.

"Can't a mother drop in to visit her beloved son?" her voice was a high-pitched squawk.

She lunged again, but I thrust both my hands towards her, palms out, and sent a jet of wind rushing at her. The air slammed into her with the force of a physical blow and drove her into a tree. Her back slammed into the trunk, her head whipped backward on her neck. A sickening, crunching thud reverberated from her head impacting the tree. Her eyes rolled back into her skull, her body resumed its human shape and she began falling from the tree.

"Which son would that be, Mother?" I asked as she bounced from limb to limb on her way to the ground. I slowly drifted down after her. She hit the ground with a bone rattling thump. I stopped my descent ten feet from the ground and let out a piercing Cr-r-ruck call. I knew it would carry back to the cabin and bring help. I watched the body of my mother; she was still breathing so I hadn't killed her yet. I looked around me to make sure we were alone. I didn't see anything but I didn't trust it. I had no idea why she was here, doubted she came alone, and had been in enough fights in my life to never trust my surroundings to not hold a few surprises.

She began stirring as I was joined by an overlarge bald eagle. I pointed a finger at her. He looked at her and then back at me. I pointed to myself then back down to the ground. My meaning was clear; I wanted him in the air watching my back. He nodded wordlessly and started circling an area about thirty feet around. I drifted back to the ground while resuming my human form. I still didn't trust this game so I kept my wings. All the times I had imagined reuniting with my mother and never once had the dreams involved a fight – or me being naked. I think my shrink would've had something to say if they had. I dropped down beside my fresh clothes and put the pants on quickly. I found a stone on the ground I could turn into a sword. She had lost the element of surprise, and I didn't intend to let her have it back.

She came to with me standing in front of her a good ten feet away. The spring was at my back and Grandfather was watching us. I held the stone sword between my legs, tip on the ground. My feet and wings were spread. I was trying to be as intimidating as possible. By the look on her face I could tell she was calculating her next move.

"How's Arik, Mother?" My voice was flat, cold.

"He's dead," she said. Her voice held resignation and sadness in it. I so badly wanted to trust her but couldn't bring myself to do it.

"From what I hear, he's done that before."

"The knight killed him."

"Did he? I knew I liked him," I said as if to myself.

"Why are you here, Mother?"

"I heard you were in trouble. I want to help." Yeah, right.

"So you pull me out from my bath by my hair?"

"I thought you were drowning." She couldn't be this stupid, I knew she was running some kind of game on me.

"I don't need your help, Mother."

"Is Ilsy pregnant yet?"

"What?" Yeah, that caught me off guard.

"Is she not pretty enough for you? I've tried to judge your taste in women but you don't seem to have one. So I went for the best I could find."

"You what?"

"I found you a mate."

"Then proceeded to kill her father and attack her uncle."

"That's ridiculous. The monk did that."

I stood silently. I couldn't figure out where she was going. It sounded as though she had no idea that I had seen Arik with my own eyes. She also seemed to not know that Darius had seen her. If true, I could use that to my advantage. She could also be playing with me and only acting innocent until one of her wolfengators could jump me from behind. Almost unconsciously, I glanced behind me but nothing was there.

"What do you know of the monk?"

"Herman wants to take over the world. He wants to use your blood to open the gateway."

"Yeah, I figured that already." If she wanted to lie, I could too.

"So he's dead."

"Not yet," I said.

"You don't know where he is, do you? I could take you to him," she said, oozing false sweetness and sincerity.

"Then what? Take me from behind so he can have me?"

"My dear son, I would never do that." I caught her eyes moving to look behind me. Either something was there or she was trying to trick me. She had to be recovered from the blow I had dealt her by now. I refused to look and hoped grandfather had spotted whatever was back there, if anything.

"That's right, I forgot about all the great times we had together. Silly me." I used to think that if I ever met my mother I wouldn't feel anything for her. In truth I felt anger, fear, suspicion, and sorrow. I never thought I would feel sorry for her, but here she was and I knew she was either completely insane or thought I was a complete moron.

"You're right. I wasn't a good mother. That's why I left you with Atlas, he was the only one I trusted to raise you. I knew he would do a better job than I would."

"I understand, Mother." I heard a ripple in the water behind me. Now I knew something was behind me. I tried to act as though I hadn't heard it. "Grandfather did a good job, but you wanna know the most important thing he taught me, Mother?"

"Of course, son." She wasn't even pretending to look at me. I was taking a gamble that grandfather was on top of things. The trap she had set was about to close. I just hoped he was fast enough to pull me out of it.

"He taught me that no matter how bad the situation, how much you mess up, or how bad you hurt the people you care about," there was an enormous splash behind me, my mother's eyes grew wide, and water rained down on me as I finished, "the people who care about you always have your back."

Grandfather flew between us, a wolfengator held in his talons. He stopped and faced her. The gator he held started to smolder, a sickly smell of roasting meat and burning hair radiating from it. The wolfengator let out a horrific shriek filled with anguish. My grandfather threw the smoking wolfengator at my mother and it burst into flames in the air. She quickly scooted away from it when it landed beside her. Grandfather took off back into the air.

"That's your first warning, Mother. Go away, do not come to this place again, leave Ilsy and her family alone, and I will allow you to live." I raised the sword and strode forward a few steps. I stopped and took a defensive posture with the sword held in front of me. I sent heat through my hands and encased the blade in a molten fire. "Leave now."

"Fine, Sean. I see you've been poisoned against me. When you decide you want fact instead of ignorant tales of self-glorification, come find me." She stood and let out a harsh call. Three more wolfengators appeared from the woods around us. Two of them proceeded directly to her side the third approached me from my right flank, growling. I stood my ground.

"Do it." I snarled.

"No!" my mother shouted as the wolfengator leaped at me. I saw its muscles bunch before the leap. I sidestepped it while bringing my sword down on its neck. The head of a young man rolled to a stop at my mother's feet. A muscular body fell to the ground in a heap between us. The head and body began decomposing immediately just like the first one I had killed.

"Looks like you'll be leaving two short," I said, resuming my stance in front of her.

"You'll pay," she said, placing her hands on the heads of the two gators at her side. She vanished.

My grandfather landed and began kicking dirt on the still smoldering ashes of the one he had killed. I let the molten flame on my sword die down and shaped it back into a stone. I dropped the stone to the ground as I walked back and grabbed my shirt.

"Thank you, Grandfather," I said as I hid my wings away and put on the shirt.

# Ragged Edge

"It was my honor, Sean. Now let's get back to the cabin in case she has something else in store for us. The woods are empty but I think we should leave soon," he said, spreading the ashes of the gator I had killed.

"I agree," I said, "I thought you were a crow?"

He finished spreading the ashes, walked to my side, clapped a hand on my shoulder and shrugged with a small smile on his face. I don't know why but we both laughed as we started walking back to the cabin.

As we approached the cabin, the smell of cooking steaks tantalized our nostrils. Getting closer we could also smell bacon, eggs, sautéing onions, garlic, and potatoes. Grandfather and I looked at each other, smiled, and then raced back to the cabin. I have no shame in admitting the old man beat me. I would say he cheated, because he did, but age has its privileges I guess. Uncle Fry was sitting at the fire pit grilling the steaks while the other smells were wafting out of the cabin. As I approached the door I detected the most ambrosial scent I have ever had the orgasmic pleasure of smelling. Freshly ground and brewed coffee sat on one of the burners of the gas stove. A longing moan escaped me as I strode to the cabinet and took down two mugs. The sound I made after the first sip was too indecent for description. Suffice it to say, I was in heaven.

The alluring scent of coffee had distracted me so much that I hadn't noticed Ilsy and Darius cooking at the stove. They were both laughing heartily. I felt a sickly, squirming, snake of jealousy try to rear its head in the pit of my stomach. A couple sips of the coffee were enough to burn it into submission. Besides that, after the trauma Darius had just gone through and the painful regrowth of his wings ahead of him, he needed a smile or two. The effect was a little creepy though. Darius doesn't laugh. In my experience, when he is happy he gives you a smile that fully details how you are an idiot and that you should have easily gotten to whatever it was that made him happy long before you did. That's what I see anyway.

"You can't be serious," Ilsy said, laughing.

"On the promise of my life, every word is true."

"What's true?" I asked feeling like an intruder into a private party. Ilsy looked over at me and started laughing so hard she couldn't breathe. Obviously, I was the butt of the joke. I stared at Darius while Ilsy snorted and used the counter to hold herself up while trying to choke down air through never-ending rolls of soundless laughter.

"Nothing much, Sean." he said casually and returned to cooking. I looked at the pan and saw a mound of onions, garlic, and potatoes frying.

"What did you tell her?"

"I was just regaling her with stories of the old days."

"Dar….," Ilsy tried to speak but choked on laughter. "You..." she squealed.

"For fuck's sake," I said and walked outside. Behind me I heard the two of them break into a chorus of laughter. I walked over to my grandfather and handed him the full mug.

# Ragged Edge

"Thank you, Sean," he said and continued a conversation with Uncle Fry.

This was the strangest morning of my life. A nice bath in the spring to clear my head followed by having my hair almost jerked out of my freshly cleared head by my mother who was supposed to be dead. A brief family squabble, the death of two of skinwalkers, and finding out my grandfather has multiple forms. That was a rarity among our kind. If we were human, we would say it was a one in a billion gift. Then we return to my cabin to find a pleasant domestic scene of early morning tranquility. At least the coffee was good.

I sat on a rock beside grandfather and tried to soak in as much of the warm feelings surrounding us as I could. I wasn't accustomed to gatherings like this. Among my kind, I'm mostly an outcast. Most of the Elders think I'm going to turn my back on the race as my mother did or just stroll off into obscurity like my father. This feeling filters down through the ranks and, as a consequence, I'm not exactly invited to many gatherings. I avoid having many human friends because it's difficult to keep lies straight and we aren't supposed to tell humans anything about us. Darius started it with Ilsy though, so I had a defense if my actions were called into question.

So I'm mostly a loner. I do my job most of the time, I do it well at least half the time, and I keep to myself. It's a lonely way to live for any amount of time but I had gotten accustomed to it over my long life. Now I was beginning to think having close friends and family was better than flying solo. My encounter with my mother would have gone differently without my grandfather being there, and I wouldn't be having one extraordinary cup of coffee without Ilsy and the others here. I began thinking I should have found a human that knew about us long ago.

What amazed me, though maybe it shouldn't have given the circumstances, was how well our two groups managed to mesh. It's said that people who go through stressful situations together often form a close bond, and I could see that bond forming in our group. Normally, I would have been the first to try severing that bond. Now, I felt an intense need to nurture that bond and, most importantly, to enjoy it. If Sir Fry participated in the upcoming battle and survived, he was still old by human standards and wouldn't be alive too much longer. Ilsy would eventually grow old and die also – if she survived coming battles. My kind tries not to think about it much, but the human lifespan is really just a blink compared to the near immortality we enjoy. So for now I let the tangible feelings of goodwill and friendship wash over me.

Soon breakfast was ready and we all sat around the fire to enjoy the meal. The food was fabulous, made better by the company it was enjoyed with. Normally I eat because I have to. Food is fuel and flavor doesn't matter. This morning was different. The act of eating had become more than the simple act of taking in nutrients for my body to burn. It was a bonding experience. None of us talked about monks, wolfengators, ancient cursed books, or the fact that Grandfather and I had just run into my mother at the spring we had been gathering water from. All of that was for later. Now it was time to enjoy each other, and the simple acts that make us human, well human-ish, I guess.

# CHAPTER 12

Eventually the breakfast was over, the dishes were washed, and it was time for business. We all gathered back around the fire pit as if we all knew what was coming without having to say it. I guess the near telepathic bond of close groups is another benefit of forming them. Then again, what else were we going to do? Decisions had to be made; we couldn't hang out here until the humans simply grew old and died. Later I would wish we had explored that option, but it seemed like a terribly boring and ineffectual course. Before we could sit, however, Uncle Fry asked me if I would take a short walk with him. A look passed between him and Grandfather. I agreed and stood up.

We walked past my car and continued down the road. I knew something was on his mind but held my silence and waited for him to speak. My cabin was out of sight before he broke the silence.

"This country is beautiful," he said, looking at the tall trees and ferns that surrounded us.

"Yeah."

"Sean, I'd like to talk to you about Ilsy."

"Okay."

"I don't know much about you, boy, but I think it's enough. You've gone out of your way more than once to make her comfortable. She tells me you even took her to see my brother before he passed. I cannot thank you enough for that. It brought her comfort, and he didn't have to die alone. So you have done a great service to my family and for that I am grateful." He stopped walking and looked up at me. I took a couple more steps before stopping and looking back.

"It was nothing."

"To hear her tell it, you about drove yourself to exhaustion."

"That's true, but it was the right thing."

"That's another thing I know about you, you don't always do the right thing." I didn't have an answer for this so I simply shrugged my shoulders.

"Sean, I know about your people. I know you are here to help us. I also know that you personally don't always do that as you should. Now, the way I look at it is that any help you do provide is good help. Though I know from Darius that you could do more than you choose. I know you don't like us humans, and I know you feel like you are little more than a babysitter." He took note of the look on my face and held up a finger stopping my denial, "I've talked with Ilsy, boy, I know the things you've said."

# Ragged Edge

I looked at my feet and shrugged again. I heard his steps approaching me.

"My point is that your actions don't speak true to your words. At least so far as my niece is concerned." I had to admit this was true but I again let my shoulders do the talking.

"Now, I don't presume to know your mind. I have seen the way you look at her though. I'm not her father but I am the closest thing to it walking this earth. I won't tell you to stay away from her; you are her guardian for now after all. I will give you some advice though."

"What's that?" I said, finally looking up.

"Leave her be, boy." I felt my face fall and my insides squirm with turmoil as he continued, "at least for now. Get this thing with the book and that monk behind you. I think you've been letting whatever you may feel for her distract you. Let it alone for now, Sean."

He reached up and placed a hand on my shoulder. "Just let it alone."

There really wasn't much I could say but I had to say something.

"Let's say you're right. Let's say that I'm facing some deep internal turmoil. We can even go so far as to say that my contempt for humans in general and my feelings for your niece are fighting each other inside me. Hell, we can also say that these hypothetical feelings are making me scared of dying for the first time in all my lives. How can I ignore them?"

"Hypothetically?"

"Yes, in the theoretical scenario that I am falling in love with your niece, what do I do about it?"

"For now, hypothetically speaking of course, keep her safe as is your job, kill the bastards that are coming for her and that godforsaken book. Then, hypothetically, you are free to pursue her if you want." He smiled at me.

"Hypothetically, how do you think she'd react to this pursuit?" I couldn't stop the words from coming out.

"In theory, I think my niece would be agreeable to the pursuit, if done properly." I let his words sink in as we both turned and headed back towards the cabin. I stopped after a few steps.

"How would you feel about it?" I asked.

"Hypothetically?"

"Yeah."

"Hypothetically, I think you are a good man deep down. I think Ilsy has made extraordinary progress at tearing down your walls and may one day manage to make you respectable. Hypothetically speaking, anyway." He laughed and started walking again. I stood looking at the trees for a minute before catching up to him. I wanted time to think but remembered my mother's appearance and knew the forest was not safe for any of us to be alone in.

We got back to the campfire and resumed our former places. I was lost in thought and didn't immediately notice that everyone was looking at me. With Darius and Grandfather here, I wasn't accustomed to being in the lead. I told myself to take Uncle Fry's advice and push my feelings down. Now was the time for the detached, uncaring Sean. I took a long drink from a fresh cup of coffee then stood and addressed the group.

"This morning, I met my Mother." Ilsy gasped, and I put up my hand to stop her from interrupting me, "We had a minor disagreement, then Grandfather and I killed a couple wolfengators that tried to jump me. So, this tells us that at least one of our groups of enemies knows where we are." I kept her words about finding me a mate quiet. Now wasn't the time.

"Until now I have been reacting instead of acting. I'm tired of reacting. It's time to take the fight to them. To do that though, I need to know where they are. I think I can find Mother easily enough. It's the mad monk I'm worried about. I still don't know if the two of them are working together. If they are, I'm sure there is discord amongst their ranks."

"I think the monk will be the easiest to deal with, so I want to take him out last. Grandfather, can the pages be destroyed?"

"They can be burned, yes, but for what purpose?"

"If I fail to kill him, he at least won't get those pages." Everyone nodded at this. I started pacing. Now that a plan was getting laid out, I was anxious to get started. Normally, I wouldn't have anyone to talk to about the plan and would just act.

"Okay, so we burn the pages and that reduces the monk threat. I believe my mother has greater numbers, so we should go after her first. Grandfather, can you make my cabin more secure? At least be able to stop her from jumping straight here?"

# Ragged Edge

"I already have, boy, why do you think she met you at the spring?"

"I thought she didn't want to make a commotion."

"Good idea, she must know I'm here and would have wanted to avoid getting me involved. The real reason is that she couldn't get closer. I don't know why she didn't send in her gators though."

"Alright, this cabin will be our fallback position. If things go wrong, we meet here. That means someone will need to stay and keep it safe." I looked at Ilsy and Darius.

"I'll stay," Darius said. "I can't fight much now anyway." He hung his head.

"I will stay with Darius." Grandfather said. I whirled around and looked at him.

"But..."

"I told you, Sean, all the help you need except the Elders. That includes me."

"But, the spring, you had my back."

"That was another matter, possibly not even directly related. Also, your mother is an outcast and violated courtesy by bringing the fight to your domain."

"Fine." I gave him a hard look then turned away.

"Ilsy, Sir Fry, I want you to wait here until I have Brother Herman located. Once I know what exactly we are up against we can make a plan for the attack. Are you sure you want to participate?" I asked.

"My sword is yours." Uncle Fry said, a bit more formally than the situation called for.

"Yes," Ilsy said. Uncle Fry turned to her.

"No, niece, you will stay here."

"Like hell I will."

"You know our family code. No fighting until you have children."

"Uncle, there are plenty of others that can carry on our family tradition. I will stand at Sean's side." Her eyes turned into shimmering green daggers as she stared him down.

"Alright, Ilsy," he said, apparently deciding discretion really was the better part of valor.

I dug my car keys from my pocket and tossed them to Ilsy.

"Take Grandfather with you and go to town. Stock up on more food and medical supplies. I'm sure we're going to need it." I stepped away from the fire, turned into a raven and jumped away.

I jumped back to my apartment first. That was the last place I knew Brother Herman had been and hoped to pick up the trail there. I landed on a flower box hanging on one of my windows. At least, anyone looking at it would call it a flower box but for me it was actually a perch. I looked in the window and saw my apartment was empty and thoroughly trashed. Books and papers were strewn all over the floor, my television lay smashed into bits, my bed was ripped apart, and my couch existed as bits of fluff, strips of leather, and chunks of wood all over the floor. An impotent rage rose in me. Sure, my apartment wasn't much and nothing that had been destroyed was really worth much, but it was my stuff. I jumped into my apartment.

On the ceiling there were scorch marks left from my fireball. I saw my cabinets had all been torn open and my specimen jars were laying on the ground in many splinters of glass. I saw no sign of their former inhabitants. The only thing I could tell for certain was that Brother Herman had been seriously pissed after Ilsy and I got away. I mean, this kind of destruction was unreasonable and I couldn't help but take it personally. I didn't bother going through the mess trying to find clues. In all honesty, I wouldn't know what he left behind and what was simply more pieces of my life he had defiled. I walked towards the door to turn into the raven once more and jump back to Ilsy's house.

From the outside her house looked untouched. Her mailbox was full and there were papers collecting on her front porch. I shifted back to my human form, collected these things, and jumped inside. I used a small fireball as light to find a light switch. Once located, I turned on the lights and looked around me. Her house had been completely untouched. I was sure this meant something but not completely sure about what. All I knew was that more wolfengators hadn't been sent here, and there was nobody to throw a hissy fit over our escape. My bloody towels were still lying on the floor beside the chair I had turned over backwards. Everything looked exactly as we had left it. I thought about snooping around her house a little, just for fun mind you, but decided I had other things to do.

# Ragged Edge

I sat down in the chair and thought about my options. I could go back to Ilsy's father's house but I wouldn't know what to look for while I was there. I could go directly to my mother, if I stayed as a bird she might never notice me and I would be able to watch her and hope she would lead me to Brother Herman. I could also try going directly to Brother Herman. The problem became names. I knew my mother's name and so I could focus on her and go to her location. I didn't know what I would find there as the bird I had to appear outdoors, so if she was inside a building I wouldn't know where in the building she was. I also didn't know how many of her skinwalkers were left. I knew of five that had been killed; that didn't help much.

On the other hand, I didn't know for sure that Herman was the monk's real name. Giving people fake names is a great way to stop them from getting too close, both literally and figuratively. All that my people have to do to find someone is know their name, and then we focus on them and jump straight to them or at least their vicinity. Without the real name, I can focus on his appearance and the name I have and might get close, but then again I may end up hundreds of miles away from him and have no way of telling. Like my mother, I had no idea of the size of his forces. He could be operating solo or he may have a few companions.

When you come to a fork in the road you have multiple ways of deciding which way to go. You can consult a map and see which fork leads to the most direct path to your destination, or you can guess and enjoy an adventure. If you know your destination, you can also pull out a compass and all that to guide you. I have a simple method. In any given life there are a surprising amount of times when you face a decision between two options with equal pros and cons. So how do you decide which option is the right one? Some say you should let your instincts guide you. While this is technically true, I have had my instincts lead me into some pretty hairy situations on more than one occasion. So I have a specific method of making these decisions. Now it's a little hard to describe, but it is a scientifically exacting method that yields favorable results only half the time. I always kept the specialized tools necessary with me in case one of these decisions stared me in the face. I reached into my pocket and pulled out the necessary tool, closed my eyes, and assigned values to my mother and Brother Herman. I took a deep breath, let it out slowly and flipped the quarter I had pulled from my pocket.

Okay maybe flipping a coin isn't that scientific, but then neither is trusting your gut instinct. I watched the coin revolve in the air, it seemed as though time slowed down. I could hear the air make barely audible whooshing noises as the coin spun, a tiny ring hung in the air from my thumbnail gliding across the surface as I flipped the coin. With a thud of impact the coin landed in my left hand, I thumped it down onto my right arm. Eyes closed, I took another deep breath, then two. I slowly opened my eyes and uncovered the coin. Heads, time to visit my mother.

# Ragged Edge

"Fucking great." I slowly got to my feet, transformed into the bird again and jumped while focusing on my mother.

# CHAPTER 13

**W**hen we use telelocation, the jump is instant. This time something went awry. Ilsy's living room swirled around me, which was normal enough. Instead of a new location replacing it, I saw only darkness. I felt wind gusting over my wings, which is unheard of as there is no wind in the between place we travel through. I could hear the crackle of flame and screams from a woman that sounded horribly like Ilsy. I heard male voices shouting, snarls of rage, pain, and cries of anguish.

I blinked my eyes multiple times to make sure they were open, but the darkness was complete. I had no reference for up or down. I was about to switch to my fighting form when a white speck appeared in the distance. I thought it might be the light at the end of the tunnel that turns out to be a train, having no other point of reference though I flew toward it. Slowly the speck grew larger. I was flying as fast as I could, but my raven form was limited to about twenty-eight miles an hour. I had no reference for distance other than the speck, so I had no way to judge how long it would take me to reach it.

As I closed in on it, the whiteness began to take shape. It was another bird, a large white dove. I got closer, all the sounds around me slowly faded away. I felt a sense of calm and peace overtake me. All at once I was flying for the joy and not with a purpose. When I got close enough to see it clearly, a pure white light began radiating from it. The light got so bright I was forced to close my eyes. It's not smart to fly with your eyes closed so I spread my wings and allowed myself to glide. To be honest I wasn't completely sure I actually was flying in this place. When the light began to dim on my eyelids, I slowly opened them.

In front of me stood, or maybe hovered, a beautiful female. She had long, flowing, blond hair, flawless skin, and eyes of changing hues. Her eyes conveyed both the love of a mother looking on a wayward child and the wrath of a mother defending her child. In one hand she held a long spear, the other a large round shield. A plate of armor covered her chest and a gown of pure white poured out from under it and down to her feet. Her cherry red lips were pulled back into a loving smile.

I stopped pretending to fly and changed into my human shape. I was keenly aware of the rags I called clothes. I knew I was unfit to be in the presence of this being. I felt tears slowly stream from my eyes as I knelt in front of her. She raised her spear and slammed it in the ground beside her. A flash of lightening lit up the world around us. In that split second I could see that we were nowhere and everywhere at once. We were in the between place and suspended in time. Her spear stuck where she had planted it. She reached out one long perfect arm, took hold of my hand, and pulled me to my feet. I realized we were of equal height. She didn't seem inclined to speak first.

"Who... who... who are you?" I murmured.

"Search your memory, child," she spoke without moving her lips.

"Where are we?"

"Not a place for asking questions when you already know the answers," she said.

"My lady, I am honored by your presence. What is it you want with me?"

"That's better. You are in grave danger, my son."

"Yeah well, what's new, right?"

"This is why I have interrupted your travel. I cannot change your course, I cannot tell you the outcome, I can only tell you the possibilities."

"How can you do that when you can't even tell me your name?" I think I have issues with people being cryptic. It pisses me off.

"Sean, you know my name, you have heard the story of my involvement with one human clan from a member of that clan."

"Thought so," I sighed.

If I was talking to a goddess, then I knew my day had gone from bad to worse, especially one this old. The beings that humans call gods usually don't take much interest in human lives. They have their own lives to deal with, their own wars, love affairs, all of the fun stuff that makes up life. Their interactions with humans are usually incidental, though sometimes they do take interest and have a purpose for involving themselves. Only once in memory had one of those beings taken an interest in my race. We were left with only thirteen survivors.

"Okay, so I'm in danger. I knew that already."

"No, Sean, you knew that you faced death. Death is not so bad; it is but the beginning of a new adventure. If you just faced death, I wouldn't bother. What you face is different, perhaps worse than death, or perhaps not – that is for you to decide." See what I mean? Cryptic.

"Alright, what's the deal then?"

"You have set your course on the perception of having only two options. Your mind was closed to your other options."

"What other options?"

"You had the choice of inaction. There is no reason for you to seek a fight with the forces aligned against you. You are capable of defending against them, but why seek them out?"

"So life can return to normal."

"What is normal, Sean?" she asked with her smile growing wider.

"I don't know."

"Correct. You also have the option of letting the one you care about know your feelings."

"Now isn't the time for that. Emotions become a distraction. I can't afford to be distracted."

"If she feels the same, you could make her one of you. Together the threats before you would be minor."

"That's assuming she feels the same way, and that she can become one of us."

"You know that she can," she said with a wry smile.

"Fine, but I won't do that. I'd still have to defend her until she finished changing."

"Correct. That is why you ignored those options."

"Look, Danu, I'm honored that you have chosen to appear to me, but where are we going with this?"

"Many hard choices are rushing towards you, Sean, but not all choices can be made by the flip of a coin. You must be prepared to accept your choices and the consequences of your actions. You will be pushed beyond what you think possible and asked to put at risk everything you are." She started fading away as she spoke.

"So what do I do?"

"You will know what's right, my son. Resume your raven form and stay quiet," she said as she vanished before me.

I took her advice and quickly changed forms. All at once there was a scene swirling around me. When it stopped I found myself flying above a dark forest in a range of mountains. I could see the opening to a cave and at least thirty people milling about. They looked like teenagers or young adults and certainly none were over thirty. Most wore only the barest scrap of clothing covering their genitalia. I thought for a moment I had been thrown into a previous time. Then I spotted a road about three miles from the cave. A winding dirt track ran from the road to the cave. I saw no vehicles on the road or track.

I guess it was only fitting that my mother's pack of skinwalkers housed themselves in a cave. It looked like most of them would have a hard time getting by in the normal human world. I knew that despite appearances, many of these kids were probably much older. I circled the encampment a few times, memorizing the land around it. I didn't spot my mother but I did see a couple wolfengators walking around. This had to be the place. As I was getting ready to leave, it felt like a baseball bat struck my right wing.

A sharp, piercing pain radiated through my wing and caused a brief cry of pain to escape my beak. I started falling to the earth and was unable to use the injured wing. I looked and saw an arrow piercing it. I jumped out of there. I didn't know who shot me with an arrow, but I did know I didn't relish the thought of falling amongst my mother's followers. During the jump I tried shifting and couldn't. I was only mildly surprised. With the arrow in place, my wings couldn't grow or fold back into me. I had to get back to my cabin.

As the world rematerialized around me I remembered two things. First, that I had asked grandfather to put up defenses around my cabin, second that I had forgotten to focus on appearing on the ground. I appeared a good twenty feet over the ground beside my spring. I could do nothing except brace myself for impact. The ground rushed up at me. I closed my eyes and tried to force myself to relax. I knew this was going to hurt and wasn't disappointed.

The drawback to turning into a bird is that your entire body becomes birdlike, right down to the light, hollow, brittle bones. I felt all the little bones in my arrowless wing shatter as I hit the ground. Pain such as I had never felt radiated through my body, sending stabs and jolts sprinting through me. I felt at least one bone stab through the flesh of the broken wing. A squawk of tormented agony escaped me. I followed that with frantic cries for help. It could only have been a few minutes at most before grandfather came to me. It felt like an eternity. He gently picked me up and carried me back to my cabin.

Ilsy let out a frightened scream when grandfather carried me into the cabin.

"Is that?"

"Yes."

I felt my consciousness fading.

"Hurry up," I cried in my harsh raven voice.

Grandfather set my broken body on the counter and looked at the arrow piercing my wing.

"This is going to hurt, boy," he said as he took hold of the arrow. I heard a snap as he broke the back of the arrow off. Another stab of pain jolted through me. To this day I swear that arrow was the size of a spear, and as he pulled it out of my wing it felt like a good five or six feet of wooden shaft slid through my wing. My voice was raw from my screams of agony. Finally, the arrow was out. Grandfather took me off the counter and sat me on the bed. I turned back to my human form. I still couldn't fold up my damaged wings. Grandfather placed his hands over the hole made by the arrow and closed it.

"I'll try to get a healer here for the other one boy," he said and walked out of the cabin.

"Can't he heal the broken wing?" Ilsy asked.

"No, he can't. Grandfather was a warrior, like me. We are only taught enough healing to allow us to survive long enough to reach help. Broken bones don't hinder our travel. They only make it painful."

"What happened?

"That's a long story. Get me a beer and I'll tell you." I hadn't noticed Darius and Uncle Fry when I arrived. Now I saw Darius get up from a chair at the dining table and walk to the fridge. A wooden chess set was on the table between them. Darius brought me the beer and opened it for me. Handing it to me, he used his free hand to pat my shoulder, he then returned to his game. I could tell they were listening as I told Ilsy of my apartment, her house, my meeting with Danu, and finding my mother's hideout. By the time I was done, I had emptied the beer and was feeling tired. My eyes drooped shut and I started thinking that I needed to be more careful in the future before drifting into an uneasy sleep. The last thing I heard was Ilsy saying, "Fucking great."

I awoke the next morning. I was groggy and unsure why I was in the bed with my wings stretched out. I remembered when I tried to fold them up. An instant crippling ripple of pain coursed through my body, ripping a scream out of me. A flutter of wings by the ceiling told me I had woken grandfather up. Darius jumped up off the couch, and Ilsy let out a frightened scream. The smell of a campfire told us Uncle Fry was already awake and outside. I writhed around on the bed, waiting for the pain to subside and bumped into Ilsy. Apparently she had slept in the bed with me. I would have been interested in this fact except for the searing pain.

Grandfather turned human as he flew down from the rafters. He walked into the kitchen and grabbed a bottle of pills, a glass of water, and a large first aid kit. He came to my bedside and handed me the pills and water. I looked at him through squinted eyes.

"The only help I could get, prescription painkillers. The Elders feel that the wolfengator problem is separate from the Codex issue and therefore are unwilling to lend assistance. Bunch of bastards. Anyway, through a human contact of mine I managed to get you those. They should help the pain a little." I read the dosage, two pills every four to six hours, and took four. Grandfather unwrapped the bandage on the wing that was shot and saw the hole had healed. Uncle Fry walked in and looked at me with a smirk on his face. I had been fond of the man, but now I wasn't so sure.

"Someone is approaching," he said and walked toward me. Grandfather walked outside to confront our visitor. Uncle Fry took over looking at my wounds.

"I thought you people healed quickly," he said.

"The wings are a little different, I need a healer."

# Ragged Edge

"Don't have one in my pocket, boy. Let me know when those pills kick in. We need to set the bones in your busted wing, and I don't think you want me to do that now." He had a knowing smile that looked like a perfect target for a fist.

"Do it now," I said through gritted teeth.

"Suit yourself." He shrugged and started poking and prodding at my wing. I couldn't answer; my mouth was full of pillow. Soon the room was filled with an assortment of snaps, pops, and muffled cries of pain. Ilsy took a damp rag and wiped the sweat from my face and tried soothing me. After what seemed like a million bones getting set, he finally stopped and started grabbing bandages from the first aid kit.

"I don't have any way to make a plaster cast for you, so I'm going to wrap it up tightly. When I finish I suggest not moving it, bumping it, or sleeping on your back." I nodded my head. I was already feeling exhausted and weak from the torture the man was putting me through.

The wrapping went quickly and he mercifully walked back outside. The stabbing, burning throb in my wing was starting to dull a bit. The pills were taking effect. I lay on my side staring at the kitchen. I couldn't believe I had been surprised. I was supposed to sneak in, see what I could, and leave. I wasn't sure how they had spotted me, and worse yet I knew that I would have to go back once I healed. I heard a merry laughter coming from outside and hated the sound of it.

"Maybe I'd be better off with final death." I didn't mean to say it. The pills seemed to be destroying what little vocal filter I had.

"What?" Darius snapped angrily.

"I said maybe I'd be better off dead. I've made a complete mess of this assignment." I felt the smack across my face without ever seeing a hand delivering it.

"Stop whining." Ilsy said.

"Exactly. So you're down for a couple of weeks," Darius said. "It's going to take months before my wings grow back. You can at least still function and help with the defense of this place. I can only run away."

"Oh shut it, the two of you. Tell me, Darius, what I have done right since you handed me this assignment?"

"You've only defended Ilsy from two attacks, gave her the chance to say goodbye to her father, made a valuable ally in her uncle, figured out that damn Codex, and found out what you are up against."

"You helped with the first fight, I ran from the monk when he showed up, and I wasn't fast enough to save her father. Grandfather told me about the Codex and it wasn't hard to find out what I'm up against when they've been coming at me every chance they get. I've been eviscerated once, torn my hands to holy hell, ran myself to exhaustion, lacked the strength to heal Ilsy's father, had my apartment destroyed, got shot in one wing, and then due to my own ignorance broke the other one all to hell. Yeah, I'm a great fucking defender." I struggled to sit up then held onto the bed as the room revolved around me.

# Ragged Edge

"Get off your pity pot. You chose to try an attack. I only assigned you to protect her and the Codex. You've been doing that. You've expended an unusually large amount of effort at keeping this one woman safe. If your task of defending her takes until the end of her natural life, who cares? You'd have done your job." He had a point, I didn't actually have to kill the monk, and I could continue avoiding the wolfengators. Ilsy would eventually grow old, die, and my task would be finished. The only problem is I wasn't sure if I wanted to watch her grow old and die. Eventually, she would want to get married, raise children, and I'd become the weird uncle that never aged and always hung around.

"If you two are done arguing, we have someone you should meet," Uncle Fry said from the doorway. I tried to stand but failed and sat down on the bed with a thump.

"Show him in," I mumbled.

Uncle Fry entered followed by a man of medium height, taut muscular build, short blond hair, and blue eyes. He moved with a casual grace that said he knew how to handle himself. Grandfather followed the man inside. The man's eyes took us all in and a smile spread on his face. He stood beside grandfather and clasped his hands in front of him. He was dressed in the exact wrong fashion to be a hiker or woodsman. He wore black leather Versace boots, or at least they looked like boots, faded blue jeans, and a teal crew neck shirt adorned by a Versace logo. I could tell immediately that he was not only confident and probably dangerous but also wealthy.

"Sean, Darius, Ilsy, this is Ben Jennings," Grandfather pointed to us in turn as he said our names. "He was apparently walking around the woods and heard your wakeup scream, Sean."

"Sorry if I disturbed you, Ben," I said.

"It don' madda', I just wanted to make sure everything was okay. What happened?" He pointed to my bandaged wing. His voice was a gravely baritone but he spoke softly with a slight Cajun accent.

"Bit of an accident. I'll be fine," I said, waiving away his concern.

"He should be fine in a week or two," Grandfather said.

"Dat's a relief. So what happened to dis finely aged specimen?" He said pointing at Darius whose bandaged stubs were poking out of his shirt.

"Not quite an accident, and it'll take me much longer to heal," Darius answered.

"Such a shame. Well, I didn't mean to bust up your fais do do here, but I'm glad I came along. It looks like you folks could use some help." He crossed the room and sat on the arm of the couch beside Darius. Darius looked down the length of the otherwise empty couch, then back to Ben with a raised eyebrow.

"Unless you know how to heal us, I think we're doing okay," Darius said.

"Oh sure, but something had to bust you up. What if it comes back?"

"Grandfather can handle it," I said nodding towards my grandfather.

"My, y'all are cranky this fine morning. May I speak plainly?" he asked.

"Well, you've walked into a room containing a man with wings, one of which is bandaged, and another man with stubs sticking out of his back. You failed to be surprised by this so I think we can drop pretense here," I said a bit more sarcastically than I intended.

"Fantastic. To begin with I wasn't exactly just walking around in the woods, I mean, look at me. Do I look dressed for a hike?"

He paused and arched an eyebrow looking us over. We were a motley-looking bunch. I was sitting shirtless in a pair of battered jeans, Darius was wearing badly wrinkled slacks with an equally messy dress shirt, and Grandfather also wore jeans with a plain white t-shirt. Ilsy was sitting next to me in a pair of loose sweatpants and a tank top, and Uncle Fry, always the gentleman, was the best dressed of us. He had on a pair of loafers, dress pants, a white dress shirt, and suspenders.

"Y'all wouldn't actually know, would you? Pity. Anyway, so no I'm not dressed for hiking, but dese rags were what I had stashed nearby, so I put them on."

"Stashed?" I asked.

"Well yeah, I couldn't come say bon jour in nothing but my skin, could I?"

"You were walking in the woods naked?" Darius asked.

"Heavens, no. I was... oh right, we haven't gotten there yet." He let out a short laugh and shook his head.

"Alright, to put it simply I've been watching you. Dis cabin of yours happens to sit in the middle of my patrol route. I don't often see anyone here so I wasn't worried about it. You've been here quite a long time now though, so I thought I might want to come say hi. While patrolling, I've seen some odd goings on here. So I knew you weren't vanilla human."

"Patrolling?" Ilsy asked.

"Well yeah, we have to maintain the land. Dat's what my pack does."

"Pack?" I asked.

"Oh my, I forgot to mention it, didn't I? Where is my head dis morning? I'm a werewolf, of course."

"Oh," I said.

"Right. So dis forest is a part of our territory, so we patrol it. Der are quite a few animals living here dat would be hunted to extinction if we weren't here protecting the place. Not to mention those damn loggers and people wanting to put cabins up here. Your cabin didn't bother us much, you obviously tried to disrupt the land as little as possible, we respected you for dat."

"Wait, so you are werewolf conservationists?" Ilsy asked, her eyes wide.

"Something like dat. I mean what else are we gonna do, right?"

"How many of you are there?" Grandfather asked.

"Oh we're a petit pack, only about fifteen of us. The question of the hour though, is what the hell happened to you two?" he asked, pointing at me and Darius.

"Skinwalkers. I've been calling them wolfengators. They look like a mixture of wolf and alligator."

# Ragged Edge

"I thought I saw something like that in the woods just yesterday."

"Why didn't you do anything?" I asked.

"Well, I wasn't exactly sure I saw what I thought I saw. Alligator head, wolf body – I thought I had eaten some bad mushrooms."

"Do you do that often?" Uncle Fry asked.

"Not so much. Anymore."

"So these skinwalkers are working with a monk, trying to get Ilsy here and a book that contains the instructions to create a gate to hell."

"Oh my, glad I found you then."

"Why?"

"Well, we've been finding some zombie-like guys slinking around the woods lately. Not real zombies mind you, just… I don't know, mindless like. They been dressed in black robes keepin' hoods over their heads. The ones we killed been shaved bald with some type of cross tattooed on their heads"

"Where?" I asked.

"Three of them were a few miles from here to the west, Jacob found another two south of here, Miss Anne found another couple to the east, and I got the other three north of here."

"How do they know where we are?" Ilsy asked me.

"My guess would be the wolfengators told them. Mother could have found me at any time and told them where to look."

"Dat sucks," Ben said.

"Ben, I guess you were right, we probably do need help," Darius said. Ben placed a hand on his shoulder.

"You can say dat again, cher. I'll go talk to the pack and see if dey are willing. What kind of help do y'all want?"

"Right now we need defense. We are down two experienced fighters. Ilsy can fight but hasn't faced real opponents like these before."

"So basically, you have two?"

"Yeah, basically," I said.

"Don't you worry, you've cared for our forest and been respectful of our land so I'm sure the pack will be happy to help. I'll be back tonight," he said, standing and moving toward the door.

"Thank you," I said to his back.

"Don't mention it, hon," he said and walked outside. A few minutes later we heard a loud wolf howl. Ilsy helped me stand and walk outside. His clothes lay beside our door.

# CHAPTER 14

After Ben left, we went about our morning routine without much conversation. I walked outside and sat beside the fire pit trying to ignore the pain of my busted wing. Despite the interlude with the werewolf, I was still beating myself up. It was stupid for me to rush into a potentially deadly situation. I got what I deserved and now I had set us back by at least two weeks. Without being able to hide my wings, I couldn't leave the forest and travel into cities. Sure, I could hide myself from humans easily enough but other entities not so much. If I got into a fight now, I'd be easily crippled by pain with one good jolt to the wing. It's always best to avoid situations where your enemies have an enormous advantage.

Grandfather took up Ilsy's training. I could see a vast improvement in her skills but she was still too slow. I knew I'd have to watch her if she joined me in battle. If she was better with firearms, I could use her as a sniper but of course she had to be good with the sword. It ran with my luck recently. Darius and Uncle Fry spent the time telling stories to each other. I was mostly left to myself. We kept a fire going throughout the day, and a part of me resented that everyone seemed to think my cabin was now a campsite. At the same time, I couldn't ignore that I enjoyed the company. Still, I wanted this day over. If the werewolves were willing, I could use them to track the zombie-like monks. If they could follow the zombie back trail, I wouldn't have to risk jumping into another ambush.

More than my wings, my pride had been hurt. I never saw the son of a bitch that shot me, but he (or she, I guess) got a good look at me. They couldn't have seen me appear, I don't believe in coincidences, there's no way they would've been looking at that exact spot. So maybe they were just shooting at random ravens. Or the cave could have been in an area that didn't have a raven population. It's possible they were also hunting, because from the look of things they were living even more primitively than we were.

That's how the day passed. Darius had found a new friend in Uncle Fry, Ilsy's training continued, and I ventured into the dark recesses of my mind. If I had known that our time as a group was coming to an end, I think I would've acted differently that day. That's how life goes though, isn't it? You never know how much time you have left. That's a difficult thought for someone like me to accept, I mean, in theory I can live forever so my time is never ending. Humans though, they have a habit of catching a sudden case of death. My kind, well, we tend to drift apart no matter how close. It's difficult to spend too much time with someone, that holds true for us and for humans. So we'll drift apart, lose touch for a while, and then come together again for a while.

Late that afternoon as we were getting ready to prepare dinner, a large red wolf approached the cabin. He moved in a familiar, languid, confident fashion. The wolf sauntered over and sat beside Darius at the fire. Darius put a hand out and allowed the wolf to sniff it. Instead of sniffing, the wolf licked the back of his hand and used his nose to push Darius' hand towards its back. Darius scratched its neck and continued talking with Uncle Fry. After five minutes of scratching, Darius patted the wolf's back and stood.

"I'll go get dinner ready," he said. The wolf yipped and nipped at Darius hand. When Darius looked down at it with mild surprise, the wolf slowly shook its head from side to side. I smiled at this. I knew we lost a vast majority of our abilities with our wings, I had no idea it took most of our intelligence too. I glanced around the fire and saw smiles and laughter hiding behind everyone else's eyes as well.

The wolf sauntered over to a tree where Ilsy had hung Ben's clothes earlier in the day. We watched the wolf began transforming into Ben, we also watched Darius' head fall as he began chuckling. Ben started laughing before the transformation was complete. After becoming a young nude man he stood and pulled his clothes from the tree limb, got dressed, then joined us by the fire.

"Thank you, cher, I simply love having my neck scratched," he said laughing. We all joined in.

"Staying for dinner, Ben?" Darius asked with a chuckle.

"Mmmm, sounds good but, alas, I must decline. I just came by to tell you dat the pack wants to meet you all, so I came by to invite you to a little cochon de lait."

"I'm sorry, a what?" Ilsy asked.

"Cochon de lait, hon, a bit of a get together. We roast a pig and basically have a party."

"Did you tell them what we are?" I asked.

"Well, yes and no. I didn't say anything earlier, common courtesy and all, but I don't actually know what you are. Never seen one of you in my entire life. So I told them you was a group of three birdmen and two humans."

"How'd you figure that?"

"The nose knows," he said, touching a finger to his nose. "You smell like a raven, Darius smells of eagle, your papaw has a bit of a muddled smell, I caught some crow, eagle, and I believe a dash of owl. The other two smell like vanilla humans though a little earthier than normal."

"What do you expect? We've been camping out here for at least a week now," Ilsy grumbled.

"No, love, not earthy as in dirty. More of a grassy, clover, flowery scent. Like freshly cut grass almost."

"Oh, is that good?" she asked.

"Oh yes, ca c'est bon."

"What?"

"It's good," he said.

"Where are you from?"

"Here and der, but I was born and raised, most of my life anyway, in the great city of N'awlins."

"I see. That explains the French then."

"Oui, I left shortly before the hurricane, haven't made my way back yet. C'est la vie," He said a little sadly.

"So this coo thingy, where is it?" I asked.

"Cochon de lait, it's a good two miles from here. No road though so we'll have to hike it."

"Sounds good, I'm game," I said. Everyone agreed and we set off through the woods with Ben leading the way.

It was a strenuous hike over two miles of a rough trail. At times we couldn't even see the path and had to trust to Ben's guidance. The hike took us at least two hours, and it was full dark by the time we got there. The pack had set up a commune of sorts. It looked like they mostly slept in tents but there were a few small shotgun houses set up around the site. Everything was laid out in a large circle with a large fire pit in the center. The smell of roasting pig hovered on the air, igniting the salivary glands into a riot of activity. To put it simply, it smelled good and I almost started drooling.

# Ragged Edge

The pack seemed to be made up of almost equal parts men and women with a few children running around. Ben led us through the encampment and stopped in front of an aggressively ugly female. Her face was scarred by what looked like crisscrossing claw marks. Long, ragged, dirty blond hair grew in patches around burn scars on her head. She looked at us with bottomless brown eyes. The look said we were welcome, so long as we didn't piss her off. Ben knelt in front of her and bowed.

"Miss Willow, it is my pleasure to present to you the visitors from the cabin." Ben spoke formally.

"Introduce yourselves." While she had a face for radio, her voice was smooth, melodious, and rivaled an infant's laugh in its beauty. I glanced at Ilsy; I could tell on her face she was just as surprised as I was. I expected a nails-on-chalkboard, train wreck of a voice. Grandfather stepped forward.

"Atlas Gryphon at your service, Madam Willow," He bowed and stepped back. Darius stepped forward, introducing himself and bowing. I followed, then Uncle Fry, and then Ilsy finished the introductions with a curtsy.

"How proper you are. Please join us and help us to enjoy the feast we have prepared. Afterward, we will discuss your situation." Miss Willow opened her arms to encompass the encampment and bowed her head. We took our leave of her and followed Ben to a sitting area.

"Ben, who was she?" I asked.

"Dat was Miss Willow. Don't rightly know if she has a last name. Anyway, she's our alpha here. The pack mostly runs itself but in matters of strangers and battle, she gives the orders."

"I see."

"Word of advice: don't cross her. I know she sounds pretty and maybe you can't tell by looking at her, but she's one fierce bitch." His voice grew reverent.

"Never could've guessed," Grandfather said.

"Any of you spent time with a wolf pack?" he asked. We all shook our heads.

"Only werewolves that I've met were ones that needed killed," I said. He nodded his head.

"Yeah, some of our cousins are ill mannered. They usually see our gift as a curse. C'est la vie, some nuts in every bunch right?"

"True."

"Well, we ain't like dat. We try to be peaceful and take care of this earth, we help those dat we can, and so on. Still, we do have a wild animal in us. Most times it's okay, but sometimes it gets heated. Y'all are being watched right now, stay in this spot till the feast begins. Someone approaches you, feel free to jabber all you like, just try not to anger no one. You wanna go somewhere or maybe need to do your business, let me know." We all nodded and look around us. I thought we had about even odds of making it through the evening without upsetting anyone.

The feast started and we were allowed to mingle with the other werewolves. Some had come and talked to us before and we heard stories of them scaring off loggers and fighting vampires and other supernatural creatures. We told them about fighting wolfengators and Ilsy's family research. This earned us some respect. Two cute female wolves came over and inspected my wings but asked us no questions. I could tell everyone gathered was curious about the winged humans but they avoided the subject.

During the feast, a few fights broke out. These were stopped in quick order, then a circle was formed around the combatants and they were allowed to continue. Ben explained that these fights were always done in human form to avoid doing too much damage. Willow presided over these. The fights usually stopped when one went down and stayed there. At times, Willow had to step in to stop the victorious combatant from going too far.

Even in human form these wolves were impressive to watch while fighting. Most of them didn't seem to have any formal training, but there was a beautifully brutal choreography in these brawls. The flesh on flesh sound of fists and feet connecting to faces, stomachs, and chests provided a primitive drumbeat that stirred the soul.

Blows that looked hard enough to crush a normal human's skull cracked like thunder. More often than not the fighter receiving the blow stayed on his, sometimes her, feet. I think most of the fights ended because one of the warriors became too fatigued to carry on. Watching these wolves fight each other made me glad I had certain advantages the times I had killed them in the past.

# Ragged Edge

We watched these fights impassively while the other wolves placed bets. I disagreed with Ben's assessment of this being a small pack, but then I hadn't been exposed to many wolf packs.

Eventually, the feast began to wind down, the kids were put to bed, and then by some unspoken signal the pack gathered around us. Willow stood facing us. She sat down slowly; everyone else followed her example.

"You have partaken of our feast, and you have been courteous and kind. I understand that you seek our assistance."

"Yes, ma'am," I said.

"I am prepared to listen to this request."

"Alright. So, I'm working on a couple of problems–"

"What problems?"

"Okay, well, I have been defending this human from dual threats. A group of skinwalkers and an insane monk that, incidentally, happens to be a necromancer. I understand you have seen some of his probable followers in the woods."

"Why?"

"What? Why? It's the right thing to do, isn't it? Beyond it being the right thing to do, the lady is in possession of an artifact that would allow the monk to create a gateway to hell. So that's one reason."

"The skinwalkers?"

"Well, I don't really know what they want. When Darius told me I was to protect her I didn't even know what from."

"Why did Darius not tell you?"

"Well, he's kind of an asshole," I blurted out. The gathered wolves laughed.

"Madam Willow, Sean is a young one of our race. His job is the protection of human kind. He's lazy in his job and hadn't been doing it. I was told by our leaders not to divulge to him the nature of the threat. He is being tested."

"I see. Continue, Sean."

"Okay, so Darius told me to go to her and protect her, only when I got there I heard a fight going on outside–"

"Did you not see this when you arrived?"

"No ma'am, I arrived inside her house. I kind of teleported there. So like I said, I heard a fight outside so I went out to help and Darius was fighting three of these skinwalkers, or wolfengators as I call them. After we were victorious, Darius left and I looked at the book. I experienced a kind of vision and that's how I know about the monk. Knowing her place was no longer safe, I took her to mine." I told her the entire story of everything that had happened to us since I met Ilsy. The pack listened to my words intently, Miss Willow interrupted me a few times with questions.

"That brings us up to Ben coming to my cabin."

"Interesting. If we choose to help you, what do you require of us?"

"Since I know where the wolfengators are, the last piece I need is the location of the monk. I was hoping that maybe while I'm out of commission you would be willing to trace his followers back trail."

# Ragged Edge

"I see." She made a steeple of her hands and held them under her chin. The wolves around us were silent while she was thinking.

"Are there any here who would be willing to work with these creatures?" She looked around the group. Ben stood up along with about five others. The others murmured amongst themselves but didn't stand.

"Only six volunteers. Mr. Gryphon, while I am the alpha of this pack, I prefer operating on a mostly democratic basis. The ultimate decision falls in my hands, but I like to take into account the feelings of the group at large." I nodded.

"With only six willing, that leaves you at a decided disadvantage."

"I'm sorry. I thought you would be happy to join an undertaking that would rid the woods of this threat." I tried to play to their cause.

"True, we could also run your group out and get the same result." I hadn't thought about that.

"So what does your group want?"

"You have told us much but told us nothing. We have your side of this story. Though your story is believable, there is something lacking."

"What's that?"

"Who exactly you are? You see, my pack has never encountered a man with wings, bandaged or otherwise. Never have we seen three men that smelled of birds. Nor have we encountered humans that smelled of a spring day."

"Okay?"

# Ragged Edge

"We would have the explanation of what sort of creatures you are or we will not help."

"I see. Okay, I'll tell you."

# CHAPTER 15

Ilsy's eyes grew wide as I spoke. We were forbidden from telling humans what we were. It was thought that if they knew what we were, they would begin searching for us. Perhaps that's true. The thing with the no telling rule is that there were a lot of us that broke that one. This was actually my second time breaking it. The first was my shrink, he didn't believe it anyway so it didn't matter and none of the Elders cared. Darius didn't even bring me an official warning for it.

This time, well what were they gonna do? Slate me for final death? Besides, if it was the only way I could get the help I needed, I saw no reason not to tell them. It's not like a pack of werewolves are going to run around telling human society that we exist. Sure there are some that believe we exist, but they are wrong in how they think we look or where we live. Grandfather said nothing about it, nor did he try to stop me. So I told

them the entire history of my race and what we were.
There were a few surprised gasps but nobody called me a
liar. Maybe the bandaged wing stood as proof of that.

"What about the other two?" Willow asked.

"Can I get something to drink?"

"Of course." She nodded and a small guy stood up
and ran to the closest tent. He came out with a bottle of
water, handed it to me, and sat back down. If this was
like a normal wolf pack the little guy had to be the low
man on the totem pole. He looked badly beaten, eager to
please, and his eyes held a haunted quality to them. I felt
anger rise in my stomach and forced it down. I don't
exactly come from a race that can throw stones at
someone else's cruelty. I drank the bottle down and
cleared my throat.

"Okay, so the story of the humans." I paused for a
moment, "Should really be told by them." I pulled Uncle
Fry to the center of our little group.

"Actually Sean, because she is still in training, the
story should be told by Ilsy." I rolled my eyes.

"Fine," I said, pulling Ilsy forward. She looked
around in surprise and asked for water. The little guy ran
for it again. After a few sips she cleared her throat,
stammered a few words, and then launched into a
beautiful telling of her family's origin. I was hoping she
would gloss over the whole wolf pack in Ireland thing
but she didn't. There were murmurs throughout the
crowd as she told of the wolves and their connection to
that long ago tribesman. When she finished, she took a
long drink of water and smiled weakly. Uncle Fry patted

her back. Willow stayed silent until the murmuring among the pack quieted down.

"The blessing of Danu graces you with the fair smell of a spring day, while the curse of Danu graces us with the wolf it seems."

"I... I don't know," Ilsy said.

"We do know child. Our stories are the same with different endings. All of us wolves are descended from that one greedy tribesman. His name was Maddock. The wealth of misfortune he received from Danu drove him mad. He saw your ancestor grow in glory and worth. He saw the children of the other greedy tribesman taken in and his jealousy grew. His anger ate him from the inside out. Then a man dressed in shadows approached him. A man that offered him the power needed to seek his revenge. Maddock accepted this gift. The gift of the wolf. The man told him the gift would pass from him to every generation, male and female, until the end of this earth. After achieving their goal of revenge, they would be free to use the gift to bring them the riches Danu denied them."

"Wait a minute," I said.

"Yes, Sean?"

"You said a man dressed in shadows. It was a man dressed in shadows that helped the monk. Could it be the same man?"

"It doesn't seem unreasonable. This man who offers gifts that become curses. So far as I know he has never again been seen to any of us."

"Go on," I said distractedly.

"Ilsy, do you agree with this man's quest?"

"Yes I do, Miss Willow."

"Sir Fry, is Miss Ilsy allowed to accept pledges on behalf of your family?"

"Yes she is, madam."

"Very well." Willow stood and approached Ilsy. She knelt on one knee before a confused-looking Ilsy.

"Miss Ilsy Hillerman, descendant of Teyrnan chief of the Brigantes Clan, I, Willow Donner, descendant of Maddock, greedy fool of the Brigantes Clan, do pledge to right the wrongs of the past. All in my pack will stand in the aid of you and yours until our curse is lifted, or until the end of this earth. This I pledge before you, these ancient winged ones, and Danu, wise goddess of old." Her eyes never wavered from Ilsy's face.

"Uh, I accept your oath?" Ilsy stammered. Willow stood and gave Ilsy a soft kiss on each cheek before backing to her original place.

"Does my pack hear the words of their alpha?" She raised her voice to a shout.

"Yes, Alpha Willow!" They all barked in unison.

"Will my pack follow the oath of their alpha?"

"Yes, Alpha Willow!"

"What will happen to a pack mate caught breaking the oath of their alpha?"

"Death, Alpha Willow!"

She nodded her head once and resumed her seat.

"Who now wishes to assist Sean in his quest?" Now every member of the pack stood, including Willow.

"Wow, maybe I should have had you talk first," I said to Ilsy.

"Sean, the pack will begin immediately," Willow said. "We will notify you as soon as a scent is found."

"Um, thanks," I said.

"Will our new friends stay here with us, or do you wish to return to your camp?" I looked up at the sky. The moon had set already and the thought of another hike through the forest at night didn't sound like much fun. We could have just jumped there but it seemed more polite to stay with our hosts.

"We will spend the rest of this night here and go back to our camp in the morning," I said.

"Very well," she said, nodding her head, "Ben, show our guests to their lodging."

"Gladly, Miss Willow."

After Ben left us in one of the shotgun houses, I fell asleep almost immediately. I don't have cause to take pain medication very often and it had worn me down. I tossed and turned through the night, waking every now and then when I rolled over on my busted wing. All in all, it wasn't a comfortable night despite the efforts of our hosts. The house was well equipped with separate rooms for each of us and comfortable beds. The fault was completely mine and was the price I had to pay for my ignorance. One thing I knew for sure was that I couldn't wait a couple of weeks for the damn thing to mend.

When we all awoke, we shared breakfast with the wolves and Ben led us back to our cabin. At the cabin I began looking over the armor I had brought with me in my cage. None of it was suitable for constant wear, nor did any of it protect my wings. My grandfather watched my frustration grow as each piece of armor was tossed aside.

"What are you doing, Sean?" he asked with a slight chuckle in his voice.

"Trying to find a way to protect these damn wings," I grumbled.

"Would you like some help?"

"No thanks, nothing here can help anyway."

"What, exactly, are you looking for?"

"I need something to cover my wings, to protect them from a blow. I could reshape what I have here but it's all too damn heavy." I walked over and gingerly sat on the couch.

"Why?" he asked as the others joined us.

"The wolves will find the trail soon, most likely before my wing is healed since our illustrious council has denied me the help of a healer. That means I will be in a fight before my wing is healed. Ergo, I need to protect it so it isn't damaged further and doesn't cause me pain at the slightest touch."

"Watch your tone. Do you have anything that can be used as padding around here?"

"Not ideal padding, I mean I have spare clothes and such. Why?" Grandfather had an idea. I could see it brewing in his eyes.

"Fine, I will go to town with Donovan and get suitable padding. In the meantime, figure out how much armor you need." He turned to walk out.

"What?"

"I can make you armor Sean, if you weren't being thick you could do it yourself. I'd recommend a chest plate at the least." He grabbed my keys off the table and walked out. I sat on the couch staring grumpily at the fireplace and listened to my car start up and pull away.

"This sucks," I said to myself.

"Stop whining," Ilsy said. Sighing, she came over and sat beside me.

"Easy for you to say, you aren't broken."

"No, I'm just the human surrounded by creatures more powerful than me. One of which keeps whining about being injured in an accident that would have probably killed me. Stop whining."

"So now you're going to complain about being a human. A human graced with a gift from an ancient god?"

"Shut up, Sean, I'm not going to fight with you."

"Then what are you doing here?"

"Well, I was going to try comforting you but you want to be an asshole." She stood and faced me.

"Comfort me how?" I asked, raising an eyebrow at her.

"Not that way, ass. Besides, I'd hate to injure your wing." She gave me a mischievous grin.

"Oh."

"In case you've forgotten, I am a doctor of archeology."

"And?"

"I know a thing or two about armor, you dumb shit."

"So, what are you thinking?"

"Stand up." She reached down and grabbed my hands to pull me up.

"What?" I sighed as I stood. She pulled me away from the couch and walked around me.

"Okay, so you're going to need a shirt underneath the armor no matter what it's made of. Your grandfather is right, you do need a chest plate, but I would recommend full torso armor."

"Why?"

"Well, you need to anchor whatever you put over your wings. If you don't, then that adds weight and tension to your, well, however the hell they are attached to you will be put under more stress."

"They are attached by bone."

"Okay, then the bone will be stressed," she said and walked behind me.

"So you need something back here with openings for your wings, here and here." I felt her hands on my back. It sent a small shiver up my spine. "If the base of your wing guards are wider than the opening, the weight will be supported more by the armor than your bones." She walked back around me with one hand tracing a circle around my waist.

"Makes sense. Except if we put more armor on me, I have to deal with more weight."

"Poor baby. What kind of metals do we have to work with?" she asked, dropping her hand back to her side.

"I have mostly steel and some brass. I can get some gold but that shit is outrageously heavy."

"Those won't work. We need a lighter metal."

"No shit," I said.

"Don't be an ass, just think of a metal as strong as steel and lightweight."

"That's easy, titanium, but I don't happen to have any."

"Could you buy it?"

"I don't think they sell it at Walmart," I said.

"Maybe Uncle knows. We can ask when he gets back, but for now come outside and quit moping around." I followed her outside shaking my head.

Grandfather and Uncle Fry returned hours later and began unloading the car. They pulled out bags and bags of gauze, foam padding, and duct tape. I grew more apprehensive with each bag they carried past me into the house. Once the car was empty, they joined us at the fire.

"So, thought about that armor?" Grandfather asked clapping me on the knee.

"Some."

"Okay, what do you want?" he asked.

"I want full torso armor. It needs holes in the back for my wings, and Ilsy thinks that the base of whatever you're going to put on my wings should be bigger than the hole in the armor, so the armor can support my wings."

"Smart girl."

"Yeah, she can be," I said as I looked at her smiling. She smacked my arm lightly.

"The only problem I see is that it's going to be heavy. I mean full torso and my wings."

"That all depends on what metal you use."

"The lightest one I can think of that would work is titanium, do you have any in your pockets?" I asked. He laughed and shook his head.

"What do you know about titanium, Sean?" he asked.

"It's lightweight but stronger than steel."

"That is correct. Where is it found?"

"Not at Walmart?"

"Mostly true. Did you know that it is the ninth most common element on earth? You can find it anywhere."

"Okay?"

"You really don't work with the earth much, do you boy?"

"Well, I mean I've turned stones to swords, made this cabin, caused a few earthquakes... why?"

"Watch and learn," he said as he stood up.

He walked away from the fire pit and knelt with his hands on the ground. He closed his eyes and stated crawling on his hands and knees. Finally he stopped, drew a circle in the dirt with his hands and marked the circle with an "x" in the center. He stood up and dusted his hands off on his pants. I stood and walked closer to him. He held his hands, palms down, in front of him, the crook of his index finger and thumb along the boundaries of the circle. Inside the circle, dust started boiling up and the dirt began cracking.

"What's he doing?" Ilsy asked. I could only shrug my shoulders. This was a trick I had never seen before.

# Ragged Edge

Steam issued from the cracks and was followed by a stream of a silvery grey-white material and a silvery material. The streams rose up to my grandfather's hands as he turned them toward each other and the metals combined. A metallic disk formed in the center of the circle, becoming a long cylinder stretching to the ground and as wide as the circle. When the cylinder was touching grandfather's hands, he lowered them, picked it up, set it aside, and repeated the processes. Before long there were three equal-sized cylinders standing in a row.

"What is that?" I asked in awe.

"Titanium, Sean. Well, actually it's a titanium alloyed with aluminum. What we have here is one of the same materials used to make the space shuttle, and we're going to use it to make you armor."

"How did you do that?" Ilsy asked.

"Simple. I reached into the earth and pulled it out."

"We can do that?" I was stunned.

"Of course we can."

"So, how do we shape it?" I asked. Grandfather smacked the back of my head.

"Damn, boy, did you hit your head in the fall? We can reshape this just like you did the stones or the trees that became your cabin."

"Huh."

Grandfather picked up one of the cylinders and motioned for me to grab the others. They were lighter than they looked, and we easily carried them over to the fire.

"So, how do we do this?"

"Leave it to me, Sean. In fact, I'd rather not be bothered. Donovan, will you grab me the tailor's measuring tape that we bought?"

Uncle Fry stood up and went into the cabin, he returned after a few minutes carrying a rolled tape measure.

"Stand up, Sean." I stood. Grandfather began measuring my chest, my waist, and my wings for width and length.

"I'll be back," he said as he placed a hand on two of the cylinders and disappeared. He appeared a moment later and repeated the process with the third cylinder.

"Do you think this will work, Darius?" He looked up when I said his name.

"Speaking to me again?" he asked. I stared at him in silence.

"Very well. Yes, it will work, junior guardians generally aren't allowed armor but your situation is a little different."

"Why not?"

"What?"

"Why aren't junior guardians allowed armor?"

"In this age it isn't necessary. People rarely walk around armored, except cops and soldiers. Even in the Middle Ages, armor wasn't worn for fun but it was more common. Junior guardians don't always understand that they can't wear it everywhere and don't usually need it."

"Do senior guardians get armor?"

"Yes, but we also deal with bigger threats."

"Fair enough," I said.

"How long do you think he's going to take?"

"Depends on how intricate he wants to make it. Simple armor shouldn't take long, maybe half an hour. Intricate armor could take him a few hours or even days to make. He'll be back when he's satisfied."

"Someone say satisfied?" Ben's voice drifted ahead of him from the side of the cabin.

"Do you have news, Ben?" I asked anxiously.

"Sure, sure, but first what's dis about being satisfied?"

"Darius was just talking about my grandfather."

"Oh? Dey got a thing going on?" He asked cocking an eyebrow. Ilsy laughed.

"I doubt it, but he does like being with my family so maybe, I guess," I said.

"Damn it, Sean. That was hundreds of years ago and just one time!"

"Yeah, and it got me a half brother I just found out about."

"Whoa, whoa der, guys. I didn't intend to step into no domestic situation, I was just making a joke is all." He held up his hands, palms facing us.

"Sorry Ben, it's just been a long day," I grumbled.

"It don madda', been a long one for us also. You know we found another fifteen of dem stinking cultists today? Dey crawlin' all over dis here forest. Willow thinks they're based pretty close by, but problem is dey trail is a bit hard to follow. Reek of death they do, it's about the most offensive smell you never want to encounter." He walked over and sat beside Darius at the fire.

"Anyway, it's fixin' to be nighttime and we'd rather not deal with dem in the night. So I'm here to tell you that we're posting a guard around your cabin. In the morning a group of us more presentable types will be going into the towns around here to see what we can find out. We got some connections in dem. Anything strange and they'll tell us about it."

"That's good to know, but why the guard?" Ilsy asked.

"You said you needed it, right? Even if you didn't though, they'd be here. Dem guys got close last night, not close enough to see the cabin but plenty close enough to make Willow worry. So if you hear fighting during the night, please feel free to help dem out."

"We will, Ben."

"Great, now what's dis I hear about you banging his mama, cher?" he asked Darius.

"It was a long time ago, Ben."

"Den why didn't you tell him about it?"

"I'm his trainer. It wouldn't have been proper."

"Ah, well dat propriety is biting on your ass cheeks now, ain't it?"

"Yeah."

"Well, c'est la vie, you can't change it now so may as well put it behind you."

"That'd be easy to do if his son wasn't coming after Ilsy."

"Yeah, you right," Ben said.

"I thought he was dead, Sean. She said he was dead and I had no reason to doubt that."

"Well, no one asked my opinion but I'm gonna give it to you. Sean, you need to cut dis man a break. Your anger is obviously tormenting him. He made a mistake, let it go. Darius, if you got anymore dirty little secrets and value your relationship with Sean, I suggest you let them out now."

"No, there isn't anything left to say," Darius said.

"See boys, it ain't hard to play nice. Now if you'll excuse me, Willow wants me to set up the scouting parties." He stood and started walking away. "I'll see y'all tomorrow, and you had best make up by den, otherwise Uncle Ben here is gonna knock some heads together."

He gave us both a stern look then walked around the cabin. A few seconds later, we heard his paws padding away from us.

The night passed without an attack from the cultists. The quiet night made me glad for our new werewolf friends. Ilsy woke me at dawn to tell me that Grandfather had returned. I slowly got out of bed and went outside. Grandfather was standing beside two tables, which I assumed he had made. Sitting on one table was my new torso armor. The rising sun glinted off it, making it look like it created its own light. For some reason grandfather had made it to resemble a bare chest and stomach. I looked at my bare stomach and saw that it matched almost perfectly. On the other table was the armor for my wings, which consisted of four pieces. They looked like they matched up precisely and would clamp shut around my wings. The bottoms had rectangles that would fit into two slots on the back plate of the torso armor. As I looked at the armour, I could see that he had carved in the form of each feather of my wings. The detail work was amazing.

"We need to try it on, Sean," Grandfather said through a wide smile. He could obviously tell I was pleased.

"Okay."

"The wing pieces will allow you to move your wings straight back, and to the side. You'd be able to flap them if you didn't have a broken wing, but for now I don't suggest it."

"Alright, so how do I put it all on?"

"Carefully," he said, chuckling. "I'm going to have Donovan wrap your wings in gauze and padding. I know only one is broken but we want them to feel balanced. I've made them as light as I can, and they should be comfortable."

I nodded my head and Uncle Fry went into the house to retrieve the gauze and foam padding. I sat down and stretched my wings straight back. The movement hurt but not too much. Ilsy held pieces of padding in place as Uncle Fry wrapped my wings. That hurt a lot and I had to clench my jaw to keep from crying out. When they were done, my wings felt muffled and constrained.

"Alright Sean, once we put this armor on, if it's comfortable, we should leave it on while you get used to it. If it isn't comfortable, then we'll take it off and I'll try to fix it. Do you understand?"

"Yeah," I nodded my head.

# Ragged Edge

Darius and Grandfather grabbed the two pieces for my right wing and snapped them together. There was a clunking sound as they closed the clamps on the wing. Grandfather told Ilsy to hold the wing so I wouldn't have to support it. The process was repeated on the left wing. I felt a sharp stab of pain when the piece closed around it and the clamps clunked shut. Uncle Fry held that wing up.

"Okay, now the easy part is done," Grandfather said, clapping his hands together. He walked over to the table with my torso armor and grabbed the back plate.

"I'm going to slip this over your wings. Don't move."

"Wait, the holes in that aren't big enough for my wings," I said, grabbing his arm.

"Oh yeah, sorry," he said and started fumbling with the plate. I heard four snaps and metal sliding against metal then he handed me two small plates.

"Hold onto these," he said. I looked at the back plate and saw two wide slats going down the back. I shook my head and held the two plates he handed me. I felt my wings being moved around and heard metallic scrapping noises until I felt the cold metal against my shirt. Grandfather reached around me and grabbed one of the plates, I heard two snaps and he reached around for the other plate. Another two snaps and he walked over and grabbed the chest plate.

"Last piece. Once this is clamped to the back plate, you should be able to support your wings with no problems. Now stand up," he said as he walked toward me.

# Ragged Edge

I stood and spread my arms as he lined up the chest plate. There was a clamp on each shoulder and two more per side. After six of the clunks telling me the armor was secure, Ilsy and Uncle Fry let go. I felt the weight of my wings pull back on the armor a little, but the plates did their work. I wasn't sure if I would ever consider the armor comfortable, but it wasn't bad.

"Move around, sit, bend, and make sure you can maneuver in it," Grandfather said.

Moving in it was pretty easy except for sitting and bending. My back couldn't arch, but after a few tries I figured out how to sit and bend over with my back held stiff.

"Are you sure this will work?" I asked.

"Well, you won't get any more damage to your wings, and they should be almost impossible to tear off now."

"Okay?"

"Oh, it's still going to hurt when you get hit, but if you man up it shouldn't be a problem."

"Shouldn't?"

"Well, I've never gone to battle with a broken wing, Sean. Want me to hit it and find out?" he asked.

I thought for a minute. I didn't want to experience the pain I was sure to feel if he was wrong, but I had to know how effective the armor was. I nodded and braced myself as best I could for the pain that I thought was sure to follow.

Grandfather was right and it did still hurt. I heard a loud clang as his fist impacted my broken wing. A jolt of pain sent a shockwave through me that caused my eyes to water and pulled a grunt from my lips. It wasn't as bad as I expected though. I remembered the pain in my jaw after I ran into his fist and knew the amount of pain they could cause even without his force behind them. I felt sure I could fight in the armor but knew I should still try to avoid getting hit in the wing.

"Alright?" he asked.

"It'll work. Thank you, Grandfather."

"It was my pleasure, Sean."

"Should I worry about water, fire, or anything else?" I asked. I wasn't very familiar with titanium.

"No, I don't think so. To melt the armor you would have to encounter a fire of at least three thousand degrees, Fahrenheit, that is. As for water, no don't worry about it. Titanium doesn't corrode like most metals so you should be good."

"Great, I can get back into battle now."

"Yeah, but I wouldn't recommend it. Yes, your wing should be safe in that armor, but do you want to risk permanent damage?"

"Not really, but if I have to I will."

I spent that day getting use to my new armor. Truthfully, Grandfather did such good work that I was used to it soon after putting it on. I just didn't want to go through the entire process of taking it off and then putting it back on when I needed it. I was hoping we would hear from the wolves soon and have something to do. The sun was setting when I asked grandfather to take it off. The process was the same as putting it on, only in reverse. Chest plate, back plate, wing guards, and then Donovan unwrapped my wings, throwing out the sweat-soaked gauze but keeping the pads to reuse. We were sitting down for dinner when a cacophony of howls tore through the still evening air.

Light footsteps were sprinting towards the cabin. We stood and faced the direction they were coming from. I prepared a fireball for our visitor, Ilsy and Uncle Fry took up defensive fighting stances, Grandfather had miniature lighting bolts circling his hand, and Darius stood behind us. I knew he felt useless, and if this came to a fight the loss of his wings would stop him from helping anymore than Ilsy and Uncle Fry. It sounded like just one person though, so between Grandfather's lighting and my fire this would prove to be a short fight.

The rushing steps came closer and closer. Grandfather and I readied to throw our blasts. The forest around us had fallen strangely quiet. No birds sang, no insects buzzed, no wind rippled through the leaves of the trees. The crackling and popping of the fire sounded like slow shots from a gun, tension built around us, and time slowed down.

A foot appeared at the corner of the cabin and then a leg clad in black. Another foot appeared. Our surprise guest was surely sprinting but it seemed to take ages for his full body to appear. A torso covered in a white cotton polo shirt appeared, then arms, and finally the face. My fireball went flying before I recognized the face. I felt a sudden rush of panic race into my heart as the ball flew towards the now-slowing man. I heard Ilsy start yelling "no" beside me.

Everything suddenly sped up and a bolt of blue flew past me. I heard a sizzling pop and saw a cloud of steam float up into the air as Ben threw himself to the ground while shouting a synonym for feces. My chest lightened as I rushed over to him. I hadn't just melted his face. I reached a hand down to him to help him up.

"Merde, what in hell are you tryin' to do to me, Sean?" His accent thickened as he grabbed my hand and I pulled him to his feet.

"Sorry Ben, we heard you folks howling, then we heard someone running toward us. I guess I'm a little jumpy," I apologized lamely.

"What happened to dat ball of fire?"

"A jet of water. You're welcome," Grandfather said with a smile.

"Thank you," Ben and I said simultaneously.

"So what brings you here in such a hurry?" Darius asked.

"Good question, let me empty my drawz and I'll tell you," he said, walking over to the fire and catching his breath.

"Would you like some water?" Ilsy asked him.

"Yeah, that'd be great," he said, sitting down.

"But damn, you scared da hell out of me, Sean."

"Yeah, sorry again," I didn't know what else to say.

Ilsy came out of the cabin carrying a bottle of water for Ben. He drained it and sat quietly.

"So what's up, Ben?" I asked.

"Ain?" he asked, looking up.

"What?"

"Huh?" I was losing this conversation.

"What's up, why the hurry, the howling, and the almost burning your face off?"

"Oh, yeah, almost forgot. Guess I shoulda' warned y'all about the howling earlier. Normally, when we have a messenger approach our camp, we howl to warn everyone. It's supposed to keep accidental attacks down."

I tried not to laugh.

"Yeah, I shoulda' warned y'all about dat. Anyway, I tink we found dem," he said.

"You think?"

"Dats what I said, isn't it?" he said with a smile.

"Where?" Grandfather asked.

"Alright, so there are little towns all around dis here mountain and dis forest. So dis morning I sent out a small group to all of dem to check in with some of our contacts. Told you we was friendly with them. So late dis afternoon, the groups were coming back and dey was turning up nothing. We were starting to think dese guys could travel farther in a night than we thought. Then the last group came back in one helluva mighty rush. They tells us we need to come quick like. Dey were sent to one of the smallest towns, maybe a hundred people in all. 'Harry,' dey says, so we rush back with dem." He paused and took a slow breath.

"Can I get some more water?" he asked Ilsy.

"Yeah," she said and went for it.

Ben sat silently waiting on her. When she came back he took a couple drinks and continued.

# Ragged Edge

"So we went to the town and it looked deserted. We started knocking on doors and no one was answering. We couldn't find the man we normally met, nor anyone else for that matter. I started getting freesôns, felt like we were being watched…"

"You were getting what?" Ilsy asked.

"Freesôns, um, goosebumps. So like I was saying, felt like we were being watched. The place just felt all wrong. Den we went to the house our contact lived in and no one answered. I tried the door and it was unlocked. That wasn't unusual though, most people around here don't lock their doors with small towns not havin' much crime. So I open this door and a god almighty stench came boiling out at me. I'm not ashamed to say I about lost my lunch. The coppery stench of blood mixed with death and decay dat hung in the air. Well, we searched the place and found our man in his bedroom. His belly had been chewed open." He took another drink while Ilsy swallowed hard.

"We didn't have time to search every house in town though, as the sun was startin' to drop. We've posted guards to watch it tonight, and we'll be going back tomorrow. I came to see if you wanted to join us." A sparkle was in his eyes that didn't fit the story. Maybe it was the predator in him, the scene he described had obviously bothered him, but the thought of closing in on his prey obviously excited him. I looked around at everyone else. They all nodded at me.

"Yes, Ben, we'll be happy to go with you."

# Ragged Edge

"Laissez les bon temp rouler!" he said, jumping to his feet. His excitement vibrated through him, and he was almost standing in two places at once.

"Come back to the camp with me. We're headed back at sunrise, and our guard will meet us on the way to update us," he said.

We gathered up everything we thought we might need. Ilsy and her grandfather grabbed real swords from my stack of weapons while Grandfather and I grabbed my armor. Ben looked at it curiously and shrugged his shoulders. When ready, we headed back to the pack's camp.

# CHAPTER 16

**W**e awoke to the sound of more howling all around us. The pack had again put us up in one of the shotgun houses. We got up and looked outside to see that the pack was assembling around the fire pit in the middle of the camp. We walked out and joined them. Willow was appointing members of the pack to go along into the deserted town and announced that we would be joining them. Everyone knew this already but I think she wanted to make sure they knew it was her word that allowed it. When everyone was dismissed, we went back to the house we stayed in, where another group effort got me into my armor.

When I walked out of the house, wings flared straight back, the wolves stopped and stared at me. I began to feel a bit apprehensive. I thought the armor looked good but maybe not. Outside I let my wings spread back out and walked, as confidently as I could, to the fire pit. My self-consciousness grew until I noticed the appreciative looks on the faces of the wolves closest to me. I felt my lips stretch into a smirk and strode more confidently.

"That is wonderful craftsmanship," Willow said, walking around me to appraise the armor.

"Thank you," Grandfather said.

"You made this?"

"That I did. Couldn't let the youngster's broken wing become a problem," he said.

"So it's like a cast?"

"More or less, it is padded on the inside. He can't stop a wrecking ball or anything, but it should keep him from being crippled by pain if something hits it."

The sun rose on the horizon and camp activity picked up. Those Willow had called to join the hunt gathered by the fire. None of them carried weapons but I guess if you have strong teeth, claws, and an innate predatory nature that you don't really need them. Ben strode up wearing loose-fitting sweats and took charge of the party.

"Okay y'all, I don't know what we're going to find but I can tell you it probably won't be pretty. Keep your wits about you and let out a good loud howl if you find any of those bastards laying in their beds. Give a shout if you find regular citizens. We don't want to be killing anything we don't have to," he said, giving everyone a stern look.

"Also, make sure not show your stomachs to anything we find," I interjected.

The wolves looked at me like I had personally insulted their mothers.

# Ragged Edge

"Cher, we don't show our bellies to no one," Ben said.

"I mean even accidently. If I'm right and this monk is a necromancer we could be facing ghouls. Long claws for fingers, sharp barracuda-like teeth, extreme speed, and even more strength. Most necromancers keep a few near them, I suspect some were the zombie-like people you mentioned seeing. Corpses raised from the grave that feed on humans to replenish decomposed skin. Most show a fondness for innards," I said.

"Right, show no belly skin y'all," Ben said.

Most of the pack transformed into wolves. I doubted there has ever been a wider variety of wolves found in a single pack. A few red wolves, some timber wolves, and a couple gray wolves. Throw in the five of us and our group totaled eleven. I watched Ilsy closely as we headed toward the town. We didn't expect to find a fight from the cultists but there are other threats. They could have turned a few townspeople into ghouls to hide them. There could be some wolfengators hiding out or any number of other surprises awaiting us. This would be her first foray onto the field of battle and I wanted to make sure she didn't crack up. So far she had shown a strong resiliency in the face of the supernatural, though her introduction to it had mostly been with people not trying to eat her.

We had gone about five miles from the camp when three other wolves approached us. They turned into humans, two males and one female, all nude. The nudity didn't seem to bother any of the wolves but it caused Ilsy to blush. They nodded to Ben and gave me an appraising glance. The armor was definitely good at attracting attention.

"Sir, we have seen no signs of any living humans still in the town," said one of the males in a business tone. He was of medium build and far more muscular than I could hope to be. His head was shaved and he had dark brown eyes.

"What of the cultists?" Ben asked.

"Twenty of them. They started walking out of buildings shortly after sunset. We expected them to head into the forest towards our camp or their cabin," the male said, nodding at my group, "but they headed south instead."

"Where did they go?" I blurted out. The wolves shot a disgruntled look at me and addressed Ben.

"We don't know, sir. They returned an hour before dawn and..." The nude wolves looked down at their feet.

"What?" Ben asked.

"They had humans with them. Mostly kids."

"Kids?" I asked.

"Yes, sir. I'm guessing for easy meals. Most of the bodies we've found have been chewed on."

"What else did you see?" Ben asked.

"After the crying of kids ended, everything was quiet until just before dawn. Then we saw cultists come out of the houses. If any normal humans come upon the town today, it'll look like business as usual."

"How could you tell they were cultists?" I asked. The male sighed as he turned to me.

"They don't smell like living flesh do they? Nor do they look it, their skin is paler than a normal human's."

# Ragged Edge

"How many?" Ben asked.

"We've counted thirty so far."

"Coño," muttered one of the wolves.

"Don't worry about it. They're dead," I said, a low growl tainting my voice. Ilsy looked at me with a worry in her eyes.

"How do you want to proceed, Sir?" the man asked Ben.

"Let's go look at the town and we'll decide how to attack it," he said. Everyone else nodded. I disagreed but said nothing and the group began moving forward. I fell behind and was joined by my grandfather.

"What do you want to do, Sean?" he asked.

"I want you to scout from above. See what you can and then come back and tell me. These wolves are cautious. I don't want to spend all day out here waiting for them to decide what to do."

"I agree, but no sense rushing into an unknown situation."

"Kids, Grandfather, they're killing kids in that town. If I knew nothing else, that alone would make me want to kill them."

"What if the monk isn't there?" he asked.

"Then we'll find out where he is from one of the cultists." Seeing the look in my eyes, Grandfather nodded, turned into his crow form, and took off ahead of the group.

It might be hard to believe, but I'm not a violent guy. I fight when I have to but I prefer to avoid it if I can. Sometimes violence seems so senseless that I think there has to be a better way. Having said that, there are a few things that can make me embrace violence like a long-lost lover. At the top of that list is doing harm to children. I believe that no child should ever have to experience the cold horrors of the world. Children should be secure in their safety. They should believe that Santa Claus, the Easter Bunny, and the Tooth Fairy are real. Their dads' are the strongest men in the world and their mothers are the most beautiful, loving women in the world. To destroy a child's naive belief that the world is basically a good place is a crime against nature itself.

I'm not the only one that feels this way either. I've seen a lot of nasty things in my life, and I've fought creatures that would give most people Lovecraftian nightmares. In general, even the bad guys of the supernatural realm are loath to hurt a child. So hearing that these cultists were using children to feed the hellish hunger of the ghouls started boiling an anger inside of me. My vision tinted red at the edges, I no longer felt any pain or discomfort in my broken wing, and I knew two things for certain. The first was that by nightfall this town was going to be empty of every last cult member and ghoul that haunted its streets even if I had to level it. The second was that I was going to enjoy destroying those monsters.

The little town sat in a small valley surrounded by cliffs and peaks with one dirt road running through the center of it. I counted at least forty houses and a handful of businesses as we watched from a cliff. I could make out the ghouls moving about the town. Most acted like everything was business as usual, a dozen were tearing down a house and stacking the wood to be reused. The rudimentary beginnings of a fence surrounded the town.

It was a pretty town, probably an ideal spot to settle down away from society but still be within a social border. Borders are important to humans – visible and invisible lines divide humans almost everywhere you look. More than once, one of my kind wanted to destroy those borders, but deep down we all knew what would happen. Complete and utter chaos. Hell, even my society wouldn't be able to function without the few dividing lines we have. We don't consider race, gender, sexual preference, or any other personal characteristic important enough to divide us. We are, however, divided by age, life cycle, and tasks. They might seem unimportant but can you imagine what would happen if someone like me were on the Elder Council?

It looked like the ghouls were setting up a border to separate this town from everywhere else. I spotted Grandfather circling the town, landing on rooftops, and listening. The ghouls were oblivious to his presence, which was good for us. It's difficult to find a scout as good as an old man that can turn into a bird. His wisdom guides his search and allows him to process the information he gathers more accurately. As a bird, most beings will completely ignore him.

After a complete circuit around the town, Grandfather flew back to us. He landed far away from the cliff and turned back to his human self. Anger flashed in his eyes and a cold steel clamped down in his voice.

"Cattle. The bastards are setting up a cattle ranch."

"What?" Ben asked.

"Some of the children are still alive, I heard them in one of the houses. The cultists are setting up a fence to keep normal humans out, and their cattle in."

"There are live children down there?" Ilsy asked.

"Yes, it sounded like ten, maybe fifteen, in that blue ranch-style house on the end."

"Any guards?" Donovan asked.

"Only the damn cultists."

"What's the move, Ben?"

"The monks should be easy to deal with. I say we hit dem hard and fast, get the kids protected as quick as possible. Once the kids are safe, we take care of the cultists," he said. I nodded in agreement.

"I'm going to make one change. I want the strongest cult member kept alive to take as a prisoner."

"Why?" Ben asked.

"If Brother Herman isn't down there, I'm going to need a messenger. The strongest cult member will also be the oldest. The oldest monster will be the most likely to know of Herman's location."

"Oh, okay." I could tell Ben wasn't use to taking prisoners.

"Let's move around to the side closest to the kids," he said, then pointed to the wolves that had been on guard duty through the night. "You three, stay in the house with the kids don't let anything in cept us." They nodded quickly and changed back to their wolf forms.

# Ragged Edge

We started walking around the west side of the valley, moving as quickly as we could while staying quiet. So far, we had surprise on our side.

We burst from the trees at a run toward the town. We got most of the way to the house with the children before an alarm started blaring. Shouts erupted around us as black-robed cultists started flooding our way. We weren't worried about being outnumbered. Sure, these unholy men appeared stronger and faster than regular humans, but they are still easy to kill. Anything that will kill a human would kill one of them. It might take more bullets, more stabs, or a farther drop, but they will die. We didn't have guns though. We had claws, teeth, swords, and all the power of the elements within easy reach.

Grandfather and I took to the skies in our battle forms. We didn't fly high, a good leap from a monk would've caught our feet, but it was high enough. The stream of cultists seemed never ending. They had to have been crammed into the houses like sardines and still it seemed there were too many coming after us. Something smelled wrong but I didn't have time to figure it out.

I started throwing balls of molten fire at random robes. The wolves had clashed with the fastest of the monks, filling the air with snarls, barks, shouts, and cries of pain. Grandfather threw bolt after bolt of lightning and the numbers didn't seem to diminish. Our party was completely surrounded but holding its own and somehow still moving toward the house with children in it. The noise of battle rose to a fevered pitch and stayed there. Grandfather dove into the first ghoul to appear and disemboweled it. Corpses were piling up.

I flew straight into the air, took a deep breath, braced myself for the pain I was about to cause myself and lunged toward the ground feet first. As I speared toward the ground, I surrounded myself with stone and soon I was more boulder than bird. I heard the wind roaring past my ears, the battle getting louder and louder, and then my feet impacted the ground. A shockwave pulsed through my body as the stone around me flew out in all directions and a cry of pain shot from my throat. A quick glance told me I landed on target: in the center of a group of ghouls. The ground rippled up from my impact and threw the ghouls off their feet. Most of the wolves managed to stay standing and pounced on the fallen ghouls. The tide turned in our favor.

I stood with a grimace. The impact shook my entire body and pain radiated from my wing. I shoved it from my mind as best I could and threw myself into the fight with the ghouls. I became a flurry of talons, lashing out at any ghouls near me. Thick blood flew from necks separated from their heads, a cloying smell of decay rose from intestines ripped from their bodies. I took back to the air and began throwing more fireballs and the stream began to slacken. The alarm had gone silent. I looked back at our group, the wolves were still fighting strong and Uncle Fry was holding his own, but Ilsy was showing fatigue. I had expected this. I jumped over to

her, grabbed her arm, and jumped into the building
housing the kids.

# CHAPTER 17

The building was dark inside. The windows had been boarded shut. I heard a gasp from the children as I brought another fireball to life in my hands. I found a light switch and tried it. The lights came on and I extinguished the fireball. The kids looked at me fearfully.

"Are you an angel?" asked a little boy of maybe seven.

"No, but I am here to protect you. Miss Ilsy here is going to keep you safe while I," I said as a scream of pain pierced the walls, "while I take care of that."

I gave Ilsy a quick peck on the forehead and jumped back to the fight. Most of the cultists were down, Grandfather had one pinned to the ground and was literally sitting on it. I helped the wolves finish off the rest and then sent them to search the town. They left Grandfather and me with the captured cult member.

"You seem to be in a pickle," I said to the cultist as I sat down beside him.

"Fuck you, winged vermin." His voice was bland, with no inflection. The man could have been anyone from anywhere.

"I don't swing that way friend, though I think I know someone who might," I offered.

"The master will take care of you. Kill me and he will kill you, let me go and he might kill you quickly."

"Oh, I'm not going to kill you," I said as I reached out and grabbed his arm. Ice crystals began forming underneath my hand. The man screamed in pain.

"No, I'm just going to hurt you. How many of you are here?" I asked. Somewhat rudely, the man ignored my question and continued screaming.

"Tell me how many and I'll make it stop." I positioned myself so I could look him in the eye. He continued to scream, so I squeezed my hand on his arm. A loud crack announced that the ice was breaking. He screamed louder, and I squeezed harder. The arm beneath my hand broke off at the elbow.

"No sense going to pieces," I said. I grabbed his bicep and started the freezing process over. "I will have my answers."

"Two hundred! There were two hundred of us!" he screamed. I pulled my hand back and watched the ice melt on his arm.

"Good boy."

"Go to hell!" I renewed my grip on his bicep.

"Is Brother Herman here?"

"No, he's not." The man was starting to cry. That's the funny thing about evil creatures: death holds no fear for them. Slow, painful dismemberment? That scares the hell out of them.

"That's fine. This is what we're going to do. Are you paying attention?" I asked, this time grabbing his leg high on his thigh.

"I'm listening!"

"Good, I'm going to let you go. You will go to Herman and tell him to meet me here at midnight tonight." The ice formed on his leg slowly.

"You fool, he'll kill you."

"Do you understand my message?" I let the ice grow faster. It was quickly approaching his groin. His eyes widened.

"Yes, I'll tell him! Maybe he'll let me watch you die!" The man said as an explosion rang through the night.

"Maybe," I said, pushing myself off his leg as I got up to my feet. I nodded to Grandfather and he stood also.

"Go now," I said. The ghoul waved goodbye with his middle finger and ran off into the woods.

"Do you believe him?" Grandfather asked.

"Oh, he'd gladly watch me die. He won't get the chance though."

I turned and started walking to the road through town. Ben was walking our way. He was bleeding from his head and a cut on his arm.

"What the hell are you blowing up?" I shouted over to him.

"Temples. We found five so far," he said when he got closer. I reached out and grabbed his arm with my hand and placed the other hand on his forehead. My hands glowed a faint blue as his wounds healed.

"You have been healed!" I declared in my best televangelist voice. He looked at his arm and felt his head.

"I'll be damned," he muttered.

"What do we do with the kids?" I asked.

"I'll have the others drive dem to a friend of ours. She'll make sure dey get taken care of," he said.

"Good man."

We gathered back at the pack's camp. I needed a nap. The day had been long already and it was only noon. The wolves prepared a lunch for us and we told them of the town. I trusted the priest to pass my message but didn't trust his counting abilities, so we had cleared the rest of the buildings before coming to the camp. Turns out his fear, or pain, caused him to tell the truth. The town now sat empty and had wolves posted around it as guards. I had every intention of meeting Brother Herman in the town that night, but I didn't want any surprises.

I tried explaining my plan to the wolves but it didn't come out very clear. I had Darius fetch the book so we could burn it. I figured if we showed Brother Herman the ashes of it, his anger would blind him. When someone is pissed, they rarely fight smart. Even at night

# Ragged Edge

I felt sure that I could take him in a one-on-one fight. I also felt sure this wouldn't be one of those fights. Willow agreed to have her entire pack around the town. Ilsy, Uncle Fry, and Darius would be hiding in the cliffs with sniper rifles. The wolves were going to rig each house to explode if it looked like I might be losing. An explosive distraction rarely failed to gain the upper hand.

When Darius returned with the manuscript, we placed it in a deep fire pit that Grandfather had prepared. The wolves looked at it and turned their noses away; it apparently smelled bad to them. I didn't bother explaining to them what I had seen when I touched it and just readied a large fireball in my hand. Standing in front of the pit, I thought about what I was destroying. Despite its wrongness, this book was a piece of history and I was about to destroy an artifact older than I was, maybe even older than my grandfather. For some reason I have a fondness for old things, and it bothered me that I had to destroy it. I almost had myself talked out of destroying it when I remembered the vision in full detail – and the fear it evoked in me.

I raised the fireball as high as I could and threw it down with all my might. When the flame contacted the pages, there was a bright blue flash like lightening and a deep crack of thunder. The smell of ozone wafted up from the pit, and the fire flashed out in sparks. The book appeared untouched. I hadn't even managed to singe it. As the ozone smell dissipated, an evil, insane laughter floated around the camp.

"Huh," I mumbled.

"This might change things," Grandfather said.

# Ragged Edge

There are few things I dislike more than getting surprised just before a fight, especially a fight that could lead to my death. Surprises throw you off your game, they cloud the mind with doubt, and, all in all, surprises just before a fight are just plain rude. Now I had to alter my plan to include a conversation. I intended to just attack and keep attacking until the bastard was dead, but now I needed to know how to destroy the damn manuscript. It just wasn't fair. It was possible that if I destroyed Brother Herman, we could hide the book. Its main danger was being in his hands, so if he were destroyed it shouldn't be dangerous anymore. So ignoring the problem would be Plan B, though it wasn't as perfect as Plan A, which was to destroy both the book and monk. And there was the possibility that he did have children old enough to understand the book, but it was all I had. I had other things to do before meeting him.

"So, we'll just deal with that later, I guess." I shrugged my shoulders.

"Maybe it can't be destroyed while he's alive?" Ilsy asked.

"That's a possibility, I guess."

"Who knows what powers the man in shadows gave him." Grandfather said.

"True, and right now I can't worry about it. I need to sleep and prepare for tonight."

"How can we help?" Willow asked.

"Hold down the fort. I'm gonna go back to my cabin."

"Want me to come?" Ilsy asked.

"Yeah, not the preparation I meant," I said with a grin. "I need rest and time alone." Her shoulders slumped. I wanted to say she could come with me but now wasn't the time to deal with personal issues. It goes back to that whole surprise thing. I saw Uncle Fry nod approvingly and knew he agreed.

"We will stay here and prepare ourselves also. Tonight we feast," Willow said.

"Good idea, party before the battle, I approve. Guys, can we get this armor off me?" I said, motioning at myself. My group assisted me out of the armor, and it felt good to be free of the added weight. Sure, titanium was supposed to be lightweight, but it added at least another fifty pounds or so. My armor was now blood stained, and I knew there would be more on it before everything was completed. I just had to hope it wouldn't be mine.

"Thanks. I'll be back in a few hours." I said before jumping back to the cabin.

It was weird being back at the cabin by myself. Everywhere I looked there were reminders that I wasn't alone. Grandfather's walking stick, everyone's clothes drying on a line in the wind, the smoldering fire pit. I frequently came to this cabin to clear my mind before jumping into battle. Some people, and werewolves it seemed, enjoy being surrounded by a group of friends or family before going into a situation that could possibly kill them. I didn't have the human fear of death, not really, but the thought of it did prickle the back of my mind.

I went inside and looked around the cabin. My friends and family had been staying with me, and here I was avoiding them. Ilsy had added a definite feminine touch to my cabin. Before her, I never bothered with decorating. The cabin was for solitude, comfort, and shutting out the world. Now it was almost possible to live here. Hell, we had been living here. She had bought a small glass vase on her last trip to town and now it sat on the table with wild flowers. I had teased her about it at first, but now those flowers brought a smile to my face. I could smell her in my cabin. Her scent was on my clothes, my bed, all around me really.

I laid down so I could take a nap. I hadn't used too much energy fighting the ghouls but I needed to go into battle with Herman fully prepared. Sleep was always necessary. Without it, the mind wanders and the reflexes slow. This man was old enough to have speed, agility, and powers equal to mine. I couldn't take him lightly.

Lying in bed, I was surrounded by the smells of Ilsy. She had been doing most of the laundry, though Uncle Fry helped a little. She had made the bed last so her scent covered it. Instead of sleeping, I lay there thinking about her: the smile on her face, the way her hair hung in her eyes, the bright spark in eyes when her anger was aroused. The wolves really were right, she and Uncle Fry had an earthy scent to them. Her scent was like a freshly mowed yard, wild flowers, and a springtime rain. Uncle Fry was more like dirt, tree bark, and animal musk. I preferred her scent.

# Ragged Edge

I knew what was happening, and that I couldn't allow it. I remembered our first night, the vision from the book, and knowing I was going to die for her. I wasn't afraid to die for her, but now, well, now I wanted to live for her. I knew I was going to die, maybe not tonight but soon. Knowing that, I didn't want to get any closer to her. I didn't want her to go through the pain of my death like she had for her father. It wouldn't be fair to her.

With those thoughts in my mind, I fell into an uneasy sleep. I guess it was only natural that I woke in a dark mood at sunset. It wasn't fair that I would finally find a human that I liked, loved, wanted to be with, and wanted to have understand me. It wasn't fair that I found her now, knowing that soon she would be ripped from me by death's cold, uncaring grasp. I walked to the kitchen and grabbed a beer before taking a shower. We had been living rough the past few weeks and I needed a real shower.

As I washed the filth away, my mood lifted a little. I knew the future wasn't written in stone, it could be changed. My vision from the book might never come to pass, and maybe I just misunderstood knowing that I would die for her. My hand rubbed against my cheeks as I washed my hair and I realized it had been almost a month since the last time I shaved. I don't know why, but it became vitally important to me that I not go into battle with a beard. Luckily, Uncle Fry had brought a shaving kit with him and left it in the shower room. I didn't think he'd mind me borrowing it.

With each stroke of the razor, I felt lighter, stronger, and more myself. The dark thoughts and mood of the past few hours weren't me. I was supposed to be confident, self-assured, and following my goal with a reckless abandon. That's who Brother Herman would be fighting. I had nothing to lose. He had an almost endless life to lose, and the absurd goal of dominating the world with whatever evil creatures he hoped to summon. Now clean-shaven, I smiled at myself in the mirror. Yeah, I'm damn sexy.

Shower over, I walked out to get dressed. Only then did I realize I couldn't get my shirt on by myself. I shrugged and put on my pants and boots. I started for the door and found Ilsy sitting at the fire pit. I paused in the doorway, took a deep breath, and walked outside.

"How'd you get here?" I asked, striving for nonchalant.

"Ben brought me. Said it wasn't safe for me to come alone," she said without looking at me.

"He's right." I walked to the clothesline, grabbed a random t-shirt, walked over to the fire pit, and sat next to her.

"What's up kiddo?" I cringed as I said it.

"Kiddo?" she arched an eyebrow at me.

"Yeah, that. I don't know where that came from." I laughed.

"Sean, can I ask you a question?"

"Sure," I said.

"What's going on here?"

"Um, well, I'm about to destroy Brother Herman in a few hours, then I'll try destroying the book again. I suppose after that, to make sure you're safe, I'll have to go find Mother and have a stern talk with her," I said.

"Not what I meant, Sean." She turned to face me. I looked at her eyes, those Irish-hillside eyes. They were moist and sparkling.

"Oh, what did you mean?" I asked and turned to the fire. I hate surprises.

"There's, I don't know, something between us. When you left the pack camp, I felt lonely. I didn't like being separated from you. That's why I had Ben walk me back. You were sleeping when I got here and I watched you sleep. Is that too stalker-like?"

"Mildly stalker-like, yeah." I nodded.

"I sat out here to think. When I heard you moving around, I thought about talking to you but I was scared. Why should I want to be around you so much? In the month or so I've known you, my life has been completely turned upside. My friends probably think I'm dead, I'm sure my job is gone, and I want to blame it all on you but I can't. Why?"

"Stockholm Syndrome," I said.

"What?"

"Stockholm Syndrome, when someone grows feelings for their kidnapper. Well, not just kidnappers, I mean it happens in hostage situations too. The point is, you've basically been a hostage out here for a long time now. It's only natural that you'd feel an attachment to the person that brought you here." It sounded reasonable to me. I was sure it was wrong but at least it sounded reasonable.

"Yeah, Stockholm Syndrome. That must be it," she said quietly.

# Ragged Edge

"Right, so now we have that sorted, will you help me get this shirt on?" I asked, holding up my shirt.

"Your bruise is gone," she said, looking at my chest.

"Of course it is, I healed from being almost disemboweled in little less than an hour, remember? Magic takes longer, but basically it was just a bigger, bloodier couch," I said with a smile.

She laughed at me and helped get the shirt over my wings.

"Thank you, Ilsy." I tried to put my feelings into that thank you. The look on her face told me I might have succeeded. I think she understood why I couldn't say it then. I hope she did.

"Anyway, it's getting dark so we should go back to the pack camp. Take my arm and I'll take us, or we could walk if you want."

She took my arm and looked up at me.

"Let's walk," she said. So we did.

# CHAPTER 18

It was midnight. I stood in the now-deserted town with moonlight glinting off my armor. Grandfather had cleaned it and polished off the stains. A slight breeze blew my hair back from my face. I walked down the road toward the center of town. In front of me was Brother Herman. We walked towards each other like two gunfighters in a western movie.

"I didn't think you'd come." His voice grated on the wind and violated my ears.

"I never issue an invite to a party I don't plan to attend," I shouted back.

We stopped about fifty yards from each other. Our eyes locked, I needed to get him talking about the book.

"Where is it?" he asked.

"Oh, it's around. I've read it you know. I think you're insane."

# Ragged Edge

"Genius often appears as madness to those beneath it."

"Sometimes, but then, madness often appears as madness to everyone. The book held madness. I destroyed it."

"Impossible," he said, laughing. I would rather have heard nails on a chalkboard.

"Suit yourself. I just thought you should know your plan won't work." I shrugged.

"If it were destroyed, I wouldn't be here. That book was given to me by the man who made me. My life and its existence are directly linked. We cannot be destroyed."

"I see. Time for you to go now. I don't feel like giving it back." He could have been lying, but I was tired of his voice. I knew he wouldn't let me leave so it was time to end it.

"Winged vermin, I will not leave this place without my book. You will beg to tell me its location and you will beg for death. Now face me." He pulled a sword from behind him.

"I am no winged vermin. I am Sean Gryphon, son of Alistair Gryphon, grandson of Atlas Gryphon. Brother of Raven, I bear the wings of my people. The people of the lost island, blessed by Gaea, protectors of humankind. I am Sean Gryphon, junior guardian, walker of the ragged edge, protector of Ilsy Hillerman and the Codex Gigas pages." My voice rose to a trumpeting cry. "I am the destroyer of Brother Herman, and a child of ATLANTIS!"

# Ragged Edge

I flung two fireballs at the houses on either side of the monk. The houses exploded and loud cries of pain rose above the roar of the fire as two humanoid forms covered in flames flew from them. Each form ran about twenty feet before falling. Brother Herman stood, staring at me. I could almost see a glimmer of fear in his beady little eyes.

"My, such fury. My young ones will be happy with your strength." He rushed at me with the sword raised. He was fast. I tried jumping behind him as he charged forward. I was a little slow and his sword came down slicing into my right arm. It was okay though – I didn't expect to end this fight without a scratch. Still, a part of me was personally insulted. I appeared behind him and threw a jolt of lighting at his back. Without waiting to see the damage, I moved again. I reappeared on the roof of a house. I sent another fireball flying at him, but he jumped to the left and the ball slammed into the ground. Before I could jump again he was beside me, his fist hit me in the chest like a sledgehammer and sent me flying from the building. If it weren't for the armor, I'm almost sure the blow would have broken my ribs. Even with the armor, he knocked the wind out of me.

I landed on my back with a loud crunch and pain seared through my broken wing. I would have yelled in pain if I'd had any air to yell with. I took large gulping breaths and got to my feet. I tried to hide the pain but I'm sure he saw it. He stood above me gloating.

"Are you ready to beg?" he asked. I shook my head.

"Not yet." I said.

# Ragged Edge

A sound a little louder than a balloon popping rang through the night. I saw a flash of flame as the incendiary round blew through his knee. He fell from the roof and I threw a fireball at a house. It exploded, sending wooden shrapnel flying everywhere as I jumped to the roof of a nearby building that was once a hardware store. The monk was engulfed in flames briefly. He streaked out of the fire with his clothes burning. The wind rushing past put them out and he stopped. Before he spotted me, another incendiary round blew through his stomach.

I had already learned a few things from this fight. He wasn't as flammable as most humans, he could move as fast as I could telelocate, and he didn't seem to feel pain. I didn't know what powers his deal had garnered him, but he was remarkably resilient.

I threw another fireball at him, and it hit him square in the back. For the first time he screeched in pain. That was when all hell broke loose. The front doors of five houses blew open and revealed a ghoul behind each. The guards had warned me about more showing up after sunset. I knew I couldn't handle six at a time, not by myself. Flying into the air, I threw another fireball at Herman and let out a raven call. From the air, I saw more ghouls exiting houses. I knew Herman had laid a trap for me, I just didn't know the scope. I hoped the surprises I had planned were enough.

# Ragged Edge

A tremendous roaring howl answered my raven call. As one body, the wolves exited the woods around the town and charged into battle. Ilsy, Uncle Fry, and Darius were firing at will with the sniper rifles. Headshots were the order of the day. Brother Herman looked up at me and screamed in rage. I shifted fully into my battle form, the armor restricted my change but didn't stop it, talking was done. I trusted the wolves and snipers to take care of everyone else; focused on Brother Herman. I telelocated right in front of him and swung one of my taloned hands in an upward swipe. My middle talons pierced underneath his chin, so I used my momentum to twist and throw him to the ground.

An inhuman screech filled my ears as he howled in pain. Dust billowed around him on impact and I jumped away. A viscous black liquid ran from the puncture wounds down his chest. I was picking him apart and his end was coming soon. Now he'd be more dangerous than ever. I dove from behind him, intending to run an arm through his back and chest. He heard the wind rushing around me and turned. Before I could change course, he ducked and, with fists engulfed in a dark purple energy, drove a crushing blow right into my stomach. The armor rang like a gong and I was thrown into the air. My armor was dented where his fist landed, I landed on a roof trying to catch my breath and threw up.

I lost sight of Herman and searched frantically for him. When a searing, slicing pain radiated from my left leg, I found him. He had gotten behind me. My leg wobbled and collapsed under me. I swiped at his neck as

# Ragged Edge

I fell and felt my talons sink in, scraping against his spine. A choking gurgling sound escaped from him as his hands flew to his throat. My leg was burning beneath me. I grabbed his leg and sunk my talons in. Heat radiated through my talons, and smoke crawled up his leg. He tried pulling away and I held tighter. His clothes began burning, the heat poured off him, I could feel my face burning from the heat. I used his body to regain my feet, always keeping one taloned hand in him.

When I was finally standing, I dug my talons into his rib cage. The heat was intense as he was burning from the inside. I pulled his face close to mine and stared him in the eyes.

"Your time is done," I growled out in my raven voice. His eyes widened as they caught fire. I grasped what was left of his heart and threw him away from me to the ground. His body exploded in a ball of purple and red flame when it landed. My leg collapsed again, but I caught myself and hovered in the air. From the sky I could see the battle raging. The ghouls were almost all dead. I threw fireballs at the remaining buildings, causing them to explode. The town was a raging inferno around us. The pack and I worked at encircling the remaining ghouls and herded them towards a burning building. I returned to my human shape with my wings out.

"Your creator is dead, you have been fed on the blood and meat of innocents, and now you will die in the purifying flame."

I thrust my hands in front of me, a gale of wind rushed towards the risen monsters and threw them into the flames. The fire flared up with the wind. A few screeches and smaller explosions later, and it was done. I landed amongst the wolves and sat down. Of the original fifteen pack members, I only counted seven left.

"Grandfather, where is he?" I asked. One of the wolves returned to human form. It was Willow.

"He's taking care of our wounded," she said.

"How many?" I asked.

"Four wounded that are expected to survive. Four others dead," she said, helping me to my feet.

My leg wouldn't support my weight. I tried looking down at it but my armor wouldn't let me.

"My leg, I can't see it, what kind of injury?" I asked her.

She looked down and let out a low whistle.

"From thigh to ankle, it strongly resembles hamburger."

"That explains it. Can you help me over to Grandfather?"

"Yes, Sean." Though much shorter than I, she was able to bear my weight with no difficulty.

"Sorry, Willow, about your pack mates, I mean," I said as we hobbled toward the wounded.

"No need to be sorry, Sean. They died in battle against a great evil. We helped save many children, and maybe our forest will be free for awhile," she said.

I couldn't argue with her logic. It was almost a given that I would die in battle, and I don't think I'd have it any other way. It's just who we are, most of us anyway.

Grandfather had set fires around the wounded so he could see better. I barely recognized most of them. The dead were laid to the side. I recognized one of them. The little haunted pack member that fetched water for us. His was untouched, his stomach was laid bare and I could see the white of his ribs. Willow helped me sit beside the wounded.

"So you lived through it, did ya?" Ben's ever-cheery voice said. I looked over and saw him on the ground. His left arm was obviously broken and he had deep claw marks through his chest, otherwise, he was okay.

"Yes I did. I'm glad you made it Ben," I said. I had grown to like this wolf. His attitude was infectious.

"Wasn't any doubt. If those had been normal humans dey would've been no problem. Dese fuckers could fight though," he said laughing.

"That they can. I think these were mostly young ones though. I hate that four died but it really should have been more."

"Yea, you right, but hey, let's be thankful for those that lived, huh?"

"Sure, Ben. How about I see if I can't fix you up?" I said, reaching a hand out toward his arm.

"Looks to me like you got some fixing to do on yourself," he said, pointing at my leg.

"It'll heal," I said. I grabbed his arm and the blue radiated from hands. Black dots swam in my vision. I bit on my tongue to push them away. When I pulled my hand back, his arm was healed.

"I think grandfather will have to take care of the rest," I said, laying back. I had pushed too far. Grandfather made setting someone on fire from the inside look easy. Turns out it's a helluva lot harder than it looks.

# Ragged Edge

"It don' madda', deres a few hurt worse den I am," he said.

He kept talking, reliving the fight, and I let my mind wander. One down, two to go. That's what I kept telling myself. The monk threat was through. Now I just had to deal with my mother and half-brother. I knew they had stronger forces, I didn't know exactly where they were. I could get back to the cave, no problem, but I couldn't bring the wolves with me. I didn't really want to either. They had been friendly and shown us plenty of hospitality. I didn't want to lead more of them to their deaths.

Grandfather worked fast and soon had all the wolves healed and headed back to camp. Grandfather's face showed how tired he was. I stopped him from touching my leg.

"You need rest, Grandfather. I'll fly."

"Don't be pig headed–"

"Sean!" I heard Ilsy yell. I sat up and looked around. She ran to my side.

"How about it, doc, think you can fix my leg?" I asked her with a wink.

"I'm not that kind of doctor," she said. Uncle Fry and Darius exchanged a look. I didn't like the look. It was a knowing look.

"Come on, guys, get this armor off me," I said.

They removed the armor and I stretched my wings out. Moving them without the armor was almost orgasmic in its mixture of pleasure and severe pain. I felt a good hundred pounds lighter.

# Ragged Edge

"Sean, let me heal that damn leg," Grandfather said. I tried to protest but the world skewed on me. My head was spinning. I reached my hands below my leg and felt a large puddle of blood.

"Fuck. Okay, Grandfather," I said and rolled over so he could get to it. I heard Ilsy scream when my leg was exposed. Uncle Fry made gagging sounds but avoided losing his dinner.

"Damn, boy, you shouldn't have been standing after this," Grandfather said.

"I wasn't, much," I said and bit down on my lip to stop the world from going black.

I felt warmth spread over my leg. The pain receded most of the way and the warmth disappeared.

"That's all I can do, boy, but you won't bleed out now," he said. I rolled over and saw Darius supporting him.

"It'll do, let's go back to camp." Uncle Fry reached down and helped me stand. We each grabbed pieces of my armor and slowly walked back to the pack camp. On the way we passed a few wolves watching the town burn. We each nodded and went on our way.

The pack's camp was mostly silent when we returned. A few private fires burned here and there and some of the pack was sitting outside recounting the battle, sharing drinks, and eating. The four dead were laid out in the center of the camp and being washed. We walked past them to the house they had given us. Uncle Fry wrapped my leg in gauze so I wouldn't bleed on the bed.

"Why isn't that healing like your stomach did at my house?" Ilsy asked.

"I wasn't tired then. It takes a lot of energy to heal wounds, and I don't have it right now. Between the busted wing, the fire I threw out there, the flying, and telelocating, I've used up most of my resources. Sleep and food will help it heal," I said and then headed for bed.

I woke late that afternoon. When I stood my leg throbbed, but when I looked down it was mostly healed. The house was empty so I limped outside. The pack was gathered around the bodies of the four fallen wolves. I joined them quietly. Willow was talking of their bravery in battle, and how they would be missed. Grandfather opened a large hole in the ground with his hands and the wolves were slowly placed in it side by side. Grandfather closed the hole over them. The rest of the pack dispersed and I was left standing at the new graves with my group.

I limped over to the table from our first night with the wolves and sat down. We should have been happy after our victory but the loss of four muted the happiness. I knew going in that not everyone would survive and still I led them in. I tried telling myself it was necessary but it didn't help.

"I tried burning the book again," Grandfather said. I looked up at him. "It won't burn."

"He said that his life was linked with the book. That they couldn't be destroyed separately," I mused.

"But he was destroyed," Ilsy said.

275

"Yeah, I watched it. He also said the man in shadows gave it to him."

"So what do we do?"

"For now, I guess we hide it." I was tired of the book. I wanted to go back to my apartment, back to my life.

"Where?" Ilsy asked.

"I don't know. Will you take it, Grandfather?" I asked.

"For now," he said.

"Sean," Darius said quietly.

"What?" I asked a little sharper than I intended.

"I hate to be the bearer of bad news–"

"Bullshit, you love it," I interrupted.

"No, I don't. Some day you'll believe that. For now though, your grandfather and I must leave."

"What?"

"It's true, Sean. The council only allowed my help in dealing with Herman, and I've done more than I should have, to be honest."

I hung my head. I felt tears welling up in my eyes. I knew it was true but I didn't want him to leave. Ilsy put a hand on my back. I rubbed at my eyes with my palms before looking up.

"Very well. It's been great being with you, Grandfather," I said.

"Remember though, in dire need you can come to me," he said, clapping a hand on my shoulder. I nodded my head.

"What are you going to do now?" Darius asked.

"I guess let my wing heal, and then have a chat with my mother," I said.

"Good luck, Sean," Darius said. I nodded my head.

"Go grab the book, Darius. I'll take it to my place," Grandfather said. Darius walked back to the house we were using.

"Now that he's gone, if you need me, Sean, call and the council be damned," he said.

"Thanks, Grandfather," I said as he wrapped me in a hug.

"I'll see you soon, boy," he said and let go. Darius returned with the box containing the book.

"I'll tell the council of your actions. Maybe they'll remove you from the threat of final death."

"Maybe?"

"Well, until your mother is dealt with, I don't know for sure. Your mission was to protect Ilsy and the book. We didn't know the two weren't connected."

"Looks like you aren't free of me," I said to Ilsy. She shrugged and smiled at me.

Grandfather grabbed the box with the manuscript and laughed. He took a step and vanished. Darius disappeared behind him.

We took our leave from the werewolves and walked back to my cabin. I told the wolves they had an open invite to my door, and they assured me the feeling was mutual. Ben promised to stop by and check on us whenever he could. We left knowing we had made new friends. It felt a little strange to me though. I had met werewolves before, but normally I was killing them. Yet now I had found a pack that were friendly and used their curse for good. I told myself that when everything was taken care of, I'd spend more time with them and try to find more to fill their ranks.

Back at the cabin, we cleaned up and then sat around. Everyone's mood was downcast and we were all feeling drained. I cooked on the fire pit outside for us and we sat enjoying the quiet. I cleaned the armor Grandfather had made and fixed the dent that the monk's fist had made. After a quiet evening with Uncle Fry telling stories, we went to bed. I think we were each feeling a need for solitude that we couldn't get yet. I intended to let my wing heal before taking on the wolfengators and my mother. I hoped we'd be able to tolerate each other until then. I wasn't sure if I could wait though. Despite the drained feeling, I was itching to get this business over with. I don't like looking for a fight, but delaying one that I know is inevitable is worse.

The next morning, Ilsy and her Uncle resumed her training. She had done well as a sniper but it wasn't guaranteed that she could stay out of the fight. I joined them in the afternoon and that's how we passed the day. Our old routine was coming back to us and we were slowly sliding back into those habits. It was comfortable. That night Ilsy and her Uncle cooked and we ate outside again.

"Sean?" Ilsy asked while sitting by the fire.

"Yeah?"

"What happens after your mother is dealt with?"

"Assuming I survive?"

"Yes, assuming you survive."

"Well, I guess you and your Uncle go back to your lives, and I return to my life."

"What kind of life did you have before this?"

"Honestly, not much different, only I didn't have any real friends. Nobody who knew exactly what I was. Other than my shrink anyway."

"Your shrink?" Uncle Fry asked.

"Yup, my shrink."

"Why did you see a shrink?"

"Because I am a functional delusional. At least, that's what he says. In reality I did it so I had someone I could talk to. I could tell him what I was, what I did, things I fought, and he never believed a word of it. He'd just prescribe me pills and think about what he was going to have for dinner or banging his wife or something," I said. Ilsy and Uncle Fry laughed.

"Why do you keep yourself alone?" Ilsy asked.

"I didn't use to. When I first started this life, I'd make human friends. Some of them I even told what I was. Then they'd grow old and die or get killed. I stopped making friends after a few hundred years. It hurt too much." I looked her in the eyes when I said this. She looked away.

"Oh."

"Darius told me you have a problem with shirking your duty," Uncle Fry said.

"Not so much shirking, at least I don't think so. It's just that you humans are so intent on destroying yourselves, I didn't see any reason to go out of my way to stop other things from destroying you."

"What?" Ilsy asked.

"Look at it: you've got serial killers, most of those are humans, your race is always starting wars and hurting each other, and very little of it has to do with things like me. We can't stop you from killing yourselves. So I'd deal with stuff I saw firsthand and let the rest happen. You've got the world overpopulated as is. From what I hear, it's getting harder to keep our homes hidden."

"Where is your home?" Ilsy asked.

"Here and there. I told you that they gathered the bits after the volcano exploded and destroyed our island. We now have four islands spread throughout the world. Grandfather lives on a piece of the island in the center of the Bermuda Triangle. Another piece is located off Japan in what's called the Dragon Triangle, and another is in the Great Lakes. The fourth is where the council meets and the Ancient resides there. I don't know where it is. I consider Grandfather's island to be my home, that's where I mostly grew up."

"Is that why things happen in those places?"

"You mean the ships and the planes disappearing? More or less. The island does have a bit of a human population on it. When a human finds the island, we can't let them leave. It's too dangerous for us."

"Too dangerous? What could we do to you?"

"I don't know the exact numbers, but you humans outnumber us by at least half a million to one. There aren't that many of us, even fewer of us that actually fight. Yeah, we can do a lot of damage in a fight but we do tire out. The mountain could have crumbled after our fight and I wouldn't have known it. Anyway, it's getting late. I'm going to bed." I stood and went inside. I was tired of the questions. I didn't want to explain my people to Ilsy. I wanted to show her my people. There was only one way I could do that, though, and I didn't know if she'd go for it. I wasn't even going to try until after dealing with my mother.

# CHAPTER 19

The days were passing slowly. It's funny how much time can stand still when you have nothing to do except wait to heal. Basically, I was bored. The pain in my wing decreased day by day, but I was still worried about going into battle with it. Ben paid us frequent visits. He was a fun guy to hang out with and filled with stories about hunting alligators, swimming in the swamps, and life in the Big Easy. Still I was anxious to move forward. In retrospect, I should have enjoyed those days more. Life was simple then. Afterwards... well let's just say it's a little more complicated now.

Uncle Fry had eased on Ilsy's training so our days were spent hiking, swimming in the spring, and reading from the books Ilsy took from her father's house. I had stopped following her everywhere, and I'm sure she was thankful I had eased up. I didn't see a need to be a helicopter, hovering over her all the time.

# Ragged Edge

So that's how time passed for the first week after I destroyed Herman. I think if I had spent more time thinking about everything that was said to me by my mother, Herman, and even Danu, things might have turned out differently. Sometimes I can console myself thinking that things turned out the way they were supposed to and I earned everything I received. Sometimes that helps.

It was a bright warm day when everything changed. I was lounging outside. Mostly I was trying to nap, but I was also listening to the birdsong and the sounds of the forest around me. Ilsy came out and asked if I wanted to go for a swim. I shook my head. She said okay and walked off towards the spring. She had done this a lot and I wasn't concerned about it. I dozed off shortly after she left.

I was jolted awake when I heard her scream. The forest was silent except her screaming. Uncle Fry came rushing out of the cabin and we went charging through the woods. When we got to the spring, Ilsy was nowhere to be found. Claw prints in the mud told us the wolfengators had been there. We found a note stuck into a tree with a stone dagger, which meant Mother had been here also. I read the note over Uncle Fry's shoulder.

*My Dearest Son,*

*Since you have been slow taking this pretty one for your mate, I have decided that you don't appreciate my gift. Like any good mother, I have decided I should return her to where she came from. I do hope that we will keep in touch.*

# Ragged Edge

Uncle Fry crumpled the note in his hands and threw it to the forest floor. I stood thinking of mother's actions. I didn't know the woman well enough to make assumptions on her next action. I did know her well enough to know that she wasn't simply taking Ilsy home. There was a deeper game here that I hadn't figured out yet and now Ilsy's life hung in the balance. I knew I couldn't give my wing time to finish healing. I couldn't let this confrontation wait any longer.

Lost in these thoughts, I never saw the punch Uncle Fry threw at me. His fist landed squarely on my chin. I stumbled backwards, barely managing to maintain my balance. Another punch was coming at me on the heels of the first. I sidestepped him but didn't fight back. I understood his anger, I was her protector – I should have been with her.

"You bastard!" he yelled at me as he threw another punch. He was fighting in a blind rage and didn't pose much threat to me. I simply dodged him.

"You could have stopped this!"

"Sir Fry, I'll get her back," I said, dodging another blow.

"She'll be dead before you get to her. Those things will tear her apart!"

"I don't think so." Dodging again.

"You don't think at all!" he was slowing down now. His grief was overtaking him.

"Sir Fry, I swear to you, I will get her back." I took the next blow on the chest.

"She's all I have left." His face crumbled as he wrapped his arms around me.

"I thought your family was big, sir?"

"Of my brother, you idiot. She's the last of us, the family continues but my line draws to an end."

"Not yet, sir, I'll get her back or die trying." He let go of me.

"I'm coming with you," he said resolutely. I wanted to tell him no. As much as he wouldn't forgive me if she died, I'm sure she wouldn't be thrilled if he died trying to save her. I did need the help though, and supposedly the Aen Sidhe would join him in battle. At least, they would if the story was true and not just a family legend.

"Where are ya'll fixin to go?" Ben said rushing out of the trees. I won't say I didn't jump but I'm sure I didn't make it a mile.

"To get Ilsy back," I said.

"The petite cher? Who took her?"

"My mother and the wolfengators."

"Well, bon ami, let's get going!"

"What?"

"I'm coming with you. Can't let my new friends get into trouble without me, can I?"

"What?" I couldn't disagree. Ben was becoming a friend, but I also knew this was the next best thing to a suicide mission.

"Sure, look you two alone, not much use, take a stout wolf like me with you and maybe ya'll got a chance."

"Ben, I can't – I can't let you do this," I said.

# Ragged Edge

"Why not? You need help, and I'm here to help. Can't bring the rest of the pack though. Dey is out looking for more of us."

"Looking for more?"

"Yeah, gotta replenish our ranks."

"How?"

"Looking for more dat don't like mindless killing. Don't change the subject. When we going?"

"Alright, but fair warning, you may not make it back." We probably wouldn't make it back. I knew it, I think Uncle Fry knew it, and I had to make sure Ben knew it.

"Fair enough. I'm replaceable. Now let's go," he said, clapping his hands together. I think the recent fight with the cult had gotten his blood up. He was itching for a fight.

"I need my armor first."

"Wing still busted?"

"Yeah."

"Den let's get dat armor and go." He turned and headed back to the camp. Uncle Fry and I looked at each other, a smile slowly crossed his face and I felt one growing on mine. We might all die in the next few hours, but at least we'd be amongst friends.

Uncle Fry and Ben got me into my armor. It wasn't as easy for two as it was for five. I felt the weight of the wing armor pulling down on my wings. It hurt, badly. Soon I was suited up and ready to go. Ben ran back to

the pack's camp and told them he was leaving for a bit.
Willow wished us luck.

While he was gone, I sent another message to
Grandfather. In my raven voice, I spread the call,
"Wolfengators have Ilsy, going to save her with Uncle
Fry and Ben. Hope to see you after. I love you." I didn't
often express my feelings. I wanted him to know that I
expected to die without actually saying it. Saying "I love
you" seemed to be the next best thing. I took one last
look at my cabin. I expected to never see it again. What
was once a place for solitude had become a home. I was
going to miss it.

When staring death in the face, I've found it's best to
smile and give him the finger. That comes easier when
you know the death isn't permanent. I hadn't heard
anything from Darius so I felt sure I was still under
threat of final death. That tends to put a damper on the
smiling and flipping the bird. This time I felt more
sentimental, like I was seeing everything for the last time.
I wasn't afraid exactly. Sure, fear played a small role in it
and mostly I felt tired. When you know that your life
may end within the hour, the years tend to weigh heavily
on you. I had seven hundred years to weigh me down,
more if you wanted to include my other lives. Never
before had I gone into battle knowing that if I died, I
was done. This was the end. I expected all of us to die,
but at least I'd be going out with friends. More
importantly, at the time, I wouldn't be living without
Ilsy. That seemed a fair trade for my life.

Standing outside the cabin, I told Uncle Fry and Ben
to hang onto me. I focused on Ilsy. I focused on

appearing a mile from her. I didn't know if my mother could stop me from jumping straight to Ilsy. If she could, then trying to jump straight to Ilsy would warn her that I was coming. I'm sure she expected me sooner or later, but I wanted to maintain whatever level of surprise I could. I should have warned Ben to close his eyes. Uncle Fry remembered from traveling with Darius. We landed in another wooded area, and Ben promptly threw up. The woods around here were more sparse, mostly oaks. I recognized the area from my last trip to find mother. I knew that we were a mile from a cave. What waited for us in the cave I had no idea.

Ben transformed to the wolf and smelled the air around us. He could smell the wolfengators. When he resumed his human form, he told us they were at least a half a mile from us. That didn't bode well. We could try to sneak in as far as we could, but we would have to fight for at least a half mile before even entering the cave. Once in the cave we had nowhere to run, we had to finish our errand and find Ilsy – or die trying. If we retreated it would surely mean death for her. I didn't think Mother would kill her while we were fighting our way to her. She seemed obsessed with Ilsy and I mating, and that couldn't happen if she was dead. I started walking towards the cave, but Uncle Fry grabbed my arm.

"Sean, wait," he said softly.

"What? Why?"

"So I can call some... friends," he said with a smile. I knew he meant the true fairies. I didn't think they carried cell phones though. I nodded and sat with my back to a tree.

Uncle Fry walked about fifty yards away from Ben and I, and made his way back in a clockwise spiral touching each tree and talking under his breath as he did so. When he got closer I could make out the words. I didn't understand them, but I could make them out.

*"Danu Ársa, Tá mé a shliocht ar an ceann ar a dtugtar Teyrnan. Glaoim ort anois in onóir an bhronntanais nuair a tugadh. Tá sé in am don cath. Éineacht liom."* His voice carried a power and authority like I hadn't heard before. In the center of the spiral he stopped, raised his hands, and repeated his words once more. A soft breeze blew through the trees and carried a voice with them. It was a soft feminine voice.

"We are with you, warrior of the Brigantes clan."

Ben jumped to his feet and looked around us. He had watched Uncle Fry with a skeptical eye.

"What in da hell was dat?" he asked.

"That, dear boy, was an ancient voice from a time long gone. We have allies now," Uncle Fry said with a smile.

"Good, maybe our chances of survival just went up," I said.

"You are some strange people, bon ami." Ben said, shaking his head.

I stood up clapping a hand on his shoulder.

"Are you ready?" I asked.

"I've said it before: lassaiz les bon temps rouler!"

"You have said that before. What does it mean?" I asked.

# Ragged Edge

"Aw man, let the good times roll!" He sounded exasperated.

"Ah, I like it. Let's go."

# CHAPTER 20

We proceeded slowly toward the cave. I knew they had the numbers for a guard, I didn't know where the guard might be. Until now Ben had always fought in a wolf form. He was larger than a normal wolf but still basically a wolf. This time he went with a wolf-man form. His body grew in muscle mass, his hands turned to claws, and his head became a human-wolf hybrid. He had the long ears of a wolf, his nose and mouth formed into a snout. His eyes stayed human.

Uncle Fry pulled two Desert Eagle hand cannons from somewhere. I had never seen the weapons before and didn't know he carried them. I had to remind myself what his family was and what they did. I suspected he had other weapons hidden – I hoped he had other weapons hidden. Even with the help of the Aen Sidhe, we were grossly outnumbered. I didn't know what strength the Sidhe had but I suspected it was diminished.

# Ragged Edge

God forms never die. They do grow weaker though as belief in them wanes. I hoped they would be enough to even our odds.

I assumed my battle form and we spread out, keeping within sight of each other. Each of us had plenty of fighting experience so we were able to operate without verbal communication. Not needing to talk was good. I didn't know if Ben could in his form, and it's not easy in my battle form. It also helped us maintain silence. We wouldn't be able to sneak all the way to Ilsy but we might be able to get close. I was sure Mother wouldn't kill her when we were discovered. I know a trap when I see one. In this case, I couldn't figure out the scope of the trap. I tried pushing my concerns aside and focusing on the task at hand. The size of the trap isn't important until you're snared in it.

I could feel the tension mounting in the air. We were being watched. None of us had seen anything yet, but we had been seen. Ben and Uncle Fry were sweeping heads from side to side, every now and then looking behind us. I kept watching forward. I knew the wolfengators could sneak around fairly well, I also knew our back were being watched by the Aen Sidhe. It helps to have backup that your opposition can't see.

The mouth of the cave came into view. I was starting to feel uneasy. We should have had opposition by now. They wanted to draw us into the cave. Cut us off from retreat, limit our movement options. I felt sure that whoever was watching us would appear at the cave opening after we went inside. I wasn't sure what to do about it. I hoped showing up with two extra fighters made them reconsider their plans, just enough to make them uneasy, but not enough to change them completely on the fly.

I remembered the cave sat in a clearing. There was a good twenty yards from the tree line to the opening. I crouched down before leaving the trees and motioned the other two over. As they approached I shifted back into a human with wings. I had to be able to talk to explain my plan. They both crouched beside me and I spoke to them in a low voice barely above a whisper. I had to hope that our watchers lacked great hearing.

"I'm going into the cave. I want you two to guard the entrance."

"No, I'm going in." Uncle Fry said.

"Unacceptable. I need you two at the entrance. Whatever is watching us is sure to attack it once we're inside. By myself I might be able to slip in and grab Ilsy. If I can, I need a way out." That was a lie. I knew the wolfengators could see me even when I tried to hide myself.

"Bullshit. The moment you grab Ilsy, they'll be all over you two." Okay, so Uncle Fry wasn't stupid. I knew that already.

"Sir Fry, if I have to create fire in the cave it's going to get really hot really fast. I don't want to risk hurting you two." This was true. I don't normally go for large fireballs but once a few wolfengators were burning I couldn't pretend to guess where they would run.

"Then don't use fire. I am going for Ilsy, Sean." Stubborn old goat.

"Okay, how about this. You two stay at the door. I'll go in. If I get into trouble, I'll call out and you can come rushing to the rescue. With the Sidhe." I had no intention of calling out. If I was in trouble, I would be calling them to their death.

"How about I have the Sidhe protect the entrance and we all three go in." I realized this was a losing argument when I noticed Ben nodding his head.

"Fine, but once we're inside, you do as I tell you, understand?" I now knew where Ilsy's hard head came from.

"What do you intend to tell us?"

"Okay, I'll make this easy. I have a few tricks up my sleeve. They can be dangerous for bystanders though. So if the situation is dire and I tell you to run, do it. You can come pick through the bodies after."

"You'll do nothing of the sort while Ilsy is in there."

"Sir Fry, do you honestly think I would do something drastic that might harm Ilsy? I am her protector. She will survive this even if one of the corpses you pick through is mine." I stared him in the eyes. He knew that I cared for Ilsy, unhealthy as those feelings might prove to be.

"Alright, Sean, if the situation is dire and you say run, I'll run," he said. From the corner of my eye, I saw Ben nodding as well.

"Good." I stood and started moving forward. The air was tense and still around us. There was an unnerving absence of sound. Even our feet on the ground seemed to make no noise. Uncle Fry was talking to a faint form I could barely make out. It was vaguely feminine in shape. I returned to my battle form.

At the entrance Uncle Fry whispered to me that the Sidhe would watch our backs. I was no longer worried about being jumped from behind. While god forms get weaker, they can't die. One or two wolfengators might slip past, but we wouldn't be facing a horde from the rear. We each looked at each other, the world around us, and stepped inside.

It's no accident that most cultures place the afterlife in the underworld. Stepping into a cave is unnerving. Stepping into a cave you know is filled with creatures that want you dead is downright terrifying. The threshold of a cave is special. It's a separation between the light of day and the dark of night. It's the closest most of us come to knowing the feeling of a grave without dying. Even with being attuned to the elements surrounding me, I wasn't thrilled about the cave.

Take away the creatures inside wishing considerable bodily harm upon my person and it was still a dark hole in the earth holding the unknown. We didn't know how deep this hole went, how wide it would be, or what we would find at the bottom. Sure, the excitement of exploration was on each of us. Then again, so was the fear of what we didn't know. The smell from the cave was a confusion of scents. Damp and musty earthen smells mingled with rancid, acidic animal musk and burnt smoky smells from cook fires. Underneath all was a steady coppery smell of blood and gut churning death. Not exactly a vacation destination.

I thought I could hear the breath of thousands of creatures around us as we moved deeper and deeper into the cave. Then again, it could have been a slight breeze moving past us to the open air we had left behind. Still within sight of the entrance, we came to a fork in the path: three openings in the cave wall. Now that we were all in the cave, I was against splitting up. We had to pick a path and deal with the consequences. Unfortunately, with three options I couldn't flip a coin. Each path was dark. Ben sniffed around each opening and I tried to peer as far as I could into the darkness. Uncle Fry looked at each opening. I almost thought he could see more than I could.

Ben pointed toward the path on the left and nodded his head. I assumed he meant we should go that way. I looked at Uncle Fry and he merely shrugged. I guess he couldn't see any better than I could. Having no other option, we followed Ben's nose onto the left hand path. The darkness became complete. I reached a hand out to either side to touch my companions. The path gradually sloped downward. The ground became uneven beneath our feet. I had no choice but to make a light for us.

Letting go of my companions, I held a hand in front of us and up toward the ceiling and created a fireball. The light from the flame lit our path. That was a good thing. We were standing mere feet from a drop off. The downside was that the longer I had to hold the fireball, the less energy I would have at the end of the path. With the light we were also beacons for any prying eyes.

# Ragged Edge

The drop off in front of us was no more than three feet in width, so we easily jumped over it and continued on our way. With the light we were able to move faster. When you go into a cave, cut off from sunlight, it's easy to lose track of time. I didn't know how long we had been walking down the path before we came to another three-pronged junction. A steady breeze came from the tunnel in front of us. There was no need for Ben to smell our way. The breeze carried all the scent we needed.

We continued this way for what seemed like hours. We had still met no resistance. We had no idea what lay before us. The tension started building in my shoulders, making it hard for me to hold up my arm with the fireball. I started switching hands trying to conserve energy. Uncle Fry was starting to slow down. We had no choice except to rest. None of us wanted to stop moving, but we all knew there was no point going into a fight half exhausted. We each sat on the cave floor and I dispersed the fireball. The darkness was complete. The only sound was our breathing. I could hear Ben sniffing at the air occasionally. I hoped he would be able to smell the wolfengators if they were coming up on us in the dark.

An unknown amount of time passed and Uncle Fry tapped my foot. I heard him stand up. I rekindled the flame in my hand and we began moving again. The cave was turning into a maze. We still seemed to be going down but the slope wasn't steep enough for me to know for sure. We arrived at another junction and could hear water from somewhere. We stopped while Ben smelled the air around the openings in front of us. Until hearing the water, I hadn't realized how thirsty I had become. I did know I was getting annoyed.

Call me crazy but I find it to be exceedingly rude to set a trap and then fail to close it. At this point they were simply teasing us. I tried jumping straight to Ilsy while Ben was sniffing. The cave blurred to black around me then reappeared, exactly like when I tried going to Grandfather's. I knew Mother definitely had her then. It wasn't hard to figure out that the stress of walking the cave, expecting an attack from every turn, and the toll it took on us mentally was a part of her plan. She wanted us exhausted by the time we got to her.

Ben came back with a problem. He pointed down one path and made drinking motions. He pointed down another and mimed fighting. I sighed and motioned for him and Uncle Fry to get behind me. Dropping the fireball also meant dropping our light. I prefer seeing what I'm doing when I mess with the earth, but I didn't have a choice. I'm sure that us rushing off without proper equipment was also part of Mother's plan.

I clasped my hands in front of me and pictured the ground beneath them. Slowly, I pulled them apart. A rumble in the ground told me I was succeeding. I stopped after a minute and brought back the fire. In front of me was a hole roughly two feet deep and three feet wide. I nodded and doused the flame. The next part was tricky. I squatted down and placed my hands over the floor, making a lazy figure eight in the air with both of them. I couldn't see the space that I wanted to fill, nor could I see the particles I was messing with. Drawing moisture from the air isn't difficult really, but drawing enough to fill a hole in absolute darkness was a little more problematic.

My hands began to emit a green glow. I couldn't recall ever having seen them glow when I made water before, but then again I had never done it in complete darkness. Soon I could see the hole below my hands had become a small rippling water hole. I stopped the water and brought fire back to my hands. We each drank from the hole. The water was cold, clean, and slightly sweet. Our thirst quenched, we headed down the tunnel with the breeze. I was sure Mother was making the breeze to lead us forward. I knew now that she wanted us to find her. I didn't know her exact plan, but killing us in these tunnels wasn't part of it. Not yet at least.

We arrived at the next intersection to find light. Well, not real light. There were another three tunnel entrances and a flickering firelight emanated from each of them. Each gave off a slight breeze. We had to be nearing the center of this cave, and now we had to decide which tunnel to enter. The breeze and light suggested that each would take us to the same place, and when you are about to get eaten by a ravenous wolfengator, does it really matter how you get to its mouth? I think it does.

# Ragged Edge

I doused my fireball and we all examined the tunnel openings. On the left, the floor appeared to tilt upwards the middle path continued the downward course, and the right hand path was level. According to Ben, they all smelled the same. The decaying stench of the wolfengators was almost unbearable, so I had no idea how he could discern any other scent but I trusted him. Judging by the light and the breeze from each opening, I felt confident that each tunnel would take us to the same general area. I knew Mother had enough wolfengators to guard each entrance. The question was, which entrance would give us the best fighting position? The answer to that question was that I didn't know.

If we stayed in a group, it would be easy for the wolfengators to surround us and destroy us. Since I couldn't telelocate from here, there was no retreat. I didn't bother telling the others of my failed attempt to telelocate. Ben didn't strike me as the retreating type, and what would be the point of running after retrieving Ilsy if they could always come and take her again? I knew this fight meant death. I just wasn't sure whose. Then I heard four little words that ended my indecision. Just four words that ran through me like a red-hot poker.

"Rot in hell, bitch!" Ilsy was maintaining her attitude. I loved her strong backbone in the face of creatures that could easily end her life in multiple horrible fashions.

I directed Ben to the downward path, Uncle Fry to the upward path, and I went level. I had to assume they knew that the three of us were here. Logic would normally dictate that we stay in one group. We could fight in a more organized fashion as one group, act in concert, and coordinate our actions better as a large group. I was banking on the unspoken communication we shared in the woods working here. We all had enough fighting experience to know what we had to do. Uncle Fry and Ben knew I had the best chance of getting to and protecting Ilsy. I knew that if I acted fast and decisively enough, the wolfengators would focus on me and give Ben and Uncle Fry a chance to get to Ilsy and get out.

Before we dispersed I gave them one simple direction.

"Wait until I act." They both nodded and walked into their respective tunnels. If any of us met resistance in the tunnel it would be easy for the other two to rush in and assist. I didn't think that was a worry though. I sensed Mother had a trick up her sleeve. She probably had a monologue ready. I hate monologues.

# CHAPTER 21

**I** slowly walked down my tunnel. The light steadily grew brighter, the air grew warmer, the stench grew worse. I thought about trying to sneak through the tunnel and keep my presence hidden until I was definitely seen. I decided that was the wrong approach. Admittedly, part of that decision came from the fact that I knew Ilsy was still alive and, if not actively fighting, at least being a pain in the ass for them. It would look bad if her protector came slinking in trying to hide. Part of it was also because I had been reacting to these damn things. From a certain perspective my actions could even be seen as cowardly. Showing a bold front wouldn't be expected. With this in mind, I ignited my arms. This was almost the same as producing fireballs, but instead of throwing balls I could now use my arms as flamethrowers. The fire wasn't on my arms strictly speaking – it was fed by a constant cushion of air protecting my arms. Neat, right?

Without that cushion, I'm just as flammable as the next guy.

The opening of the cave came into view. Actually, to be completely accurate, a large wolfengator came into view. Behind him, though, I could see the cave. The wolfengator took a step forward and I matched his step with a smile on my face. I've been in a lot of fights against various creatures of the nightmare realm. I've been outnumbered often. With numbers comes confidence. I didn't have numbers on my side, so I faked it. The trick in a situation like this is to make your enemy think you are either crazy or have a secret. I didn't have much in the ways of secrets. Sure, I knew their backup probably wouldn't be joining the party, but that wasn't enough for confidence. And according to my shrink, I am truly crazy.

I kept walking and smiling until I was maybe five feet from the wolfengator. I could see light dancing on his face from the flames on my arms.

"Move," I said in the hardest voice I could summon.

It growled.

"Move, please."

Another growl.

"Move, now!" I yelled as I thrust my arms forward. Two bolts of flame flew from hands and hit the gator square in the chest. I knew the flame wouldn't kill it. The smell of burning dog hair told me I was turning it into some kind of mutated hairless Chihuahua. More importantly, the force of impact knocked it off its feet and threw it a good twenty feet out of the opening. I entered the cave through the hazy smoke from its burning hair.

The chamber I entered was large and I mean large. I could almost make out the tips of stalactites hanging from the ceiling. The floor was clear of stalagmites, as far as I could tell anyway. It was covered in wolfengators. A brief count caused me to lose interest in the number after a hundred. I mean once you get to one hundred against three, do the remaining numbers really matter? The fact was, unless I could pull something spectacular out of my ass, we were screwed.

The roar of the flames I shot out echoed around the cavern, the smell was impossible. Think of a sewage treatment plant, burning, with stink bombs exploding around it and maybe add, just for fun, an undiscovered mass murder decomposing next door. In other words, it smelled bad. I tried breathing through my mouth. The smell didn't taste any better but at least my eyes weren't watering. If we managed to save Ilsy, I was sure she wouldn't smell properly for years to come. In the center of the room on a stone platform stood my mother. Ilsy stood beside her tied to a post. I estimated at least a football field between us. On the other side of my mother, sat two people in chairs. I recognized both immediately. The shock of seeing them almost took away my crazy swagger.

Sitting in one chair was the man I now knew was my half brother. Sure, Mother had said he was dead, but even then I knew that was a lie. The other chair was occupied by an impossibility – the necromancer Brother Herman sat with a twisted smile. His smile grew wider as

I looked at him. His mouth was moving, talking in a whisper to those around him. I swallowed my confusion and strode forward.

"Hi, Mom," I shouted. My voice reverberated back to me from a thousand directions at once. No shouting then.

"Oh, it's Mom now? I thought you were done with me, child." Her voice floated to me. I'm not familiar with acoustics and what makes them good or bad or how echoes are caused, but her voice failed to echo. For some reason, I was a little creeped out by that.

"Aww, Mom, how could I not be nice to you? You gave me such a wonderful gift as a mate."

"What?" Ilsy shouted.

"Quiet, honey, grownups are talking here." I laughed inwardly. I hoped Ilsy knew me enough by now to understand I was acting. Otherwise, if I did save her, I was never going to hear the end of it.

"I thought you didn't like her," Mother said. Ilsy apparently decided to listen to me.

"I never! Did I say that? No, I merely had to take care of a pesky little problem before I could make her mine." I kept walking forward, looking around me. I saw the openings to the tunnels holding Ben and Uncle Fry behind me. With my entrance, they were unguarded. Good.

"So you do intend to give me a grandchild?" Why would she want a grandchild? She didn't even want me.

"Is that what you want, Mom?"

"Of course, child, all parents want grandchildren."

# Ragged Edge

"What about Arik? Can't he give you a grandchild?" If I could keep her talking, I'd be able to approach the platform before attacking.

"Arik was born with... problems."

"Doesn't look like anything a few hours in the sun wouldn't fix."

"Fuck you!" Arik's grating voice assaulted me. Apparently his complexion was a sore spot. Interesting.

"I don't understand why you kept him, Mother. Darius said he wasn't one of us, why keep a broken child?" Arik stood and stepped to the edge of the podium. Mother grabbed him and whispered something in his ear. He laughed and resumed his seat.

"Not broken, son, just not finished."

"Oh, so he's slow?" I was halfway to the platform now.

"No, he just needs more life than I could give him." So yeah, that made no sense.

"More life?"

"Arik is the next step in our evolution. No more wasted years with dying repeatedly."

"How's that?"

"Brother Herman made it possible. Did you know, I'm sure you didn't know this, we Atlanteans can feed from the dead with no ill effects?"

"Not even uncontrollable regurgitation?"

"No, son. When I went to Darius so long ago, I was going to kill him. I wanted to devour him as Brother Herman devours his prey. Only, no matter how hard I tried, I couldn't do it."

# Ragged Edge

"So why sleep with him?" I wasn't interested in these details. I had another twenty-five yards to the platform.

"Well, that was mostly just for fun. A woman has needs. I should have known the damn fool didn't have kids yet. I wanted to kill the child in me. Brother Herman stopped me. He told me of ghouls that had gotten pregnant, their children were ghouls but stronger."

"My brother is a ghoul?" I guess it made sense.

"No, he's something more, and soon he'll be the first Atlantean ghoul." She laughed then. If I didn't already know she was insane, it was made perfectly clear in the shrill cackle of her laughter.

"So why the grandchild?"

"Brother Herman has done me a great service, child. I must repay him." Twenty yards to go but I couldn't ignore that. She wanted my child for the monk. I knew what use he was likely to have for it. Anger boiled inside me, the flames on my arms grew hotter, my blood grew cold. I rose into the air and slowly flew towards the podium.

"What could he want with a child?" It took every ounce of my will to keep the anger from my voice.

"Not just a child, Sean, an Atlantean child. He wants more children as well."

I nodded my head. I was over the platform. Staying three feet off the platform I moved in front of Ilsy, back to her, as though she were unimportant. I glanced around the cavern. Ben and Uncle Fry were crouching in their tunnels.

# Ragged Edge

"Never!" I shouted as I slammed myself down onto the platform, sending the earth rippling up and away from me. Arik and Brother Herman were thrown from their seats into the crowd of wolfengators. The echoes of my voice mingled with the thunderous rapid firing of Uncle Fry's guns and an earsplitting howl from Ben.

Mother looked away from me toward the tunnels. Stupid and insane, maybe this would be easy. I shot a jet of flame roaring for her. It caught her in the chest and slammed her into the wall behind her, a good hundred yards away. Alone on the platform with Ilsy, I let the fire on my arms die and turned toward her. Our eyes met. Everything between us lay bare. I nodded and sliced the ropes holding her with my talons. She gave me a brief hug then reached down and grabbed a stone that shook loose with my earthquake. I formed it into a sword and we prepared to fight.

Mother was flying toward us. I caught sight of Arik and Brother Herman running toward Ben and Uncle Fry. Ben was slicing through soft bellies with ease, and Uncle Fry was reloading. Bodies already littered the floor. Ilsy jumped off the platform and ran toward Uncle Fry. She was great with a sword. The wolfengators attacking her would have had better luck attacking a table saw with their tongues. Limbs flew everywhere. The noise was deafening.

Mother tried following Ilsy. I dove from the ledge and threw an electrical bolt at her back. She jerked when it struck her and fell to the floor. With her stunned I looked for Brother Herman. He should have been dead already. I spotted him behind Ben about to attack. I hurled a fireball at him. My aim was off and I only hit his leg. Ben jumped to the side when my fireball passed as Brother Herman jumped into the slashing claw of a wolfengator. Black ichor flowed from the wounds. He lashed out and took the head off the gator.

Arik was rushing toward Uncle Fry with Ilsy on his heels. Waves of wolfengators were rushing towards the tunnels. Our initial attack had gone off great. The attack surprised them and at least thirty were already dead, but they had the numbers. I didn't know about Ben's stamina, but I knew Ilsy and Uncle Fry wouldn't be able to keep up the feverish pace for too long. I also knew I couldn't keep throwing the elements around indefinitely. We had to consolidate and get ready to run. If we could draw them outside, the Aen Sidhe could help us so long as they weren't still engaged.

I headed toward my allies and looked back for my mother. Now I was the stupid one. She wasn't on the ground where she fell. I was looking around when I felt a sledgehammer blow to my back. My armor rung out like a church bell and I flew forward, off balance. My wings roared with pain, I was sure the broken one had just re-broken. I turned and caught my mother rushing toward me. I lashed out with my talons and tore three ragged gashes in her face. Her mouth opened in a screech. I think. The riot of noise had killed my hearing. I followed the slash with a punch. My mother may have been a good warrior with her clan, but she was rusty and the blow knocked her backward. I sent a jet of air at her and pushed her toward the ceiling. I had hoped to hit one of the stalactites with her. Impalement was a fitting punishment in my mind. I missed.

Keeping an eye on her as she fell, I rushed toward my group. Brother Herman was apparently fighting on our side. Or maybe the wolfengators were fighting for us. Either way, they were keeping him busy and he was helping kill them. I guessed the alliance between my mother and the monk was shaky at best.

Arik had drawn a sword and was engaged with Ilsy. They seemed evenly matched, he had more technical skill but she was more pissed off. Mother was rising back into the air. I expected her to rush me again. Instead she sent a jolt of electricity at me. I dodged it and sent a fireball at her. She dodged and sent another one at me. This game wasn't going to work out in my favor. It was distracting me from my group and wasting my energy. I could feel fatigue in my wings already. We needed to speed things up.

I knew I didn't want to physically engage the wolfengators. I don't have to tear up my hands more than once to learn a lesson. Instead, I flew to the ceiling, covered my hands in stone, and began hitting stalactites. Each stalactite was at least the size of a man. The physical force to knock them down was less draining than the elemental force needed to throw fireballs and wind everywhere. The spears falling to the ground slowed the wolfengators down and impaled a few. Before heading to my group, I ignited my arms and threw a wall of flame across the room, hoping it would be enough to give us some breathing room.

Mother was throwing bolts of electricity and balls of fire at me. I was dodging them easily until I zigged when I should have zagged. An electrical bolt caught my wing. Electrical fire ignited my brain and disconnected it from my body. I fell two, three, four hundred feet and slammed into a group of wolfengators. Sure, they broke my fall, but alligator hides aren't exactly soft. I heard Ilsy scream over the din of battle as I blacked out.

I came to with Ilsy pulling on my arms. Ben and Uncle Fry were keeping everyone off us. My wall of fire was still burning. Brother Herman and the wolfengators were still fighting. Ben was engaged with Arik, and Uncle Fry was firing and reloading faster than I would have thought possible. He had to be running low on ammo though. I shook my head and immediately regretted it as pain radiated throughout my body. I fought it down and used my legs to help push. We were headed toward one of the tunnels.

At the tunnel mouth Ilsy let go of my arms and helped me to my feet. The wall of flame was dying. I threw a bolt of fire at Arik that sent him flying through the remnants of the flame wall. Ben nodded at me, put his claws on his knees and took deep breaths. We were going to be overrun quickly. My legs were wobbly beneath me, and Ben was wearing down. The focus was off us for a moment, so Uncle Fry stopped shooting.

# Ragged Edge

"I'm almost empty!" he shouted over the noise. I thought so. My body was hurting, my mind was fuzzy. I wanted sleep. There was no way we could fight our way back to the daylight. There was no way to know what waited for us if we made it there. I had one last trick up my sleeve. It was tantamount to suicide for me, but it might save the others. I didn't see any other way for us though. I looked at Ilsy standing next to Uncle Fry, her sword at the ready. A tear rolled down my cheek.

"Fall back!" I shouted.

"What?" Uncle Fry looked back at me.

"Get out of this cave. I'll hold them off," I said.

"You're almost out on your feet!" Ilsy said.

I stepped forward and threw more fire around the cave. I heard a shriek as Brother Herman went up in flames. He streaked around the room until the flames went out, exactly as his look alike had done. If I thought I was going to live, I wouldn't have wasted the energy.

"I can wipe them out, but it might splash back on you three. You need to get out." An idea struck me. "Hold them off a little longer."

I took to the air. My wings hurt, my body hurt, and I was about to hurt it more. I slammed into the floors of the other two tunnel openings, they collapsed into heaps of stone. Now there was only one way out. Through me.

Scanning the cavern I saw my mother rallying more wolfengators around her. She was getting ready for another push. We wouldn't be able to stand against it. I went back to my group.

# Ragged Edge

"Now go," I said, grabbing Ilsy from behind and pushing her toward the opening. I didn't have much strength. She came back.

"No, I will not leave you," she said through clenched teeth. A tremendous roar shook the floor. The wolfengators were coming.

"Get out of here!" I roared.

They spotted the forces coming at us. I watched the realization of defeat creep over their faces. Ben and Uncle Fry nodded and they began moving toward the opening. Ilsy stepped up beside me.

"Damnit, Ilsy, get out of here!"

"Come on, Ilsy!" Uncle Fry shouted. She ignored us and stood beside me.

I can't explain what happened next. Uncle Fry walked over to her, hugged her, and handed her one of his guns. Tears were streaming down her face. The old man's eyes sparkled with tears that hadn't fallen. I felt comfort flowing through me. I knew I was going to die, but for the first time in my life, I knew I wasn't going to die alone. Then Uncle Fry raised a taser and stuck it in Ilsy's back. She dropped like a rock. Uncle Fry clapped a hand on my shoulder.

"It's been good knowing you, Sean. I'd like to know you longer," he said and rushed into the tunnel. Ben gave me a little salute, picked up Ilsy, and rushed after him. I was alone.

"Whatever you're going to do Sean, do it fast." Uncle Fry's voice floated down the cave.

I didn't know if what I was about to try would work. A charred and blackened Brother Herman separated himself from the group heading toward us. His hands blurred with the purple black light and the dead wolfengators began to rise. It didn't seem fair that I had to kill him again. Assuming it was him that I had killed the first time.

"Hurry, Sean," a voice said in my head.

I nodded and shut my eyes. I wanted fire, massive amounts of fire. Normally, when we create fire, the heat isn't much more than any other fire. But we can create more. Grandfather had reached into the earth to pull out the materials for my armor. I worked on the same principle. I reached towards the magma beneath the earth's crust. I had used that for fireballs in the past. Now I needed more. I kept reaching until I found the molten core of our planet. I wouldn't be able to pull all the heat from it. Not even a large amount of it, but I thought I could pull enough.

I focused on that heat. I felt it burn through me. I focused it into my wings. The titanium would help hold the heat for a short while. I heard the wolfengators rushing toward me. The ground rumbled with their steps. I felt my wings already burning within my armor. I didn't have much time left.

I turned my back to the cave and hunched over. A scream involuntarily escaped my lips as the heat in my wings grew more and more fierce. Pain audibly leaving me, I unleashed the fire. My armor began melting and I felt each feather burning, every bone in my wings burning, white-hot titanium dribbled onto my back. I felt like I was burning from the inside out. I threw the flames as far from me as I could. I felt lava pouring from the stubs that were once my wings. I hoped it would stop before my power to control it stopped. The flame was me and I was the flame. My clothes were bursting into flame. My ears filled with screaming. I couldn't tell who was screaming. I felt blackness overtaking me. I felt the last nub of wing burn off and the lava stopped.

"I love you, Ilsy." I think I got the words out before blackness overtook me.

# CHAPTER 22

I had spent an inordinate amount of time unconscious recently. Other than sleeping, I had been knocked out, electrocuted, and run myself to the point of exhaustion more than I had done in at least a century. Other than when I'm sleeping, I don't normally have dreams when I'm unconscious. This time was different. I knew blackness had overtaken me. I knew I had passed out from the heat, the pain, and the exhaustion. You don't channel lava from the center of the earth without wearing yourself down; you just can't do it.

This time a soft blue light slowly grew around me. I tried blinking my eyes, in my mind it worked, but my body informed me that I was still blacked out and I should mind my own business. A familiar female form took shape within the blue light. Danu was visiting me again. I wondered idly if the Elders would have given me this task had they known I would be dealing with god forms. I think they would have been worried about me making a bad impression. They don't normally trust me to be diplomatic. I'm not sure why.

Danu reached out and stroked my cheek. Another short argument ensued between my mind and body. This was seriously the strangest dream I'd had in a long time. I assured my body that I was aware it was still blacked out so it could stop interrupting. In the middle of the argument Danu smiled at me.

"Is this what comes next?" I asked. She laughed.

"No child. Unfortunately you will wake up. I'm sorry," she said.

"For what?"

"The pain you will go through."

"Bad?"

"To put it mildly."

"Ilsy?" I had to ask. If I failed then I would rather die. If I succeeded in protecting her, maybe the pain would be worth it.

"She will live." I heard a "but" in her voice.

"I hear a 'but' in there."

"But she too will eventually be in great pain. You did your best to get her away from harm. The heat was too great; it blossomed up and out of the tunnel. Unfortunately, Sir Fry and Ben had to drop her body at the entrance. I have taken steps to make sure she does not feel her injuries for now. There are things left to be done."

"Like what?"

"She must wake you. If you do not wish her permanently disfigured, she must travel with you. To save your life, she must tell your Elders what you have done on her behalf."

"Why can't you do that?"

"I can do nothing for your pain," she said softly.

"Oh." I stood quietly looking at her. I felt pressure on my chest. "Why are you here?"

"One of your enemies still exists in this chamber. Do not overlook him. Finish the fight."

"What?"

"I have protected Ilsy as best I can from your flame. Your friends are returning to you. Do not leave until it is finished."

I felt my heart start pounding in my chest, and before I could say another word she was gone. The blue light faded to black.

I opened my eyes and saw Ilsy above me. She was pressing on my chest, performing CPR. The back of her hair was burnt almost to her scalp. The back of her neck and arms were blackened. Blood oozed from her wounds. I had to be quick. I didn't know how long Danu could hold the pain away but once it came she would surely die. I had to get her to a healer. I moved to sit up. My head spun.

"Don't move, lay still," she said softly.

"Can't. Someone survived," I said, rolling onto my hands and knees. Every move was an exercise in anguish. My head throbbed, thrummed, hummed, and stabbed with pain. A million shards of glass violated every inch of my body. Tears sprung to my eyes. I forced myself to move, to ignore the pain as best I could.

"Nobody survived that," she said.

"Someone did. She said so." I looked around the room. Hundreds of tiny fires burned around piles of ash. I heard footsteps rushing down the tunnel towards us. Instinctively, I tried to ready a fireball. I couldn't manage. My wings were gone. The tears spilled from my eyes.

Ben and Uncle Fry burst from the tunnel and skidded to a halt.

"Bloody hell." Uncle Fry stammered.

Ben looked around the cavern dragging his jaw through piles of ash.

"We've almost won. Someone survived. Find him," I said.

Uncle Fry spotted Ilsy's wounds. He stood in shock.

"Hurry, damnit, we don't have time." I still couldn't regain my feet.

"Who are we looking for?" Ben asked, now back in his human form.

"I don't know. Find the only body amongst the ash." I said. My stomach suddenly revolted and I vomited. Fresh red blood was mixed with everything else. I shook my head.

"Uncle Fry, quickly."

He looked at me in a daze. He clearly didn't understand how Ilsy was moving or maybe how she had been hurt in the first place. I didn't have a mirror handy but I'm sure neither of us looked like we could win a beauty pageant. I felt a heavy weight on my back that wouldn't move. I remembered my armor melting. I didn't let myself wonder how I was going to get the remnants off.

Ben began searching the cavern, Uncle Fry stumbled along behind him. I used the wall to force myself to my feet, and Ilsy stood beside me. I could barely look at her. Everywhere her skin was exposed had been blackened. I knew if I could get her to a healer fast enough, and if they would help her, she would survive. Probably wouldn't even scar, but we had to hurry. I heard a clock ticking in my head and tried to help search. My body didn't agree with me. Later, after I had mostly healed, I was going to have a long talk with it.

"Here!" Ben shouted halfway to the platform. He rushed back to me and supported me so I could walk. It took us forever to get to the one remaining body. I recognized it immediately. The unassuming face, though now lined with wrinkles speaking to its true age. I shook my head. Even blacked to little more than charcoal, this damn monk just would not die.

"Hi there," I said.

"Don't kill me!" he pleaded. His cowardice caused anger to well up inside of me. This creature, so sure of its superiority only minutes ago, now begged for mercy. If I had my wings I would have disassembled him, piece by piece, with ice.

"I don't want to kill you," I said. His eyes widened.

"You don't?"

"No." I shook my head. My anger pushed the pain away. It still existed, I still felt all of it, but it wasn't important. I bent down and picked up a large stone with both hands, raised it over my head, and slammed it down onto one of his hands. There was a sickly splattering sound as his hand burst, staining the ground with his black blood. He shrieked and writhed in pain.

"What are you doing?" he cried.

I picked up the stone again and slammed it onto his other hand.

"I don't want to kill you. I want to hurt you," I said through gritted teeth, picking up the stone again.

"I want to cause you pain." I slammed the stone onto his knee.

"I want you to understand the torment you and your kind have caused." I felt my anger boiling over, dancing in glee as I slammed the stone on his other knee.

The others looked at me as if I had grown a second head. I didn't care. All of my fear, pain, and rage had a focal point.

I shattered his left foot.

His voice had grown raspy from screaming. Still he started chuckling.

"Does this make you feel better?" He rasped.

The stone came down on his other foot forcing another scream from him. He started to chuckle again. I cut off it off by slamming the stone into his groin. Black bile erupted from his mouth turning his scream into a gurgling bubbly sound.

"No more." He rasped.

I looked at him and saw an orange flash flood my vision. My anger soared further out of control.

"Now you want to die?" I said, standing over him. I raised the stone for another strike when the thunderous roar of Uncle Fry's gun erupted around us. The monk's head exploded and, startled, I dropped the stone on his body. His remains puffed out in a cloud of ash.

"Why did you do that?" I yelled at Uncle Fry.

"It's not sporting, boy. We cannot become as bad as them." I took a step towards Uncle Fry, my hands balled into fists.

"Not sporting?" I spit out as I advanced on Uncle Fry. He trained his gun on my chest.

"He killed children, for millennium he has caused pain and suffering, and in case you forgot. He helped kidnap Ilsy!" I yelled as I grabbed his gun and put it against my chest.

"This isn't a sport." I growled staring into Uncle Fry's face.

His grip loosened on the gun, I took it from him and threw it across the cavern. I knew it was irrational, I knew I had no quarrel with Uncle Fry, every fiber of my being was screaming at me to hit him.

Ben grabbed my arm and pointed at Ilsy. She had collapsed onto the floor shaking.

"She needs a hospital," he said.

My anger broke as I saw Ilsy crumpled in a heap on the floor. I rushed to her side and grabbed her hand.

"Come here, we're leaving," I said to the other two.

They hurried over and grabbed my other arm. I focused harder than I can ever remember focusing. The cavern blurred and winked out of existence around us.

# Ragged Edge

A deep forest appeared around us. I collapsed when my feet were on solid ground. It takes a helluva lot more energy to telelocate without wings. I was sure I wouldn't be able to do it again. A path stretched out in front of us, weaving through the trees to a clearing. In the clearing stood a cabin. The cabin from my dreams. My grandfather's cabin.

"Ben, go to the cabin. Get my grandfather. Hurry," I said, lying down beside Ilsy. She had passed out, her breathing ragged and shallow. I kept a hold of her hand.

Ben took off at a sprint for the cabin.

"Atlas!" he yelled. I couldn't look at the cabin. I knew what was inside. My dreams told me. Life, death, or both. I would have to face it.

"Atlas!" Ben yelled again.

Uncle Fry crouched beside Ilsy and took her other hand. He spoke to her softly. Assured her she would be safe. Danu was right, we didn't have much time, and I had wasted it embracing my anger.

I heard footsteps rushing back up the path. Grandfather landed beside Uncle Fry as Ben returned. Without a word he rolled her onto her back and spread his hands out over her. A bright blue-green light issued from his hands as he moved them over her barely an inch above her skin. The blackened skin turned an angry red. Ilsy's breathing settled into a slow rhythm as if she were asleep. The angry red softened and then looked like nothing more than a severe sunburn. Grandfather dropped his hands and took a deep breath.

"She'll be okay," he said as he rolled her onto her back and picked her up. Uncle Fry was weeping as he helped me to my feet.

"Thank you, Sean." Uncle Fry said.

"For what?"

"You saved her."

"Are you a fucking idiot? I damn near killed her!" I shouted at him.

"Sean! Come inside." Grandfather said angrily.

I took a slow deep breath, let it out, and followed him, Ben and Uncle Fry followed me silently.

Grandfather's cabin was more comfortable than mine. He had expanded it since I had last been here. It appeared to hold at least four bedrooms, a bathroom and a nice kitchen. He had running water, matching furniture, statues and artwork from all over the world, hell, from all over time as well. I sat on a stool beside an island separating the kitchen from the rest of the cabin. My pain was coming back as my anger dissipated.

"What happened?" Grandfather asked as he entered the room after placing Ilsy in a bedroom.

"Mother," I said through clenched teeth. He looked me over. I knew the back half of my armor was now a shapeless lump on my back. My clothes were tattered, burnt scraps, my hair was scorched, and I was sure I had blackened spots just like Ilsy.

"Tell me," he said as he walked over and began running his hands along my back. I felt the pain ease up.

# Ragged Edge

As he worked, I told him about my lapse in judgment that caused Ilsy to get kidnapped. I told of Mother's plan for Arik and her desire for a grandchild to give the monk. After seeing how badly we were outnumbered, I should have tried to avoid the battle in the cavern. I told of my inability to best Mother and my lack of focus allowing her to hit me with an electric bolt. Sending Ben, Uncle Fry and Ilsy away. Ilsy's fight to stay with me and Uncle Fry using the taser on her. Then I told of reaching into the earth's core, sending molten fire all over the cavern, losing my wings, and almost killing Ilsy and myself. Then I told him of my visit with Danu, how she warned me about a survivor and the limited time she could hold off Ilsy's pain. I told him about losing control of my anger and wasting that little bit of time.

I hung my head as I finished my story. This was my fault. I knew it, he knew it, everyone knew it. If I had been smarter, faster, or more vigilant, none of this would have happened. As a result I almost doomed the woman I now knew that I loved and was supposed to protect to a horrible burning death. Grandfather reached out and lifted my head. He studied my face for a long moment and then nodded his head.

"I will call the Elders," he said, then walked out of the room and vanished.

# CHAPTER 23

Hours passed and grandfather didn't return. Ilsy slept, Uncle Fry and Ben made themselves comfortable. I stewed in a burning, boiling, inner turmoil. Herman was finally dead. I felt sure Arik and mother were dead as well but had no way of knowing. My attack had left no bodies other than the monk. I was now mostly human like Darius and beating myself up for the pain I caused.

As the sun was setting grandfather finally returned with an Elder I didn't know. A stately old woman, tall and proud with flowing white hair and dark, almost black, eyes. She walked to Ilsy's room without a word. Another hour passed. The Elder and Ilsy walked into the living room. Ilsy rushed over and threw her arms around me in a tight hug, I didn't feel I deserved, but was grateful for just the same. After releasing me, Ilsy approached Uncle Fry and gave him a resounding slap. Anger briefly flared in his eyes but then he hung his head. Saying nothing, Ilsy sat away from the both of us. The Elder approached me and stared into my eyes. I felt myself getting lost in the depth of her gaze.

"Young Gryphon, while misguided, you have acted admirably." Her silvery voice flowed out with musical charm.

"With respect, Elder, I have acted foolishly."

"You have made mistakes on your way, I agree, but when the time came you were willing to lay down your life to protect this one in your charge." She glanced at Ilsy then returned her gaze to me. I had no idea what she was looking for.

"Atlas, I will speak with you outside," she said and walked out. Grandfather followed her.

"What was that about?" Ilsy asked.

"Beats me," I said.

Uncle Fry walked over and gave Ilsy a hug that she accepted like a statue.

"I was afraid we were going to lose you," he said.

"So was I, but Sean did it. He stopped Arik and his mother." She hugged me again.

I felt an unexplained anger rise in me. I started suspecting something was wrong. Normally, I am slow to anger and am in control of myself. Now my emotions were flying all over the place. I chalked it up to fatigue. Ilsy told what she could remember after Ben and Uncle Fry left her at the mouth of the cave. Watching them fight the remaining wolfengators until a blast of heat exploded from the cave's opening. She didn't blame me for anything, she even called me a hero. I totally disagreed with her but they wouldn't hear it. I suddenly felt as though the room were closing in on me. I needed air but didn't dare go outside for fear of interrupting two Elders. For all I knew, they could have been deciding my future.

Grandfather came back in without the Elder.

"Who was that?" I asked.

"Elder Samsi Messias. The greatest healer of the Elders, next in line for Ancient," He sounded distracted.

"Sean, we need to talk," he said, wringing his hands. Fear boiled up inside me. Grandfather was never, ever, nervous.

"What is it?" I asked.

"We should really do this alone," he said and strode back outside. I looked around the room at the others. They all shrugged their shoulders. No help there, I followed him outside.

Grandfather had walked a little way down the path we had appeared on. I caught up to him and we walked side by side. I hadn't been on the island for centuries, and I remembered many of the trees as saplings. We walked quietly for what seemed like forever. Nervous energy burned inside of me. I wanted to know what was wrong, I wanted to talk, and I wanted to sleep.

"Sean," he said quietly.

"Yes, Grandfather?"

"You're sick."

"What? No, I'm tired but that's natural," I said, waving away the suggestion of illness.

# Ragged Edge

"No, Sean. What you did in the cavern is impressive. It also threw you out of balance."

"What do you mean?"

"I mean the elements are no longer balanced within you. Fire reigns in your soul."

"Okay, so I will realign myself." I didn't understand the melodrama here. It wasn't that uncommon for an Atlantean to find themselves out of balance. From what I understood, it was a relatively easy thing to fix. They had to stop using whatever element had become dominant and focus on the others. Eventually, everything would balance out and they would be okay.

"It's not that easy, Sean. You lost your wings, so you can't use the elements."

"So I wait for my wings to grow back. That's going to take at least a month, I certainly won't be using fire in that month. When they come back I'll stop using it for a while. What's the problem?"

He stopped walking and turned to look at me.

"You don't have a month, Sean."

"I... wait, what?"

"The fire is burning too hot. It's going to consume you. Elder Samsi believes you have a fortnight, maybe a little more."

"So I could make it a month?"

"It's doubtful," he said, putting an arm on my shoulder.

"So, I'm going to die?"

"Yes."

"Well, what's the big deal. I'll start another life, we're born in balance with everything. They are lifting final death aren't they?"

"Elder Samsi says yes, but she doesn't make the final decision."

"Okay?"

"The entire council has to vote on that, and you know that you don't have many friends there."

"Why not?"

"Something to do with the hundreds of years of shirking your duty," he said.

"But Darius said that if I completed this mission, the final death would be lifted," I pleaded.

"Did he?" I thought about that for a bit. It had been so long since that conversation. My shoulders slumped.

"Not exactly, no."

"Correct. It has to be voted on, and while you did remove a great threat from this world, that may not be enough."

"Alright, so you're saying I might die because of bureaucratic bullshit."

"In so many words."

"When will the Elders vote?"

"I don't know. Elder Samsi is going to speak with the Ancient. She will then call the Elders together."

"So we wait?"

"Yes."

I took a deep breath and closed my eyes. Emotions were whirling around inside me at a furious pace. I turned to go back to the cabin.

"Sean."

# Ragged Edge

"What?"

"Your father would be proud of you." I think he meant for this to mean something to me.

"What about you?"

"I have always been proud of you." He clapped a hand on my shoulder and we walked back.

I must have been looking downcast when we reentered the cabin. Ilsy immediately looked worried.

"What?"

"What?"

"What's wrong?"

"Oh, well, apparently I might die." I tried being flippant.

"The hell you say?" Ben asked.

"What?" Uncle Fry asked.

"No!" Ilsy shouted covering her mouth with her hands.

"I made a slight error in judgment," I said, shrugging my shoulders.

"What error?" Uncle Fry asked.

"Well my last burst of fire was apparently too strong."

"Yea, you right. Melted dat fancy armor onto you."

"Yeah, so anyway, I'm out of balance. Being consumed by flame you might say."

"Not dead dead, right?" Ilsy asked.

"I don't know. The council has to vote and see if I've earned the right to keep living."

"When?"

"I don't know that either."

There was silence around the room as my new friends digested this information. I didn't have anything else to add. In my experience, the council normally acted slowly. I'd be lucky if they were able to vote before I died. Still, I wasn't dead yet.

"Anyway, you guys don't need to stay. If I live, I'll come see you." I meant it, too.

"Are you sure?" Uncle Fry asked.

"Yeah, no sense having all of us wait around. I'm sure Ilsy would like to get back to her life, and your pack needs you, Ben. I don't know what you do exactly, Sir Fry."

"I do need to finish getting my brother's affairs taken care of."

"I'm staying," Ilsy said.

"You don't need to do that, Ilsy."

"I know. I want to," she said, smiling. I couldn't help myself and smiled back.

"Alright, so how do we get back?" Ben asked.

"I'll take you," Grandfather said.

As they stood to leave Uncle Fry stared at me for a moment then approached me and grabbed me by the shoulders.

"I could have killed you in that cave, Lad." He said quietly.

"Yeah." I whispered.

"You weren't you, I saw flames in your eyes."

I didn't know what to say so I just shrugged my shoulders.

# Ragged Edge

"Be careful Sean. No matter what happens, you can't lose yourself fighting these things."

He pulled me into a hug. I closed my eyes and rested my face on his shoulder hoping his shirt would soak up the tears in my eyes.

I'm not good at goodbyes. I haven't had to say it very often. The upside to not getting close to humans is that after my job is done I can leave without a word to anyone. In this case there were handshakes all around and promises to keep in touch. It seemed like we had been together for much longer than a couple of weeks. When they disappeared with Grandfather, I found myself hoping that I would see them again.

A week passed and there had been no word from the Ancient calling a meeting with the Council. Grandfather had removed my armor. He was able to reshape it on my body easily enough, but the flesh on my back had fused with the metal. You can't rip metal off skin like a band-aid. He had to cut it off with a long knife then heal my flayed open back. I started thinking that there wasn't even going to be a vote. Then the messenger came and Grandfather left for the meeting. I was out with Ilsy showing her around the island. We had become very close that week, what with no monsters chasing us. My emotions were still furiously boiling inside of me and Grandfather had noticed I was becoming very hot to the touch. There were times I thought I could feel the fire eating me from the inside.

# Ragged Edge

Ilsy enjoyed walking the island. It wasn't a big island so we could walk around it in maybe five hours. There were places that had some original buildings from before the volcano destroyed the island. I call them original, but they had actually been rebuilt. Besides my grandfather, there were only three other Atlanteans living there with a few dozen humans. The Atlanteans tended to avoid the two of us, I guess I was something of a pariah. The humans were friendly and some wanted news of the world off the island while others wanted to know more about us. I started trying to avoid them. For me there was only one human on the island worth spending time with.

A few days after Grandfather left, I started feeling hot, and my skin took on a reddish hue. For the first time I really thought about what it meant to be consumed by fire. My death wasn't going to be a pretty one. I no longer had full control over my mood, bouncing from happy to sad to pissed in the blink of an eye. I didn't want Ilsy to see my death, but I didn't want her to leave. I wanted to tell her everything I felt for her, but if this was to be my final death, why should I burden her with that? I knew by then that the feeling was shared though unspoken. Sometimes on our walks, her hand would slip into mine or we'd end up sitting on a beach, my arm around her and watching the sunset. Those were the best days of my life and I hated knowing I was going to lose them. Finally, with two days left of Elder Samsi's prediction, Grandfather returned.

"What did they say?" I asked excitedly.

"Nothing yet. I have been excused from the voting because I cannot be impartial. Ben, Donovan Fry, and Willow were all brought in to talk on your behalf. Darius spent a lot of time recounting your deeds and misdeeds. They did not total up in your favor."

"Oh." I was crestfallen. Smoke had started escaping my mouth whenever I exhaled. My insides were constantly burning and I was definitely turning red. Constant pain was my companion as much as Ilsy was.

"When will the vote finish?" Ilsy asked.

"I don't know," he answered.

That evening, Ilsy and I went back to the beach. I couldn't touch her without burning her anymore.

"I think it's time for you to go, Ilsy," I said as the sun painted the ocean orange.

"What? Why?" She grabbed my hand and immediately pulled her hand back. There was a brief sizzling sound when she touched me.

"I don't have long. I don't want you to see it. I want you to remember me the way I was."

"I don't want to go," she said, tears springing to her eyes.

"If the final death gets lifted before I die, I'll come find you as soon as I can."

"But, Sean, I..." She looked away from me.

"I know, Ilsy."

"When we were in that cave, I heard you say something."

"I said a lot of things in that cave, Ilsy." This wasn't going to be a fun conversation.

"While I was at the entrance, I heard your voice or thought I did. I was still groggy.

"Oh, yeah."

"Did you mean it?" she asked, her eyes sparkling with the last light of the sunset.

"Yes, Ilsy. I love you. I have for a while now. I thought we'd have time to, I don't know, I just thought we'd have time."

"I love you too, Sean. It's why I stayed. It's why I want to stay."

"Ilsy, I'm burning up."

"I know, Sean."

We sat silently watching the ocean darken as the sun disappeared. I didn't know what else to say. I hoped my death would be quick, painless, and temporary. So far, I knew it wasn't going to be painless, two out of three wouldn't be bad, but I had almost convinced myself it wasn't going to be temporary.

That was the last real conversation we had.

The rest of that evening was filled with faltering conversation. How do you act when you've just professed your love yet knew you were going to be dying soon? I didn't know then. Even now I have I no idea. Grandfather tried to keep the mood light but my flaring temper wouldn't allow for much joviality. I hated that time. It wasn't fair to have my life start meaning something while knowing it would soon be over.

I went to bed that night in a tub of water. Steam rose from my body as I lay in the quickly warming and evaporating water. I felt angry, no, I felt pissed off. I was being cheated out of the best thing that had happened to me because the old fucks on the council wouldn't pull their heads out of their asses and do something about my final death. Grandfather was right about my enemies, but they didn't need to vote against me. They just needed to delay the vote. I had to turn the faucet on to keep a stream of cool water on me. It was the longest night of my life.

When I woke in the morning I was too weak to move. My skin had blackened overnight; my fingers and toenails were gone. At some point, my hair had burned off, leaving nothing but ash. Grandfather started bringing in ice to try to keep my temperature down. The pain of the freezing ice and my burning body was indescribably horrid. I could barely speak. Smoke boiled out of my mouth whenever I opened it and flowed from my nostrils when I breathed, and my vision was marred by waves of heat. I knew that would be my last day. I was right.

That afternoon a messenger came to check on me for Elder Samsi and to tell grandfather that the vote would be taking place that evening despite protestations that I might not be alive that evening. The messenger was unsympathetic, suggesting that if I didn't last until the matter was decided it was my own fault. I wanted to strangle him. Hell, at that point I could have just held my hands on him and burnt him alive. Grandfather left after the messenger.

"I may not be able to vote, but I can damn well make sure they know who they're killing," he said as he stormed out.

I think they knew who they were killing. Sure I had changed but it had been too late. Now I was going to be forced to pay for my past. All I could really say was that it sucked. I felt I had paid for it enough, not to mention the fact that they were torturing the very human they had forced me to protect. I don't think I ever want to be on the council. It's not that I have a soft heart. It's just that I know we can change. I think some of the relics on the council can't accept that. I wish I had been able to tell Grandfather what he meant to me. I don't care what you are: when you are a young child without parents, whoever takes you in, takes care of you, and shows you love becomes important.

An hour after he left, I burst into flame. I was trying to talk with Ilsy, it was the only thing that wasn't agitating my temper. She had a calming effect on me that I had grown to depend on. In the middle of a word, a foot long flame spewed from my mouth followed by a weak, rasping scream from me and a loud piercing scream from Ilsy. The ice and water surrounding me began boiling furiously until the tub was empty. Ilsy tried to keep up putting more and more ice on me. It instantly melted, boiled, then evaporated. I stopped her with my last words.

"It's time," I croaked out. Ilsy stood in the door, tears streaming from her eyes, sobs breaking out from her chest. That was the last thing I saw before my world became flames. The odd thing is, it wasn't as painful as I thought. I don't know if my heart burnt too quickly or my brain fried before I could notice. I remember looking at Ilsy, wanting to say more, then a bright red-orange flash and nothing else. That was the night I died. I knew it was going to happen the moment we came back to Grandfather's house. The dream that I had talked to my shrink about had finally come true.

☐

# CHAPTER 24

Obviously, I didn't really die since I am telling this story. Grandfather told me later what had happened. He came home to find Ilsy sobbing in the bathroom, the tub was dry and filled with ashes. Between sobs, she explained my death. My grandfather carefully scooped up my ashes and placed them in a vase. Ilsy stayed with him for a few days before he took her to Uncle Fry. After explaining everything to Uncle Fry, he visited the wolf pack and told them of my passing. They held a feast in my honor. I was touched by that.

I, however, was somewhere else. I found myself on a hill covered in clover, the air smelled sweeter than any I could remember. It was fresh and clean, no pollution had ever touched this place. Around me I could see tall and mighty oaks, elms, willows, birches, alders, and many other trees whose names I didn't know. This pure, untouched forest stretched around me as far as I could see. Before I could remember I no longer had wings, they were stretched behind me and I was flying over the forest. The loveliness of the place took my breath away.

"Enjoying the view?" asked the sweetest voice I had ever heard. I looked to my left and found Danu gracefully flying beside me.

"Yes, dear lady, I am enjoying the view."

"I thought you might like it," she said with a broad smile.

"Where am I?" I asked.

"Ireland, dear boy. Where else?"

"No, I've been there and this isn't what I saw."

"Let me be more clear, this is the Ireland that was. In fact, at this very moment, you are being born. Not here, of course, but somewhere."

"How did I get here?"

"I brought you here."

"So, I'm alive?"

"No."

"I'm dead?" I looked away back to the trees.

"Not precisely."

"What?" I asked, jerking my head back toward her.

"Your body is dead, but surely you are familiar with rebirth."

"Well, yeah, but the council and the vote."

"Oh, your silly Elders. They don't have nearly as much power as they think. You and your kind are not gods, Sean."

"Yes, I know that."

"For now you do but when you reach thousands of years, perhaps you will forget."

"I suppose I could." I shrugged.

"That forgetting is a foul thing, but it happens. We allow it to happen because it keeps your society stable."

"Okay."

"Sean, this is but a repast. You have free will and can choose to remain here."

"But?"

"But, you can also choose to go back."

"Then I want to go back."

"If you go back, you will have a great task."

"I want to go back, what's the task?"

"You must find and destroy the cloaked one."

"What?"

"The one who created Brother Herman, the one who created the werewolves, the one who poisoned your mother's mind. You must find him and you must destroy him."

"Okay, who is he? How do I destroy him?"

"Those are answers you must find for yourself."

I glided silently on the wind. If I went back, I might have an impossible task to perform. Then again, I'd get to be with Ilsy. This place called to me, however, and I wanted to enjoy it. But knew I would soon grow tired of it without someone to enjoy it with.

"I want to go back," I said firmly.

"Very well."

I felt warmth surround the crown of my head. I looked at Danu, panic rising in my chest. She smiled at me and nodded her head. I tried to ask what was going on but my voice failed me. The warmth slowly moved down my head, my sight and hearing left me. My body felt constricted like I was being forced through a tunnel. My chest constricted, and I couldn't breathe. I felt coolness replacing the warmth. As my head cooled my sight returned, blurry at first. I heard a shattering crash and my sight cleared. I saw Grandfather's cabin from floor level. I inhaled my first breath and got a mouthful of ash. Choking and spluttering, my head rising from the floor. I looked around me. My body was growing from a pile of ash on the floor. Small flames rose around me without burning.

I saw Grandfather, standing at the doorway with one hand over his mouth, watching me grow. All I could do was smile. When I finished growing, I felt a silky smooth warmth on my back. I spread my wings. They stretched to their full seven feet, radiating cool flames. I thought about my former wings and the flames died, replaced by my raven wings. I was back, I was alive, I was... something.

"Phoenix," Grandfather whispered.

"Yes, I am the phoenix," I said. I felt strong, I felt powerful, I felt a soaring happiness I had never known.

"Impossible."

"Why?"

"The final death."

"Well, maybe they voted in time."

"Sean, they voted not to repeal the final death."

While Darius and Grandfather lobbied hard in my favor, the majority of the council had refused to vote in my favor. I felt anger rise in me, but a more important thought came to me.

"I have to go to Ilsy," I said.

"Sean," he said quietly.

"What?"

"You died eight months ago."

"What?" I exclaimed.

"It's been eight months. I haven't talked with Ilsy since. She may have moved on."

"Grandfather, she loved me. I love her. I have to go to her."

"No! You have to see the council."

"Fuck the council! They wanted me dead. Now I'm not and I'm going to find the woman I love, please understand, Grandfather. I'll be back." I focused on Ilsy and telelocated to her.

I appeared outside of Ilsy's house. In her driveway I saw my car, behind it a Prius. Some people never learn. I walked to the door and prepared to knock. Then I heard laughing. I moved to one of her front windows and looked inside. Ilsy was sitting on her couch, a guy sat beside her. His arm was around her shoulders and they were laughing. I don't know how long I stood at her window watching them.

Eventually, I shifted to my raven form and perched on a tree limb outside. I watched them until they went to bed. I watched them when they woke up. I watched them as they left. My heart was shattered. Ilsy had kept my car, but Grandfather was right, she had moved on. I was getting ready to go back to Grandfather when a voice spoke beside me.

"Poor little birdie, sitting in a tree, watching his lady love K-I-S-S-I-N-G another man." The low melodious voice said in a singsong manner.

I looked beside me and saw a man crouched on the limb, a man cloaked in shadows.

"I can return your lady love to you. I can give you the power to keep her," he said.

"Who are you?"

"You haven't guessed yet?"

"This is your free pass. Leave me now," I said.

"Have it your way, pretty bird. We'll meet again." In a puff of smoke, the man disappeared.

I took one last look at Ilsy's house and felt two tears roll down my cheeks. They hissed and smoked when they hit the ground. I had been a phoenix for one day. So far, I knew my wings and tears could burn. I focused on the inside of Ilsy's house and jumped there. Her sweet scent surrounded me, mixed with the musky masculine scent of the man she was with. Looking around her house I found the key to my car, a pen, and a piece of paper.

*"Ilsy, thank you for taking care of my oldest friend. I hope to see you again soon. I love you. Sean."*

A tear fell and singed a hole in the paper. I placed my note on the coffee table and jumped back outside. A smile grew on my lips as I climbed in the seat of my car.

I was alive, I was going home, I was a phoenix. The world was wide open.

# THE END